I heard

phone.

It's about time!

I hurried down the stairs, trusting the banister to keep me from tumbling forward. In the kitchen I turned on the light and picked up the receiver. The line was alive, crackling with static as it had been before. Between gasps, I managed a breathless "Hello?"

"Linnet..."

It was the same soft, lightly accented voice. The same woman.

"Yes, this is Linnet."

"I'm sorry. We were cut off before. Sort of."

"Who are you?" I demanded.

"That's not important," she said. "I need to tell you something. Listen carefully. We're almost out of time."

"Then tell me before we get cut off again." I raised my voice above the static, praying that the caller would stay on the line.

"It's about your death," she said. "There's a slight chance I can help you prevent it."

★

Previously published Worldwide Mystery titles by
DOROTHY BODOIN

THE CAMEO CLUE
A SHADOW ON THE SNOW
SECRET FOR A SATYR
SNOWHEDGE

Love, Deadly Love

Dorothy Bodoin

WORLDWIDE®

TORONTO • NEW YORK • LONDON
AMSTERDAM • PARIS • SYDNEY • HAMBURG
STOCKHOLM • ATHENS • TOKYO • MILAN
MADRID • WARSAW • BUDAPEST • AUCKLAND

To Emilie Bodoin, my niece, goddaughter, and dear friend.

LOVE, DEADLY LOVE

A Worldwide Mystery/March 2011

First published by Hilliard & Harris

ISBN-13: 978-0-373-26743-9

Printed in U.S.A.

Acknowledgments

I wish to thank my friends and critique partners, Marja McGraw, Shirley Schenkel and Susan Shaw for their invaluable help with the first draft of my book, and Stephanie Reilly for making *Love, Deadly Love* a reality.

Love, love, tender love,
Where are you tonight?
Moon and stars shine up above,
But without you, there is no light.
Love, love, tender love,
Hear my lonely cry.
Moon and stars die up above,
And without you, then so will I.

—Cajun folk song

ONE

THE PHONE WAS RINGING.

Its incessant shrill sliced through the afternoon silence that hung over Beechnut Street. In the thick June air, the sound was unnaturally loud, as nerve-wracking as any sudden disturbance in a quiet place.

One more annoyance, I thought as I turned the key in the lock.

Then, *What phone?*

The only phone in my newly-purchased Victorian cottage in Maple Creek was a vintage black dial tone landline, mounted on the yellow kitchen wall. It had been disconnected, or so the Realtor, Dinah Deering, said.

Therefore it couldn't ring. Still, it did. Three times; four times; five…

Turning the knob, I pushed open the front door and dashed through the dining room to the kitchen. As I reached for the receiver, the ringing stopped, leaving a lingering echo in the close air.

Still I picked it up, surprised that it felt so heavy and cold against my ear. Feeling foolish, I said, "Hello… Hello?"

No one answered. The echo faded; welcome silence returned. I heard the muted hum of the refrigerator, the faint *drip drip* from the faucet, and the ticking of the clock in the living room. All familiar sounds. I was home—*Home Sweet Home*—in my own house, a mile from the clamor and chaos of Louisa M. Alcott Middle School. Nothing could touch me here.

I replaced the receiver and brushed a speck of dust from its top with my finger. How could a disconnected, dead phone ring? The answer was simple. Dinah Deering was wrong.

I had never questioned her. I'd never even taken the receiver off the hook. In the age of cells and BlackBerry smartphones, landlines were extraneous. I'd only given the phone a passing thought. When I painted the kitchen a softer shade of yellow, I would remove it and fill in the hollowed-out space. Until then it could stay.

Besides, who would call Violet Julaine, the previous owner? She was dead, murdered a long time ago in this very house. Anyone wishing to contact me knew my cell phone number. I'd probably just missed a telemarketer.

Setting my purse and school books on the table, I told myself, *It's Friday. Forget the phone.*

But it wasn't that easy. Wouldn't Dinah know whether or not the phone was working?

I lifted the receiver again and listened. There was no dial tone. Nothing but dead air. Well, then, Dinah was right.

Still puzzling over the mystery, I climbed the stairs to my bedroom to change out of my white blouse and navy skirt into a silky peach dress with an empire waistline. For the first time all day I felt comfortable and cool.

The rest of the afternoon was mine.

EVERY DAY AFTER SCHOOL I drew a heavy black X through the date on my kitchen calendar. On Friday, I counted the days left until June seventeenth and the end of the school year. Then I celebrated the survival of one more week with a fabulous dinner at the Blue Lion Inn on Main Street. They offered prime rib, fish, spirits, and the best desserts I'd ever eaten.

Usually I dined alone. Still relatively new in town, I hadn't met many people yet, and most of my school friends had their own lives.

I always walked the half mile to the Blue Lion, reveling in the fresh air and scenery. The leaves on the trees along the way were fully developed now, vibrant green and russet red. They rustled in the breeze and cast shadows on the gleaming sidewalk. Stray sunbeams filtered through their canopy and danced off the geraniums and impatiens in my neighbors' yards.

This was one of those rare days in June that inspires poets and revives the weary; when vegetation is young and fresh, not yet weighted down by the summer heat, and pesky insects are still hatching. Feeling free and grateful for my life, I breathed air filled with the scents of freshly-mowed grass and spicy stock.

I still marveled that I had found a unique fairy-tale home in this picturesque town. Known to the locals as Valentine Villa, the nineteenth-century Victorian cottage was the soft pink color of strawberry fluff. Beneath the highest gable, a heart-shaped stained glass window glowed in the light like a rosy jewel.

The Victorian was exquisite, a veritable jewel itself, yet it had languished in Michigan's dying house market for over a year. I couldn't understand why no one had snapped it up at its incredible twice-reduced price.

On that sunny day last month when Dinah Deering had showed me the property, she'd offered an explanation. "That's because of the murder that was committed here. It's part of the house's colorful history, but some folks don't want to live with…" She paused, looking away. "With unfortunate associations."

"Well…" I'd let my gaze rest on the heart window and thought about my savings that would cover the down payment; about the affordable mortgage; and, most important of all, my present long commute. If I lived in Maple Creek, I'd avoid snowy weather and road rage on the freeway. My drive time would shrink from an hour to ten minutes, and I'd save hundreds of dollars on gas. "If this murder happened some time ago…"

"It did," Dinah said quickly. "And it wasn't a bit gory."

"If the murder is part of the past, then it won't bother me," I said.

An historic murder. A Valentine window swimming in a light May mist. Cascades of pink blossoms on the weeping cherry tree in the front yard. Delicate gingerbread trim, a spacious front porch. Here was everything I had ever dreamed about; more than I ever thought I'd have.

I gazed at the white picket fence that enclosed the yard and thought, *Now I can have my dog.*

"Let's walk around to the back," Dinah said. "The flowerbeds need a little work. With all the rain we've been having, the weeds have taken over."

They had, but against the west fence, tulips and hyacinths bloomed in the shade of the closely spaced maple trees that gave the yard the look of a forest. Wild ferns and lilies of the valley threatened to choke the weeds Dinah had mentioned. I'd never had a chance to work out of doors. Neatening this unkempt garden would be a pleasure.

"The back yards on this street are unusually deep," she added. "You could plant a vegetable garden if you like."

"Not in all this shade," I said.

"In containers then?"

The first half of the property was level; then it sloped slightly downward to what might have once been a grape arbor. A white aluminum tool shed with a pink roof and doors was the sole structure in this extensive space.

"The last owner left a few tools and gardening supplies in the shed," Dinah said. "There's an old manual lawn mower. I think it still works."

Behind my property a white house sat diagonally on its lot. The largest weeping willow tree I had ever seen shaded a pond bordered by huge rocks. From the small back porch of the pink Victorian, the view was breathtaking.

"You've decided, haven't you?" Dinah asked with a smug smile.

"Yes. I'm going to make an offer today. Do you think it'll be accepted?"

"Count on it," she said.

So, after the traditional inspections and paperwork, after the hassle of packing my belongings and moving up north, I became a first-time homeowner, a resident on the street called Victorian Row.

I'd never regretted my hasty decision.

"Lynette?"

A deep masculine voice calling my name cut through my reminiscing. A vintage blue Cadillac convertible as sleek and gorgeous as a prehistoric winged creature had landed gracefully at the curb.

The man behind the wheel was gorgeous too. Incredibly handsome and tanned, with eyes the color of a cornflower opening to the sun, he wore a deep blue shirt rolled up to his elbows. The color matched his eyes and the car's custom paint.

Out of uniform and away from his intimidating cruiser, Lieutenant Dalton Gray of the Maple Creek Police Department looked like a different man, friendly and approachable.

I had met him at school on the worst day of my teaching career. Then his handsome features had been chiseled into a grim mask, and his eyes were as unyielding as stone. His presence had commanded instant silence from my class, the first I'd ever experienced. I could almost have been afraid of him myself.

"Hello!" he said again. "Lynette, isn't it?"

He pronounced my name incorrectly, as almost everybody did.

"It's Linnet," I said. "Like the bird. Accent on the first syllable." Then, realizing how pedantic that sounded, I added a smile and a compliment. "That's the most beautiful car I've ever seen, Lieutenant Gray. It looks like you just drove it out of the show room."

He beamed with pride. "I found her rusting away in an abandoned barn and restored her from scratch. She doesn't look a half century old, does she?"

"Not at all." I touched the shining fender. It felt warm and smooth, kissed by the sun.

"What are you doing in this part of the country?" he asked. "Don't you live somewhere downstate?"

"Not anymore. I moved to Maple Creek last month. That pink house down the street is mine."

He smiled. "The one with the stained glass heart. I know it. We're almost neighbors." He hesitated a moment, his eyes bright with excitement. "Would you like to go for a ride? This baby is as swift as a missile and soft inside. Like marshmallow." He patted the pristine upholstery.

The temptation was strong, but something made me hesitate. His well-known reputation with the ladies, perhaps. And spontaneity wasn't one of my virtues.

"Thanks, Lieutenant, but after being cooped up in a classroom all day, I like to walk."

He glanced upward at the small patches of blue sky that managed to break through the leaves. "It's going to rain any minute now," he said.

I couldn't see the clouds, but the sun burned down on my bare arms. There wasn't a hint of rain in the air, nor in the day's forecast.

"Not till this evening, I heard."

"Believe me, Linnet. Police have access to secret weather information. What do you say? I can raise the top, and we'll stay snug and dry."

Now my stubborn streak took over. "Some other time, maybe."

He shut off the ignition, apparently settling for a casual exchange on the street. "How are the little monsters at Alcott Middle School?" he asked.

His question dragged me back to my fourth hour class and its rogue students, the ones I wished fervently to forget when I didn't have to deal with them.

"They're under control," I said. "Sort of."

"No sinister plots against authority?"

"None that I'm aware of. The principal suspended the two ringleaders for the rest of the school year. That helps a little."

"Let's keep it that way," he said. "School's almost over, isn't it?"

I nodded. "Just about. For students, on the fifteenth. Two days later for staff."

"Next fall you'll have a whole new bunch of kids. I hope they'll be better."

"They can hardly be worse," I said.

But next fall's freshmen would have heard of what I referred to as the Plot. Unfortunately, now I had a reputation too.

Lieutenant Gray slid over to the passenger's seat and laid his hand on the door handle. "How about joining me for a coffee?"

I glanced down at my wrist and realized I hadn't worn my watch today. "I'd love to, but I'm on my way to dinner. I'm already late."

"What can we do about that?"

This man didn't take defeat lightly. Being unable to think of an appropriate response, I felt at a disadvantage.

From school gossip, I knew that the handsome Lieutenant Gray had several girlfriends. He thrived on variety. Many women hoped they could snag his interest on a permanent basis, but the word 'commitment' wasn't in his vocabulary.

My friend, Beverly Lyle, also in the English Department, had summed him up in three words: "He's a player."

To be truthful, I wouldn't have minded joining the ranks of the favored few for a date or two, but it didn't seem prudent to initiate a social relationship with a man I might meet again on another official occasion.

Don't be so stuffy, Linnet, I thought. *The man asked you out for coffee. It's not as if your engagement calendar is filled, and if you're late for dinner, who cares?*

I started to speak, but Lieutenant Gray appeared to have accepted my decision.

"How about a rain check then?" he said. "A welcome-to-Maple Creek drink. Sometime when you're not so busy."

A loud crash of thunder overhead underscored his words. His eyes held a glint of triumph, and he winked. "Change your mind?"

"I'll take a rain check, and I'd better be on my way. It was nice seeing you again, Lieutenant Gray."

In a stern policeman's voice, he said, "It's Dalton…Linnet. Don't keep him waiting. Whoever he is."

I smiled, ignoring the wave of warmth that broke over my face, and began walking briskly toward Main Street. A few raindrops fell on my bare arms, then a few more.

I should have brought a cardigan, should go back home for an umbrella. Should have accepted Dalton Gray's invitations. But I walked on. A little water wasn't deadly.

Behind me, the Cadillac's ignition purred into life. Soft music drifted into the humid air. The melody was vaguely familiar, a jaunty little tune from an earlier era, the sixties, perhaps, to complement the age of the convertible. It practically demanded that the listener sing along and be happy.

The music lent me an illusion of newfound energy. Or perhaps it was something else. An invitation from a man like Dalton Gray was a dose of spring tonic. Even if I didn't need one. Even if he was a player.

DALTON'S RAIN proved to be a gentle spring shower. By the time I left the Blue Lion with a take-out container of strawberry cheesecake, the sun had reappeared, and the sidewalks were already drying. Raindrops glistened in the grass and dripped down from the trees. The world smelled even fresher than it had before.

We were both right about the weather. A severe thunderstorm, complete with lightning, made its appearance at ten o'clock as I lay in bed, thinking about the pleasant after-school encounter with Lieutenant Gray and berating myself for not accepting one of his offers. Why did I always do the opposite of what I really wanted to do? It made no sense.

"Would you like to have your piano lesson on the spinet today, Linnet?"

"Uh, no." I sat down at the Baby Grand and opened my Bach.

I was seven years old.

Of course, I wanted to play on the little piano. As it turned out, I never had another opportunity.

But with Dalton, there was still that rain check, if he was serious about it.

I turned on the bed and listened to thunder rolling over my roof. It seemed close. Too close. The rain pounded against the old windows. Intermittent lightning flashes illuminated the room's shadows.

I wasn't afraid of electrical storms, but I didn't like them.

In the humid air, my light cotton gown felt like wool. The one amenity the pink Victorian didn't have was air-conditioning, and I couldn't afford another expensive purchase, only a pair of humble fans, one for each floor.

This had been the warmest, rainiest spring in my memory. People planted their flowers between showers and postponed their barbecues and outside projects. A rained-out weekend would be bad enough. But a rained-out summer? Unthinkable.

On the other hand, dismal, wet weather would keep the kids from going wild on these last hectic days of school.

My eyelids grew heavy. I wished I lived in *Camelot.*

Rain for school days, sunshine for vacation time, and a handsome blue knight riding down Beechnut Street on his azure winged steed…

Downstairs, the phone rang, yanking me out of my doze. Its impervious, persistent sound was so loud that it might have been in the room with me instead of in the kitchen. I counted ten rings. My heart rate speeded up and my hand closed around the sheet.

Someone knows you're home. Someone's waiting for you to answer.

Eleven. Twelve. Silence.

I stayed in bed. It was dangerous to rush down the stairs at night. In any event, I could never have reached the phone before it stopped ringing.

TWO

I WOKE THE NEXT MORNING with a nagging sense of apprehension. A small element in my universe had fallen out of its appointed place. Something was wrong. Again.

Even with the circulating power of the fan, the air in the room was stifling. I pushed back the crumpled sheet. The break of sunlight through the sheer curtains was too bright, and a headache throbbed behind my eyes. Pushing my hair back from my face, I massaged my temples.

It was Saturday. The first day of the weekend. I needed to feel well, needed to feel energized.

Then I remembered the dead phone. Yesterday it had come to life twice—which was impossible. Nevertheless, this had happened, and it might happen again. Today I intended to solve the mystery. I had enough aggravation in my life and didn't need more from an inanimate object.

I got out of bed and opened the windows halfway. The breeze that rushed in was hot. It felt more like July than early June.

A half hour later, I stood in front of the phone, daring it to disturb the morning silence with that shrew's-voice ring. It didn't. I picked up the receiver and listened to silence. The phone might have been an antique child's toy whose whimsical recorded message had broken down.

Dead as the traditional doornail.

Still, I couldn't forget yesterday's double disturbance. On an impulse, I rummaged through my purse for my cell phone and dialed the number written in blue ink on the landline's dial.

It didn't ring. That was progress.

Stay dead, I said, chagrinned that a black plastic box could unsettle me to the point where I was talking to it.

I dropped the cell back into my purse and filled the teakettle with water, turning my focus to my pretty country kitchen. I loved everything about it except the walls. They were a blowsy dandelion yellow that could blind the person who stared at them too long.

The cupboards were white. They glistened in the sunlight like silk. In spite of the shade cast by the trees on the east side, the kitchen was the brightest room in the house. Apparently it was the only one that had been freshly painted before the house went on the market. The only change I'd make was the color of the walls. I'd be happier with a softer shade of yellow. Daffodils rather than dandelions.

While I waited for the kettle's whistle, I dreamed of all the decorative touches I wanted to add to the kitchen: Cobalt canisters on the counter to catch and hold the sunlight, a novelty cookie jar, an old-fashioned glass hen, and a pitcher filled with wildflowers for my new oak table.

Home sweet home, I thought. *I was so lucky to find you.*

AFTER A BREAKFAST of cereal and blueberries, topped with two pain pills, I felt better and able to tackle my planned activities. Dressed in jeans and a low-cut tank top, I opened the side door and stepped on tangled sweet pea vines that had flopped down over the walkway.

Tie it back before it blooms. I began to make a mental list. *Stake the black-eyed Susans, inventory the tools in the shed, pull any plant that even looks like a weed…*

That was an ambitious list of chores for a hot day when all I really wanted to do was admire my property. I walked slowly around to the back. The grass sparkled with dew, and white clouds floated languidly above the treetops, forming fantasy shapes in a deep blue sky. The day was spring perfection, except for unseasonable heat and humidity.

My neighbor, Bonita White, was pruning the shrubs that grew along her side of the fence. She stood ankle deep in branches, her copper red hair shining in the morning sun.

Petite and trim, Bonita reminded me of a bright butterfly, flitting from one place to another without a single wasted effort. She was always coming or going, impossible to catch. Sometimes she stayed away from home for days at a time.

Bonita seemed friendly enough if you merely wanted to exchange simple greetings and weather observations in passing. Every now and then she skidded to a halt and initiated a real conversation—the butterfly landing.

She was the best kind of neighbor.

When I approached the fence, she glanced up and smiled. "Good morning, Linnet. You're up early for a Saturday."

"I'm going to do some yard work," I said. "It's a good day for it."

Bonita nodded. "This spring you have to seize the moment." She set her pruning shears down and began to toss cuttings into a tall grocery box, taking occasional sips from a can of orange soda set on the ground.

I leaned against the picket fence and let the breeze blow my hair back and up and into my face. Wherever it chose. How luxurious not to worry about a windblown coiffeur or wrinkled dress. How glorious to be home in mid-morning with a whole day before me.

"Are things going all right at school?" Bonita asked.

Like practically everybody else in town, Bonita had read the story about me and my killer class at Alcott Middle School. Although the reporter had withheld my name, anyone could guess my identity from the selected facts she gave.

"It's a madhouse, but so far, so good," I said.

"I could never be a teacher," she said. "With kids the way they are these days, it's hazardous to your health."

I nodded. "School can be a battleground. It's sad."

Bonita owned a riding stable north of Maple Creek and managed a vintage dress shop, an unusual combination. She seemed happy.

"It's nice to have somebody living next door," she added. "I thought that house would never sell."

"Because of the old murder?"

She frowned. "If you're referring to the Violet Julaine case, that's not so old. It happened a year ago last February."

"But the Realtor said..."

I broke off, puzzled, trying to remember. What *had* Dinah said about the house's past? The murder wasn't a bit gory. What else?

I couldn't recall anything, but my imagination, fired by the house's old-time atmosphere, had suggested the early 1900s and given me an image of a gracious lady in a long pink gown. I had held on to it.

"I must have misunderstood her," I said. "How did Ms. Julaine die?"

Bonita set the pruning shears down and took a long drink of soda. "She was poisoned. Somebody gave her a box of cherry tarts for Valentine's Day. They were laced with arsenic. She ate one, maybe two, and died."

Well that wasn't gory. Only insidious and deadly. And ironic that a Valentine gift intended to be a symbol of friendship or love should carry death.

"I can't imagine anyone doing such a terrible thing," I said.

"They never found the killer, but Violet must have known him—or her—because she opened the door and ate the tarts."

"So a lover or friend?"

"My guess is a friend, a woman, because the tarts were homemade. That's a sexist comment, I know." Bonita picked up her shears again and snipped a branch that had grown through the space between the pickets. "Some folks think it was a copycat killing."

When Bonita chose to converse, she became a veritable treasure trove of information. I listened eagerly, hungry for any crumb if it concerned the house's history or my new town.

"Was there another murder involving poisoned food?" I asked.

"A few years ago one of our townspeople, Cora Valentine, ate a poisoned caramel apple at the Apple Fair. Now, *her* killer is locked up. Whoever murdered Violet was luckier."

My hand tightened on the picket's sharp point, felt it wearing an indentation in my palm. I had taught at Alcott Middle School for two years but had never heard of either murder. "I thought Maple Creek was such a quiet little town."

"Oh it is, pretty much," Bonita said. "Killers ply their trade in country hamlets, too. We've only had two murders here in recent history. That's not so bad."

"Unless you're the victim. Or the victim's family."

My thoughts shifted to the fancy desserts I loved. To desserts in general, a whole cart of them—tempting, irresistible—sometimes and in the wrong hands, deadly. Poison in a caramel apple; arsenic in a cherry tart.

Who would dream that a slice of cheesecake topped with fresh strawberry sauce like the one I'd brought home from the Blue Lion last night could kill? With just one added ingredient.

A memory surfaced, giving rise to new fears. Last week, Candace Ann Clayborne had brought a box of brownies to class, one for everybody, including me. "I baked them myself," she'd said with a blush and a shy smile. "Today's my birthday."

After the Plot, I'd resolved not to give the fourth hour students a single inch. In this instance, I could fall back on the school's rule, and fall I did. Hard and quick.

"Remember there's no eating or drinking in class. Save them for lunchtime."

"But we won't be all together then," Candace Ann said.

"You'll find a way to distribute them. We can't break the rule."

At the girl's stricken look, I hastened to add, "Happy birthday, Candace Ann."

As she'd stashed the box under her desk, the class fell uncharacteristically silent for a moment. Then they reverted to their usual noisy, disorderly state.

Poison in a caramel apple; arsenic in a cherry tart. *Strychnine in a brownie?*

At the time I hadn't thought of the incident as another fledgling Plot. But after what had happened a few weeks earlier, I should have. This was Maple Creek where my self-absorbed freshmen students would have heard of the murder at the Apple Fair and a copycat poisoning on Valentine's Day, even if I hadn't.

Each brownie had one of our names written in vanilla icing on the top.

And the biggest one is for you, Ms. Shellwin.

Young people, too, can be copycats.

Candace Ann wasn't part of the group of seven boys I suspected of concocting the plot, though. She was one of the few good girls in fourth hour, quiet and fairly studious. Her greatest transgression was reading her romance novel during class.

Bonita brought me back to the present. "Is anything wrong, Linnet? You look pale."

"I'm just thinking about what you said. About the abysmal state of teaching."

"Don't think about it till Monday when you have to."

She was right, of course. "I'd better get to work if I'm going to accomplish anything this morning."

At the tapping of heels on concrete, Bonita snapped her pruning shears shut with untoward force. "Tansy Stewart," she said in a whisper. "Darn."

I turned around to see a small, chunky woman in a slimming chocolate-brown and white dress crossing the street, heading in our direction. She looked neither to the right nor left, apparently assuming that the way was clear. Fortunately for her, it was.

"Good morning, girls." The newcomer cut across the grass and came to a stop at the fence. Her hair, a striking mix of brown and white, like her dress, was rapidly losing its sleek shape in the humidity. "I came over to tell you how beautiful your azaleas were this year, Bonita," she said.

They'd been bright and abundant, but now, like the cherry

blossoms, were gone—faded, dried, and blown away in the winds of May.

Bonita smiled. "To everything its season. Have you met our new neighbor, Tansy?"

"No, but I know all about her." Tansy's lips and her smile were too bright, scarlet like the vanished azaleas. Like the sun. I felt like shading my eyes.

I didn't have to guess what Tansy knew.

"Linnet Shellwin, right? You teach ninth grade English at Alcott Middle School."

"That's me. I… Me."

Bonita said, "This is Tansy Stewart, Linnet. She lives across the street."

"In that big white house," Tansy said.

Most of the structures on Beechnut Street were white and all but one could be described as large. Tansy pointed to an elegant Queen Anne with an extravagance of landscaping and riotous color in the front yard.

Bonita shook the orange soda can. "If you two will excuse me for a minute, I have to go in for reinforcements." She practically ran into her house.

Tansy shook her head. "Not very sociable, is she?"

"Bonita's probably just thirsty. It is hot for this early in the morning."

"Well it's almost summer, and thank heavens for that. Now we can get out and visit our neighbors."

Sensing a new source of information, I said, "We were talking about the woman who used to live in my house. The one who was murdered."

"Poor Violet," Tansy said with a discernible shiver. "Did Bonita tell you that I was the one who found Violet's body?"

"No, she didn't. How awful for you."

"I still think about that terrible day. February 15th." Tansy gazed off in the distance as if seeing a slow-motion reenactment of it. "Violet and I watched out for each other, both of us living alone and being friends. Before the murder happened, I hadn't seen her for three days but didn't think anything of it. Remember how cold and snowy it was two winters ago?"

I did. Treacherous lanes on the freeway. A major blizzard. An ice storm. Three snow days. Every time I turned onto the I-75 entrance, I thought, *I'm going to die on this stretch some day.* That was the year I thought spring would never come, the year I began to think seriously about moving closer to Alcott Middle School.

The next winter was milder, but once the idea of moving occurred to me, once I knew it was feasible, I started poring over ads in the real estate section of the papers and checking out properties in the area.

"Would you like to sit down for a while?" I asked, indicating the pair of wicker chairs on the front porch. "I'd like to know more about the murder, if you don't mind talking about it."

Tansy didn't need any further encouragement. "I hadn't seen Violet leave her house for three days. She didn't shovel her walk. That should have tipped me off, but ah, well..." She shrugged. "It didn't. Anyway, no one went outside unless they had to.

"I usually keep an eye on who's going where, but I didn't see anyone coming up to Violet's house with a box. I blame myself. I might have been able to save her."

"Or she might have invited you to join her for a tart and you'd be dead yourself," I said. "Besides, you can't be on the lookout every second."

Could she?

"Did you see any tracks leading up to her house?" I asked.

"No. None."

"Then how could someone have visited her?"

"The night after Valentine's Day we had three inches of new snow." She glanced down at the front walkway, now swept clean. "Anyway, I called her but kept getting a busy signal. Finally I got worried. I let myself in..."

I looked at her, wondering if I'd heard her correctly. That was my house she was talking about.

Apparently noting my dismay, she said. "We had keys to

each other's places for emergencies. Violet was always locking herself out." She added quickly, "I turned mine in to the police."

"I wish someone had given it to me," I said.

I'd have to ask about the extra key at the police station. I didn't like the idea of anyone having easy access to my house, especially the law. Especially Lieutenant Gray.

Dalton's face appeared before me, his handsome features, more clearly defined, his cornflower blue eyes brighter. Dalton who had issued invitations as if they were orders.

On second thought, maybe I'd better have the locks changed.

Tansy eased back into her narrative. "I called Violet's name. When she didn't answer, I knew something was wrong."

She pressed her hand to her eyes for a moment and continued.

"I saw the box of cherry tarts on the counter right away. There was a teapot on the table and a plate filled with crumbs stuck to some dried red gook. It looked like blood, but it turned out to be syrup—from the tarts. I haven't been able to eat a tart or pie since."

"Well…" I couldn't think of anything to say except "You will, one day."

"The phone was off the hook," she said. "Violet must have tried to call for help, but the sickness overcame her."

"Where was she—when you found her body?" I asked.

"In her bedroom, just off the kitchen. She was lying on the bed, fully clothed. Not covered. Dead. I didn't touch her, but I knew. It must have happened quickly. So I got out of there as fast as I could. I've never been back, and I'll never set foot in this house again. No offense, Linnet."

"None taken," I said.

"It has bad vibes." Tansy peered through the bay window, her obvious curiosity belying her words. "But you're all settled in. Nice furniture, from what I can see. You're brave to live here."

I refused to let Tansy's gruesome account diminish my pleasure in the pink Victorian. However bizarre and tragic the murder of Violet Julaine, it had nothing to do with me. Still, I was glad I'd chosen a room on the second floor for my bedroom. The room in which Violet Julaine had died at present held boxes waiting to be unpacked.

"I'm not very brave," I said. "It's just that what happened here doesn't touch me. It must have been a vendetta or something. Someone had a grudge against Ms. Julaine. She had an enemy."

"And that person is still at large. But you're right. The murder doesn't affect you. Let the past die." Tansy rose. "Enjoy your new home, Linnet."

As she said goodbye and walked back to the street, I had a strong feeling that she didn't think it was possible.

THREE

AFTER TANSY STEWART went home, my desire to work outside evaporated, but I tackled the yard anyway, taming sweet pea vines and pulling clumps of clover and tiny maple seedlings out of the rain-dampened earth. The hardier weeds clung to the ground as if their roots were trapped in concrete. These I cut at the base with scissors, knowing full well they'd soon bounce back.

Bonita came out and finished trimming her shrubs. She didn't say anything more about the murder, didn't say anything at all beyond a brief comment on the high humidity.

The temperature rose, and I felt my bare arms burning. It was too hot for strenuous activity, and the breeze did nothing to cool the air. Perhaps I should rethink my plan. If I pulled just a half dozen weeds every day for the rest of the summer, eventually I'd have the beds cleared.

At noon, I showered and changed into a yellow sundress. Buoyed by a fresh burst of energy, I took a walk that ended on Main Street. When I'd lived downstate, I rarely ventured beyond the school grounds. Now that Maple Creek was my home, I was determined to familiarize myself with it.

My particular destination was the park. This was a tranquil, shady parcel of land in the heart of town with fountains, ponds, and a small stone dinosaur that little children could sit on. Lush beds of annuals and fruit trees provided color, and stone benches invited strollers to sit awhile and contemplate nature's serenity.

Today seven boys had gathered around the statue of a Civil War cavalry officer mounted on a horse. They ate ice cream cones, tossed balls to one another, and behaved in a civilized, albeit rowdy, manner. They appeared to be a year or two younger than my fourth hour miscreants.

I found an empty bench with a view of a large rock-bordered pond. Two ducks swam close to the water's edge, looking for chunks of bread or tastier fare. I wished I'd brought something to give them. More to the point, I wished I'd brought a lunch for myself.

Even with the breeze and proximity of the water, the day was hot. This was the kind of oppressive summer weather that makes you wonder where spring has gone.

Through a stand of lacy willows, I could see a new storefront on the street that ran parallel to Main. Squinting in the brightness, I made out the shop's name. The Tea Room. Suddenly a cup of tea seemed like the most desirable drink in the world. There would most likely be sandwiches and pastries inside—and air-conditioning.

That was a place worth investigating. Leaving the bench, I walked the several feet to the park's edge and crossed the street.

A woman in a blue shirtwaist dress sat at a table under a crisp green and white striped awning. Two high stacks of paperback books rose high on either side of her. Everything about the woman was soft—her blond hair with its narrow swath of silver to the left of her part; the merest hint of makeup, a strand of pearls, and misty pink fingernail polish. Incredibly her shoulder-length pageboy held its shape in the humidity and brisk breeze.

The sign behind her said, *Buy a book and Madame Milla will tell your fortune.*

I stopped at the table and glanced at the paperback's red and gold cover. It depicted a rugged sheriff and his titian-haired lady locked in an ardent embrace. Was there any other kind in the world of romance? The title was *Capture My Heart;* the author was Ludmilla Schoenherr. No doubt Madame Milla.

The woman smiled; recognition flickered in her gray eyes.

I looked at her more closely. I'd seen her somewhere, around the neighborhood possibly.

"Did we ever meet?" I asked.

The woman's smile deepened. "No, but we teach in the same district. I saw you at the spring In-Service. I'm Milla Schoenherr from the high school. And you're…" She hesitated and a faint blush spread over her face.

"Linnet Shellwin. The teacher whose class tried to kill her. It's all right. You can say it."

"Sometimes you get a group that defies control, even for a master teacher, and those Hogan boys have always been bad news."

Hogan was the name of the Plot leader. Carl Hogan.

"There's more than one?"

"Carl has an older brother. We're going back ten years or more. He was constantly in trouble, but he never pulled a gun on a teacher."

"Kids are getting bolder today," I said.

I warmed toward her at this expression of empathy. "My other classes aren't so bad, but that fourth hour is impossible."

"When they move over to the other side of the hill in the fall, the seniors will whip them into shape."

Because Alcott Middle School was built on a small hill and the high school was a mile down the road, or up the road, depending on one's perspective, "the other side of the hill" was a common expression in the Maple Creek lexicon.

"The computer will shuffle them up into different sections," I added. "They'll be older in September, too. What do you teach, Milla?"

"English and German," she said.

"You might have some of my students then."

"Heaven forbid."

Waving away the prospect of inheriting members of a killer class, Milla laid her hand on one of the stacks, presumably to draw my attention to them. She wore a lustrous pearl ring in a silver setting. It matched her necklace.

"Is this your first book?" I asked.

"It's my first *published* book. I've been writing forever. When Gabrielle opened the Tea Room, I asked her if she'd let me do a signing and sell copies of *Capture My Heart* on consignment."

"How does the fortune telling fit?"

"My heroine meets the hero on the same day a gypsy tells her fortune. Hence the gimmick."

"It's a clever one. Did you sell many books?"

"Only two so far."

"I'll make that three. Do you have a crystal ball? Or cards?"

"I work with Orange Pekoe." Milla signed the flyleaf of a book. "All you have to do is drink a complimentary cup of tea. It has to be black. Cream and sugar interfere with the patterns."

She rang a silver bell. Immediately a young waitress with a plump blond braid and a name tag identifying her as Janice appeared in the doorway. In one hand, she carried a tray containing a cup of tea and two shortbread cookies, which she set in front of me, along with a spoon and napkin.

"That was fast," I said.

"We're well organized." Milla thanked Janice, and I regarded the loose leaves in the plain white cup with interest. They had settled at the bottom, although a few floated on the steaming surface.

Being accustomed to tea bags, I said, "I hope I don't swallow them."

"You won't. Give the leaves a stir and drink. I'll tell you what to do then."

Like the day, the brew was too hot. I sipped it slowly and nibbled at a shortbread cookie.

Milla tapped her ball point pen on the table as if encouraging me to hurry. "You bought Violet Julaine's house, didn't you?" she asked.

"Yes. How did you know?"

She looked down. "Violet was a good friend of mine. I still miss her."

Which didn't answer my question. Then I remembered that I lived in a small town now. People knew their neighbors' business. They probably knew exactly when Dinah Deering had taken down the For Sale sign; and everybody must have heard about the murder.

"Violet loved her house," Milla said. "She always worried about who would live in it when she passed on. She'd be pleased to hand the keys over to you."

What a strange observation! An equally strange image of the lady in pink formed in my mind. Now her dress was shorter. In her outstretched hand she held a gold key.

Letting the image dissolve, I said, "I think she'll approve of me. I haven't changed anything."

But I would. A pale shade of yellow on the kitchen walls and a smooth surface at the site of the old landline. These innovations shouldn't distress Violet Julaine. Anyway, I owned the pink Victorian. Violet lived in some far-off otherworld—as a spirit.

I took the last swallow of tea and started to ask Milla what she knew about the murder, but she said, "Drain the excess liquid in the saucer. Turn the cup toward you three times. Let the leaves form their own patterns. Make a wish."

Awkwardly, I followed her directions, wished for a sweet little collie puppy, and watched the tea leaves arrange themselves into tiny clusters that looked like ink blots.

"Is that all I do?" I asked.

"That's it." Milla took my cup and turned it slowly around, studying the leaves with a slight frown and long silence that unnerved me. Finally she said, "You're going to meet a dark and handsome stranger."

All the fortune tellers said that. But surely Milla didn't mean for me to take her prophecy seriously. It was only a gimmick to sell her books, intended for fun.

Everyone needs a little fun. For these few minutes, I'd believe in the power of the leaves to predict my future.

"This dark, handsome stranger," I said, thinking of Lieutenant Gray. "What if I already met him?"

"Then you'll form a closer relationship with him." She stared into the cup again. "I see storms ahead. Severe storms…"

"Literal ones?" I asked.

"No. They're figurative. Your life is about to be thrown into turmoil."

Well, I thought, *this isn't fun. Is Milla a secret sadist?*

"But here's an overflowing basket," she said, pointing to a tiny formation. "Your wish will come true. Unless you change professions, you'll never be rich, but you'll attain your heart's desire."

I thought of Dalton, then of Ned Glint. Not dark but very handsome, Ned was my colleague in the English Department. My school crush.

"Now, if I could only be sure what that was," I said.

Milla smiled. "That's a universal problem for the undecided."

She set the cup down, apparently finished with the reading.

"You didn't see anything bad besides the storms?" I asked. "Nothing like death?"

"Not today, but that can change."

I decided not to dwell on change. "I can't ask for anything more than a handsome man and my heart's desire, but I don't like the idea of those storms."

"Everyone has troubles," Milla said quietly. "You can't avoid them."

I knew that. My personal storms blew into my classroom every day as soon as the bell rang for the beginning of fourth hour. My life was already in turmoil.

I rose, picked up my book, and said, "Thanks for the reading, Milla. I think I'll check out the Tea Room."

If I didn't have anything to worry about except an occasional storm and my class—and they'd soon be moving on—I could turn my attention to lunch in a quaint place and something larger and sweeter than the shortbread cookies.

THE TEA ROOM WAS SMALLER inside than I'd imagined, its half dozen café tables covered with cloths in rainbow colors. Dried bouquets arranged in teapots served as centerpieces, and framed reproductions of Chagall's art decorated the walls.

Two women chatted over their tea companionably and in low tones. Another sat alone, swiftly turning the pages of *Capture My Heart.* Janice was busy polishing glassware.

The tea choices were extensive. Domestic and Imported. Decaf and herbal. Tempting combinations I'd never heard of. There were clear canisters filled with loose tea for those who didn't want to deal with tea bags.

The day's menu featured minced ham and chicken salad sandwiches on sesame buns. The dessert shelf held trays of Danish, muffins, and tarts with delicate fluted crusts. Strawberry rhubarb, blueberry, and raspberry. None were cherry.

I ordered an apricot Danish and Garden Peach tea and found a seat near the window. Unbidden and out of nowhere, an old nursery rhyme came to my mind: *The Queen of Hearts/ She made some tarts,/ All on a summer's day;/ The Knave of Hearts/ he stole the tarts/ And took them clean away.*

The Queen's story didn't strictly apply to the murder at Valentine Villa, but it captured my imagination. As I sipped my tea and ate the Danish, it kept replaying through my head. Seized by a perverse spirit, I substituted a chilling line of my own: *The Queen of Hearts/ She made some tarts/ And stirred the arsenic in them...*

Then I couldn't think of anything that would rhyme with "them" and also make sense. Apparently neither had Anonymous because, like many of its kind, the little tale lacked a proper ending.

What happened afterward? Did the Knave eat the tarts? Did the Queen call out her men to pursue the thieving Knave? Did she cry *Off with his head!* when they dragged him back to the castle? Incidentally, how many Queens descended to the castle kitchen to do their own baking?

Well, I didn't need to critique Anonymous' work. Just my own. And here was something interesting: None of the Tea Room offerings had cherry filling. Was the baker out of cherries, or had the denizens of Maple Creek lost their appetite for them?

WEEKEND DAYS HAVE a tendency to race by. Sunday's weather was gray and disheartening with intermittent rain. I stayed inside at the kitchen table and wrote lesson plans for every week until the end of the year. These were the last ones until fall when we would all enjoy a fresh beginning.

With a sigh I closed my notebook. September was two months away. I still had lessons to teach, reviews and exams to write, and grades to figure out. Some of them were certain to be challenged.

It was already six o'clock. Nothing untoward had happened since last night. Still, I found myself edgy and restive, waiting for the landline phone to ring again.

Some time after dinner, while I was reading, it did. Closer this time, I hurried into the kitchen and lifted the receiver. It was cold, as cold as the arm of one who has been deceased for days. As I'd anticipated, there was no sound on the other end of the line.

But I imagined an entity waiting breathlessly for my response. If I spoke, said even a fraction of what was in my mind, maybe the caller would get the message.

"Who's there?" I demanded in my uncompromising schoolteacher tone. "If you want to talk to me, stay on the line. If not, stop calling this number."

What an exercise in futility—talking to the air. But it made me feel better.

I hung up and rubbed my right hand. The chill of the

receiver had somehow transferred itself to my fingers. They were practically numb.

What was going on here? And when would it stop?

I almost looked forward to going back to school tomorrow. Rogue students were a shade easier to deal with than a rogue telephone.

FOUR

SHADED BY STATELY maple trees, Louisa M. Alcott Middle School sat serenely on a small hill, its sun-washed bricks fading gracefully into old age. A gray gravel path wound down to a white farmhouse that served as the cafeteria. On the grounds, redwood benches reserved for the staff offered fresh air lunching in warm weather.

Plans to raze Alcott and build a new structure to rival three year old Maple Creek High School had been shelved as the economy worsened and taxpayers rebelled at yet another unnecessary millage. Alcott should last well into the new century, they argued.

Would that the same could be said of its teachers.

I looked for Ned Glint in the crowd of early arrivals. He sat at one of the outdoor tables unofficially reserved for the coaches. His fair hair, practically spun gold, shone in the sunlight. Not everyone would consider him conventionally handsome, but to me Ned was magnificent. Why was he teaching business and English in Maple Creek when he could have been a Hollywood leading man?

He was eating pizza and drinking a large Coke.

I bit into my sandwich, surprised that the turkey wasn't the bland deli variety. To encourage staff satisfaction, the cook prepared special healthy lunches for us: On Monday salads, roast turkey or chicken sandwiches on whole wheat bread, fruit for dessert, and iced tea or coffee. Today, as a concession to the temperature, which had stalled at eighty-nine, she'd added orange sherbet and lemonade.

I yearned for the children's fare: Hot dogs, potato salad, pizza, and blueberry pie.

Annabelle, my usual lunch companion, trailed a straw lazily through her lemonade. "What are you looking at, Linnet?" she asked.

"Nothing in particular," I said, forcing my eyes back to my plate. "I was just thinking."

The petite blonde taught ninth grade biology. I admired her extensive knowledge and envied her easy way of dealing with young people. Annabelle's classes seemed to love her. She had all of my most difficult students and swore that she never had a problem with them.

I consoled myself. Kids, boys especially, like science better than English.

"I wonder why nobody ever mentioned the Julaine murder to me," I said. "I just found out about it this weekend."

"But didn't you say the Realtor told you there'd been a murder at the house?"

"I assumed it happened way back in the past."

"Would it have made a difference if you had known?"

She raised a point I'd never considered. "No," I said.

In my eyes, the pink Victorian with its Valentine window would always be the most beautiful house in Maple Creek. With its gingerbread trim that reminded me of strawberry frosting, the nostalgic white picket fence, and the vast green backyard, it was easily the star of Victorian Row. That house and I had been made for each other.

"I'm curious, though," I said. "Especially since the lady's killer apparently got away with murder."

"So far. Do you know about the poisoned tarts?"

I nodded. "My neighbor told me. She said the police never found out who did it."

"She's right, but I have faith in them. They will, even if it takes twenty years."

No doubt she was referring to an incident we'd discussed last week. A Maple Creek detective who refused to give up on a cold case had nailed a child killer, now masquerading as an ultra-respectable family man. He'd even discovered where the little girl's body had been buried.

"There must have been some suspects in the Julaine case," I said.

"The members of Violet's writing group were questioned. They used to meet every month for potluck dinners. Luckily for them, no one brought cherry tarts to their last get together—on February 13th."

"What about opportunity and motive?" I asked.

"Just about everyone had opportunity, but there was no clear motive."

"Maybe it was random. A thrill killing."

"That could be, but giving a victim poisoned tarts wouldn't serve up much of a thrill. Not like chopping a body up with an ax."

She looked down at her sandwich and shook her head. "According to the papers, Violet Julaine didn't have any known enemies. She led a quiet life, especially after she got laid off from her job at the *Tribune*."

"It looks like I moved into a mystery," I said.

The bell rang, signaling the end of our lunch period. We had seven minutes to return the trays to the cafeteria and walk back up the hill to our classrooms on the second floor. After fourth hour, the rest of the day was the proverbial piece of cake: One small amiable group and my conference period.

Annabelle wrapped her dessert apple in a napkin. "Good luck with your fourth hour class today."

She always said that. If one day she forgot, I felt that the status quo would break apart and something terrible would happen again.

THEY WERE ALWAYS NOISY.

Shoes stamping and squeaking; books slamming onto desk tops, some hitting the floor. Shouting, laughter, an ungodly shriek. Anyone would think that Room 207 had been set aside for recreation.

In the interest of survival, I had created a list of rules, some for students posted on the bulletin board, some intended for me alone, known as Linnet's Rules For Herself. Like Rule #1, which had two parts: Never leave them alone in the classroom. Never leave chalk where they can find it and scribble something inappropriate on the blackboard.

I'd written the assignment on the board before going to lunch, pushed the chalk to the back of my middle desk drawer, locked the door, and was, as always, the first one back.

Not that I didn't trust my class.

Now I stood in front of the room, grade book and seating chart in hand, trying to appear stern and implacable as a riot of teenagers scrambled to their assigned seats.

My weapons in this daily battle were simple. A professional appearance, today a long beige skirt and white silk blouse. A facade of bravado. No acknowledgment that not so long ago a pair of ne'er-do-wells from this class had seized the reins of authority in their grubby hands.

The Plot was forgiven, more or less, but not forgotten.

Into a welcome lull, I said, "Everyone. Take your seats."

"Where do you want us to take them?" Janie Ferris asked.

I ignored that. Naturally the class didn't.

Taking attendance, a serious matter at Alcott, was relatively easy today. Everyone was present except for the two boys who had been suspended. Whoever wasn't sitting down when the second bell rang received a "tardy". Accumulated "tardies" could lower grades. Because most of the class aspired to A's and B's and even scholarships, they generally cooperated.

The majority of my students in fourth hour were unusually bright, which was good. Still this made them more dangerous. Dull students throw paper wads, scribble and draw on desktops, and talk back. Intelligent ones devise plots.

Gradually the noise level subsided, but individual voices managed to break through the post-bell buzz.

He broke my pencil. Miss Shellwin! What are you going to do about it?

Can I borrow a pen?
It's so hot!
Are they going to send us home?
Aren't you hot in those long sleeves, Miss Shellwin?
Pass it on!

That last was a bright red flag. Pass what on? I couldn't determine who had uttered those three inflammatory words. Nor did I see a note. *It* could be something as fairly innocuous as textbooks falling to the floor in unison or an overturned desk. Or something lethal.

I sighed. One more hour of waiting for something to happen. The need to be constantly on guard combined with the heat made me feel ill. Yes, it was so hot! Yes, I was hot in my long-sleeved blouse. But I couldn't afford a moment's distraction.

The noise continued, building to a crescendo, rising higher still. How would I ever keep this rowdy bunch orderly for a two-hour exam?

"Quiet! Everybody settle down." I was shouting myself. Not the right approach.

Rule #2: Don't try to drown them out. Wait until they're quiet, even if it takes all hour. And hope the clamor doesn't carry down to the principal's office on the first floor. Or that my across-the-hall neighbor, Murielle Evans, doesn't stroll over to my door and glare at them, chipping away bit by bit at my authority. Just hope.

Setting my grade book in the top drawer of my desk, where presumably it would be safe, I surveyed the group, letting my gaze linger on certain individuals who required watching. Jimmy, with his spiked red hair and mock innocent grin. Kevin, his cousin and faithful follower. Bill, husky and handsome, the class bully. Dale, whose polished looks and manner were deceptive.

And the girls. Azalea, who wore her blond hair long and her denim skirt short and tight. Even with her distinctive apparel and appearance, Azalea was adept at slipping out of the room the moment I looked away. Debby, the perennial whiner. Laurie, the future model who at present was surreptitiously applying red lipstick with a heavy hand.

I reached down to pick up my textbook, ironically titled *Enjoying English,* and, without turning around, pointed to the board. "Open to page 699, please." Rule #3: Never turn your back on them.

After a seemingly endless uphill trek, we'd reached the end of Charles Dickens' *Great Expectations* without a day to spare if we were going to review before the final exam.

I read the two endings aloud to them, anticipating their indignation at an author who couldn't end his novel properly.

"But that's stupid," Debby cried out when I'd finished. "What *really* happened? Did Pip and Estella ever get together?"

I had an answer ready. "Dickens was an obliging author. He gave his readers what they wanted…"

"Not like you, Ms. Shellwin," Jimmy said, and his audience laughed.

Unfazed, I continued. "And what they wanted was a happy ending. Think of an alternate universe. In one universe, Pip leaves Estella. In another, existing alongside it, they live happily ever after."

"That's stupid," Debby said. "The whole book is stupid."

"It's a soap without sex," Azalea added.

Rule #4: Don't ever let them rattle you.

"Stupid or not, that brings me to today's assignment," I said, realizing that my segue didn't make sense. "Here's your chance to put your thoughts down on paper."

I'd written the topic on the board: *Discuss which ending you prefer. Write two and a half pages. Be specific. Use examples. Give your paper a title. Write complete sentences. Due at the end of the hour.*

"*This* hour?" Jimmy and Bill said that together.

"This is the last paper of the year," I said, trying for a cheerful note. "You have thirty minutes. Let's get started."

"Are you going to write one too?" Bill asked.

"It's too hot to write," Debby wailed. "All those words. It's too much work." She ripped a page out of her notebook and began to wave it back and forth in front of her face, stirring up the warm air.

"Why don't they put air conditioning in this school?" demanded Kevin.

"Bring a fan tomorrow, Miss Shellwin. Please?" That was Carrie Rawson, who seldom said anything.

Grumbling and pathetic references to the weather gradually subsided into a snapping of binders being opened, a rustle of paper and a scratching of pens. Relative quiet settled over the room. My reference to the Double Endings assignment as the last paper, the last chance for an A, had its intended effect. The clock was ticking, the hour winding down.

Rule #5: Plan to fill every single minute. Don't give them a chance to get into mischief.

I walked up and down the rows. Kevin was doing his Algebra homework.

"This isn't math, Kevin," I said.

"Don't I know it?" he muttered.

A fleet of paper airplanes lay on top of Jimmy's literature book, ready to launch.

"Put those away, Jimmy," I said.

Mumbling a protest, Jimmy complied, stashing them in his backpack, but Kevin was still scowling over an algebra problem. Apparently I hadn't been specific enough for him.

Carrie yelped. She held her long pony tail in her hand, smoothing its ribbon, as Bill, seated behind her, smirked in triumph.

"What happened?" I asked.

"Nothing," Carrie said. "Sorry, Miss Shellwin."

I glared at Bill who picked up his pen and opened his book.

In the last desk in the middle row, Candace Ann glanced from the literature text to her paper. She had already written a half page. I stopped to read it.

"That's a good beginning, Candace Ann," I said.

Moving to the back of the room and over to the open windows, I stood for a moment, letting a hot breeze wash over me, wishing I could sink into the hard wood teacher's chair.

Rule #6: Don't sit down. It communicates inattention and indifference. Keep moving. Like a carousel pony. Round and round. Stop, read, compliment, encourage, move again. Until you melt.

A paper airplane whizzed through the air and landed on my desk. Jimmy bent his head low over his paper, writing as if a Fury were whipping him on.

Rule #7: You have to be quicker than they are. And Rule #8: Realize that you have to overlook some misbehavior.

"Five more minutes," I announced. "Be sure you write a conclusion. Don't forget your title or your name."

These last five minutes proved to be the most productive of the hour as the class rushed to finish the assignment. Finally the bell—the blessed bell—rang.

It hadn't happened.

"Put your papers in fourth hour's folder," I said.

They stamped and squeaked and scuffled and screamed their way to the front door and out into the hall, bound for their fifth hour classes. Papers landed like windblown flyers in an untidy heap on my desk.

In the interlude between fourth and fifth hours, I filed them neatly in the proper folder. One page was an ink drawing, an unflattering caricature of myself with flyaway hair, bug eyes, and antenna. Printed in block letters was a legend: *Shellwin is stupid.*

I crumpled it and dropped it into the wastebasket.

In all, this had been a fairly peaceful fourth hour class, better than most. Thank God it was over.

AFTER THE ECHO of the last bell died away, quiet descended on the school. Usually I left when the other teachers did, five minutes behind the students. Lingering in a dim, deserted hall was unwise. But tonight the Let's Go Green Club was meeting across the hall. With approximately fifteen members and two male sponsors. I should be safe.

I had already corrected the *Great Expectations* papers and transferred them to the Hand Back folder. For the most part they were well-written and perceptive. I'd known from the first day that, with a few exceptions, the fourth hour group was bright, hungry for newness and challenge. In a former day, they'd have been labeled Accelerated.

Maybe *Great Expectations* was too old-fashioned for these children of the twenty-first century. We should revamp the English curriculum. *To Kill A Mockingbird* was our only relevant novel. Even that revered classic hadn't appealed to all of them.

I'm out of tune with my students, I thought.

How could that be? I was only twenty-six. Ten years ago, I had sat in a ninth grade English class, mesmerized by the majesty of a Shakespearean play.

Of course not every student is enamored of Shakespeare. Not even intelligent ones.

In any event, revising the required readings list was the privilege of the English Department head, stodgy, stuck-in-the-past Jarrod Charles.

I had a chance to shape a new class, though. This summer, Ned and I, along with four other teachers, were going to put together a new course designed for the new millennium. We were scheduled to start work on it the week after school ended.

I'd volunteered for the project before I knew that Ned was interested in combining English and business skills.

"Hey, Ms. Shellwin. You busy?"

Startled, I closed my hand over my souvenir letter opener and looked up. Candace Ann stood in the doorway, eyeing the manila folder I'd just closed. A slender girl with brown hair and golden-brown eyes, she wore a pretty T-shirt today. The array of glittering sequins in no particular pattern transformed her wren-like appearance dramatically. It was a birthday present,

I supposed, as it looked fresh and bright, unlike the faded tops she usually wore.

"No," I said. "I'm just getting ready to leave."

"Did you correct my paper yet?" she asked.

"Yes, I did." I leafed through the folder. "You got an A-."

"A minus?" She bit her lower lip.

"You have a few run-on sentences and fragments. Those problems are easy to correct. If you like, I can give you some extra help before the exam. Could you stay after school tomorrow?"

"I guess so. I might have to babysit."

She made no move to leave but hovered around my desk, examining the snow globe I used as a paperweight. Obviously something troubled her. Surely not her grades. The rejected birthday brownies, maybe?

"I wanted to tell you something, Ms. Shellwin, but you can't let anyone know I said anything."

I waited. An icy band coiled around my heart, no doubt detected by my antenna.

"A few of the kids are planning to do something mean to you on the last day. I heard them talking."

I tried not to react. Rule #9: Be cool. Pretend, if you have to.

Having experienced last days before, I was prepared for anything. Forbidden water pistols, papers torn into confetti, bursting balloons, even firecrackers. But something mean?

"You know who they are," Candace Ann added.

Well, not Carl and Adam. They wouldn't be allowed back in the building. But those others…

"I can guess," I said. "What is this new plan?"

She shook the snow globe, her eyes transfixed on the white flakes that swirled around Bambi. "I don't know yet, but I can find out for you."

And I could be on guard. But then I was always on guard.

"You stay out of trouble, Candace Ann," I said, knowing the universal fate of informers. "I can take care of myself. Let me know if you're free tomorrow, and we'll tackle those writing problems."

"It'll probably be okay." She walked slowly to the door. "Goodnight, Ms. Shellwin. Don't worry."

"I won't," I said with a smile so bright anyone who knew me could tell it was false. "Thanks for trying to help, Candace Ann."

After she left, I closed the windows, shutting out the hot air, wishing I'd driven to school instead of walking. But I'd soon be home where I could relax and forget about all my problems except for one.

Something mean.

What fresh hell is this? I wondered as I locked the classroom door.

FIVE

ALL THE WAY HOME, A five-block walk from Alcott to Beechnut Street, I fretted about fourth hour's mean plan. What could they be concocting?

Student threats were commonplace nowadays.

I'm going to let the air out of your tires. Smash your car's hood in. Trash your room. Kill you. You'll be sorry if you fail me.

Mindless promises made by mindless malcontents who never remembered that there would always be a day of reckoning, that it could come as soon as tomorrow. They rarely caused any real mischief. Often they settled for a rude retort. I remembered one from last year. As my third hour had stampeded out the door after their final exam, I'd wished them a nice summer.

"It will be without you, Shellwin."

The speaker melted into a crowd gone mad with the joy of summer freedom. I let him go. Chances were good I'd never see him again. Today I couldn't recall his name.

But this year's fourth hour was different. They had far surpassed rudeness, and I would be foolish not to take them seriously. Assuming Candace Ann was right.

I frowned, remembering the sincerity inherent in her warning. Of course she was right. Never having believed that only two boys were involved in the Plot, I should have anticipated a final defiant gesture.

Unmindful of the bright landscaping in my neighbors' yards and the familiar dogs who ran to the fences to greet me, I let myself relive the nightmare of the twenty-fourth of May, one of the first warm days of spring.

Fifth and sixth hours had been cancelled to make way for

the annual Honors Assembly, followed by an early dismissal. Fourth hour was uncharacteristically subdued, which should have tipped me off. Any deviation from the norm bore watching. Even Carl Hogan, who enjoyed his well-earned reputation as the class bad boy, had opened his book. Carl hunched over a textbook was an anomaly.

When the bell rang, they trooped out of the room, all except for Jimmy Jamieson and Dale Sands who tried to convince me to let them stay in the room so they could do their English homework.

"You can stay too," Dale said. "It'll be fun."

"I want to go to the assembly," I said. "So should you. Aren't you two expecting honors certificates?"

Jimmy grinned. "We can pick them up in the office tomorrow."

"Go," I said. "Now."

They tossed a few more arguments at me, then, looking grieved and rejected, picked up their books and went.

Some students always tried to skip assemblies, providing they could slip by the teachers assigned to hall monitor duty. Extra time and their own brand of freedom were infinitely more enticing than sitting on hard chairs and applauding their classmates' achievements.

A purse lay on a desk by the windows, forgotten in its owner's haste to exit the room. A denim clutch decorated with sequins, it belonged to one of the McElroy twins, Brandy or Sherry. Although high school freshmen, they still dressed alike and owned identical accessories.

I'd take it to the front office since I would never find them in the assembly crowd.

One by one, I closed and locked the old windows, sympathetic with the desire to run free rather than sit in the stuffy gymnasium auditorium for two hours.

Stealthy footsteps outside in the hall drew my attention. Someone trying to elude the hall monitors by jumping down from the second floor? Unlikely. Probably a straggler, like me. Or Brandy or Sherry returning for the purse.

But some inner warning system clicked on.

I walked over to the door. The hall was quiet except for a sound that might be breathing or the old building settling. I didn't see anyone. All the classroom doors were closed and presumably locked. I'd better hurry.

Still, I was spooked. I considered leaving the rest of the windows open, but that was begging for a bitter complaint from McGregor, the chief custodian, and an infamous yellow note from the principal, Dwight Dunlap.

I picked up the abandoned purse and closed the last window.

Behind my back, the door slammed shut.

Alarmed, I rushed to the front of the room just as it opened again.

A male figure wearing a black ski mask burst into the room. He brandished a gun, or what looked like a gun.

"Back! Get back!" the figure said in an unnaturally high-pitched voice.

I backed up a few feet, and he came closer. I knew him. Did Carl Hogan think I wouldn't recognize that weird skull ring he always wore and his grime-encrusted fingernails? Not to mention his stained Cedar Point T-shirt? A strong odor of liquor drifted across the space between us.

Another boy materialized behind him, his features also hidden behind a ski mask. This could only be Adam Perkins, judging by his husky build and distinctive warlike stance. He carried a length of rope and a black trash bag.

Making a snap decision to ignore my racing heartbeat and the gun, I said, "You boys better hurry along to the assembly, or you'll be marked absent."

That was a bluff. No teacher took attendance at assemblies where classes promptly scattered to sit with their cliques or friends. They depended on the hall monitors to keep the students from roving.

"Yeah, sure, Shellwin. We'll do that. You get in that closet."

I stared at him aghast. "What?"

"You heard me. The closet."

"Is this some sick joke?"

Carl raised the gun. "There ain't no joking in this class."

It *had* to be a toy, one of those realistic facsimiles that are always getting pulled off the shelves.

But what if it were real? I couldn't take a chance. What *could* I do?

At that moment, it wasn't my life that flashed in front of my eyes. It was newspaper headlines, all whirling about in a mad dance:

Students spike teacher's coffee with sleeping pills... Boy to serve jail time for plan to blow up school... Malfunctioning brakes kill coach, ousted player suspected...

The world's young people had gone insane. Why did I think peaceful little Maple Creek, Michigan, would be different?

Distract them, I told myself. *Call them by their names.*

"Carl," I said. "Adam. Why do you want me to go into the closet?"

Carl laughed, the most unnerving sound I'd ever heard. Abruptly he dropped the phony high-pitched voice. "We're going to wall you up alive."

Like in *The Cask of Amontilldo,* last week's story. I could have sworn that Carl had slept through the reading and discussion.

"And I ain't Carl Hogan," he added.

Adam punched him in the ribs. "Shut up, moron."

I shuddered at the thought of the small musty closet where McGregor had recently set a trap for a mouse. But they couldn't lock the closet door without the key, and after opening the door in the morning, I kept it hidden in my Vocabulary File, the last place Carl or anyone would look. At the moment, it was in my purse.

In the warm, close room, I felt as if ice cubes had replaced my blood. This was serious. Deadly.

What was the rope for? What were they going to do with that trash bag?

"Move it," Carl said.

That can't possibly be a real gun, I told myself.

Of course it could. I saw another heading: *Disgruntled student opens fire in cafeteria. Ten die.*

I tightened my hold on the purse, wishing it were a gun of my own.

Another headline danced giddily before my eyes: *Louisiana assistant principal advocates arming staff.*

If only I had a buzzer to press. A panic button. A hotline to the principal's office. Every classroom needed one. The principal, Dwight Dunlap, would be at the assembly handing out certificates, but surely he would have left his assistant in charge to take care of emergencies and murderous students. Matt Dilland, nicknamed Marshall, was an administrator and wannabe cop.

"I'm not going to do it," I said. "Hand over the gun, and we'll go along, nice and quiet, down to the front office. Maybe we can sort all this out."

Carl raised the gun.

"What did I ever do to you?" I demanded, searching my memory, finding nothing but the occasional well-deserved detention or zero.

"You're always looking at us," Adam said. "You're stalking us."

"You're boring." That was Carl.

Boring, am I?

I zipped open the purse and hurled it at Carl. Its contents flew through the air—lipstick, compact, brush, wallet, keys, a glittering green necklace whose tiny beads broke from their string and rolled away in every direction. A bottle of nail polish shattered on the floor and splattered the edges of Carl's tattered jeans with splotches of hot pink.

He swore, backed away from the onslaught, and slipped on a bead.

I ducked behind the desk just as he regained his footing and fired the gun. A hole opened up in the window behind me. The deafening noise of the retort seemed to go on forever. He lunged at me.

I picked up the heavy *Thesaurus* and flung it at his head. Then *Webster's Dictionary.* Next *Prose and Poetry for Enjoyment. Bartlett's Familiar Quotations* caught him in the stomach. With a howl of rage, he slipped on another bead, and the gun fell out of his hand.

As he reached for it, an indignant voice broke into the melee. "Here now! What's all this?"

McGregor dodged *Understanding Grammar* and hauled up a surprised Carl roughly by the arm. I hadn't realized until now that Adam had disappeared.

McGregor gave Carl's arm a vicious yank. "I'll take care of this slime for you, Ms. Shellwin."

"And I'll call the police," I said. "There's another one."

THE MOOD AT ALCOTT the next day was somber and tense, practically funereal. Everyone was appalled at what had happened at our school. After all, any one of them could have been a victim of Carl Hogan's madness.

There was talk about Carl following in his bad sheep brother's footsteps and speculation about his family life and his future.

McGregor was a sudden new hero. I was poor Linnet Shellwin who was holding up well, considering.

To my chagrin, nobody thought of me as a heroine.

In the morning, before the first bell, I met Lieutenant Dalton Gray of the Maple Creek Police Department in Mr. Dunlap's office. The principal looked drawn and pale, not his usual buoyant self.

"We caught the other boy," Lieutenant Gray said with grim intensity. "He tried to hide out in a video store. They're both in custody. We have enough to hang them."

I looked at him, startled by his choice of words.

"Well, not literally." His grim expression softened with a half smile. "I'll be in to talk to your fourth hour class later on today," he said.

"Good. I've always wished I could have a policeman aide."

His smile widened. "I don't plan on changing jobs, Ms. Shellwin."

"Maybe you can find out who else was involved," I said.

I was convinced that Carl and Adam hadn't acted alone in hatching their plot. I remembered Jimmy and Dale pleading with me to let them miss the assembly and do their English homework. How odd was that! And the purse that had saved my life. It belonged to Sherry. Had she truly forgotten it or left it behind as a decoy?

In truth, my suppositions didn't make sense. How could the presence of Jimmy and Dale have aided Carl? Everyone knew that teachers were the last to leave their rooms. The purse would only take me a minute to retrieve.

But I couldn't change the way I felt. Every unusual detail fed my growing paranoia.

After lunch, Lieutenant Gray stood in front of my class looking tall and powerful in his uniform, trying to impress on them the gravity of what had occurred. The room had never been so quiet except when it was empty.

"Two boys ruined their lives because of a senseless violent act," he said. "Now they have to pay the price, and it's going to be high."

He encouraged anyone with information about possible accomplices to contact him at the police station, assuring them that no names would be revealed.

It was all very official.

The faces that swam before my eyes were pale, with shocked expressions. But I couldn't look at a single boy or girl who had ever caused trouble in my class and wonder if he or she had had a hand in planning my demise.

Candace Ann raised her hand. "We're sorry, Miss Shellwin."

"Yeah, you're nice, kind of," Jimmy added.

"Thank you," I said faintly.

"Does anyone have any questions?" Lieutenant Gray asked. "Anything to add?"

An uneasy silence greeted his questions. Who would speak up in class? We'd see if this Secret Witness program yielded any names.

I walked out to the hall with Lieutenant Gray. He laid his hand on my shoulder and said in a low voice, "This must have been an ordeal for you, Miss Shellwin. Throwing that purse at the Hogan boy was inspired. Dangerous though. *You* could have stopped that bullet instead of the window."

He had said something similar yesterday. Now that we were alone in the hall, I had a regrettable urge to throw myself into his strong arms and cry and keep crying until my eyes ached. I couldn't do that. I'd only just met him. Besides, I had two more classes to teach. One more rule: Never show them a sign of weakness.

Instead I said, "I didn't have time to think. I just acted. What's going to happen to Carl and Adam?"

"They're underage. They'll be tried as juveniles, and suspended, of course."

"Carl would have killed me," I said. "Shot me, stuffed my body in a plastic bag, and then what? What was the rope for, I wonder?"

He shook his head. "We can only guess. Adam appears to have been the mastermind, but the plan wasn't very well thought out. How were they going to get the body—that is, you—out of the building? How would they dispose of it?"

His words reminded me anew of my narrow escape. I felt ice cubes forming in my veins again.

"Carl was the kid with the gun," Lieutenant Gray said. "He says they only meant to scare you."

"Well, he accomplished that. He said something about

walling me up alive in the closet, of all places. We'd just finished Poe's *The Cask of Amontillado.* But then he had the gun."

"Put them out of your mind," Lieutenant Gray said. "They won't bother you again." He gestured toward the half open door of my room. "You have a lively group in there."

"They're too lively."

He smiled, and I noticed that his eyes were as blue as cornflowers. My favorite color, one of my favorite flowers. Yesterday I must have been in shock because I didn't notice anything about Lieutenant Gray except that he was the law and had guns of his own. I had felt safe then; I felt safe now.

"Don't make the mistake of blaming the whole class for what two individuals did," he said. "I don't think anyone else was involved."

I did. That was why I'd told Milla that I was the teacher whose class tried to kill her.

I realized that Lieutenant Gray's hand still lay on my shoulder.

A buzz erupted in my classroom. It was loud but not the usual fourth hour roar. Lieutenant Gray's power and hold over them appeared to be wearing off.

"They shouldn't be left alone," I said. "Not even for a minute."

"I'll see you again, Linnet." The lieutenant walked briskly down the hall to the staircase, and I went back into the room.

They wanted to talk about the incident. I didn't. I yearned for routine and longed to escape into the orderly world of Dickens where children knew their place. But we couldn't pretend that nothing had happened. So we talked. A little.

"What's going to happen to Carl and Adam?" Dale wanted to know.

"I'm not sure. We'll have to wait and see."

"They shouldn't have done that."

"No. It was foolish and self-destructive."

"My purse saved the day," Sherry said, not even trying to

disguise the pride in the role she had inadvertently played in the drama.

"Yes, Sherry, it made an excellent weapon."

They laughed. For once we seemed to be on the same wave length, my class and I. Sadly, even that was suspicious.

I had offered to replace Sherry's nail polish and necklace, but she declined with an unaccustomed blush. "That's okay, Miss Shellwin. I have a new bottle at home and those beads were already broken."

"Do you like Lieutenant Gray?" Brandy asked with a sly grin.

"I don't *know* Lieutenant Gray," I said. "He seems nice enough."

"Well I do," Brandy announced. "He's cute."

"Let's..." I searched my mind for my day's lesson plan. What were we going to do? Read. What page? Usually I wrote it down on a post-it note. I'd forgotten to do that yesterday. I'd forgotten all of my rules.

"We left off on Chapter 10," Candace Ann said.

"Yes. Chapter 10." I opened my book.

That was the last time I spoke about the Plot in class but certainly not the last time I thought about it, and one night, soon after that day, I had a dream. I stood alongside Farmer Jones from George Orwell's *Animal Farm.* All the barnyard animals were advancing on me with unadulterated hatred in their eyes. Suddenly Farmer Jones vanished, and I was alone. The animals turned into the members of my fourth hour class.

Unlike most nightmares, this one stayed in my memory.

SIX

DURING MY SHORT WALK HOME, the sky had darkened perceptibly, and the air smelled of rain. Puffed-up gray clouds appeared to lean heavily on the treetops. They threatened to burst at any moment.

That was a teacher's life in Maple Creek. Always under a cloud.

As I approached my house, I spied a solitary man standing in the driveway, his eyes riveted on a point high above the weeping cherry tree. He was staring at the Valentine window. Passersby frequently stopped to admire it, especially when sunlight turned the heart to pink fire.

Dressed in blue jeans, a fringed camel-colored vest, and a Stetson hat, the man looked like an actor who had wandered away from a western movie set. He was a dark and handsome stranger whose deeply tanned complexion attested to hours under a hot sun.

My heart began to pound. I didn't see a nearby car with an out-of-state license plate. Perhaps the stranger was only taking a walking tour of the neighborhood, but the fact that he was standing on my property, that he was observing my house with such intense scrutiny, made me uneasy.

As I came up beside him, I said, "Can I help you find someone?"

"I was just looking at the heart window." He glanced at the keys that I had begun to jingle. "I'm glad to see it's still there."

So he wasn't a stranger to Maple Creek.

"That's what first attracted me to the house," I said, beginning to relax a little. "That and its soft pink color. Did you used to live in Maple Creek?"

"Once. I've been out of touch for a while. Where did Ms. Julaine move to?"

I told him what little I knew of her murder, adding that her killer remained at large.

A look of shock crossed his face. "I can't believe it! Ms. Julaine never hurt anyone. She was the kind of lady who would shoo a moth outside instead of squashing it."

"I wish I'd known her," I said.

"When I was a kid, I used to deliver papers here. She always gave me a generous tip and a glass of lemonade on a hot day."

Raindrops splashed down on my head and arms, large warm splatters. I was curious about the stranger. Who was he and why had he come back to Maple Creek? But it began to rain in earnest, and the man said, "I hope the cops catch the scum who killed Ms. Julaine and lock him away for life."

We parted then, he walking briskly into the rain, I cutting across my lawn and hurrying up the walkway to the porch.

Only a little wet, I stood in the vestibule, savoring the knowledge that I was home. The house always seemed to welcome me at the end of the workday, offering balm to a survivor of the school wars.

I dropped my purse on the sofa and switched on the fan. Its blades began to turn, coaxing the still warm air into motion. As the soothing whirr worked its spell, I stopped obsessing about fourth hour's mean plan and wondered how to fill the hours of a long rainy evening.

Nothing came to mind except reading, my favorite pastime on a night like this.

In the kitchen, I filled the teakettle with water and set it on the stove to boil, as I did every afternoon after school. Then I searched the refrigerator for a substantial leftover from an earlier meal. Nothing appealed to me, and I didn't want to go back out in the rain. So, what was I going to eat?

I sat at my kitchen table and contemplated the sugar bowl and creamer as if they held the answer. Gradually, my mind drifted from lackluster dinner choices to Violet Julaine's deadly Valentine gift.

I imagined her exclaiming in delight over the tarts and deciding to sample them without delay. I could see her scooping out a cherry with her fork, turning the fork sideways and cutting through the crust. One bite. Delicious. Another bite and another until all that remained on the plate were crumbs and thick cherry syrup.

How long did it take arsenic to kill its victim?

Eventually Violet would have felt ill. Not suspecting that she had been poisoned, she might have started to call a friend or her doctor. Tansy Stewart had found the receiver dangling off the hook. Either Violet had changed her mind or the sickness had begun to overtake her.

I could visualize the scene, as if it were a movie reel unrolling in my mind. The film had a red tint, the color of fresh blood.

Outside, intermittent thunder crashes reinforced the lurid image. Rain battered the windows, pounded on the roof, and gushed down from the gutters, no doubt creating a small lake around the house's foundation. I could see that, too, without looking out the window.

When Violet ate her poisoned tart, it was snowing. Cold and snow keep people inside, or she might have sought help at an urgent care center. Instead, she had gone into her bedroom on this very floor, lain down without undressing, and died. Although dead and buried, she still seemed to hover around the table where I sat, recreating her last night.

Never eat anything you haven't prepared yourself, she might have said. *Not even if a friend gives it to you.*

I didn't think I would.

In spite of Alcott's strict policy on eating outside the cafeteria, kids always wanted to bring food to class. Candace Ann's birthday brownies. Cookies and candy to share with their friends and the teacher. A cake to celebrate the end of the school year. But surely no one at Alcott would initiate another killing plot. The new plan was just plain mean.

Surely I could deal with mean. But why had I come full circle back to vindictive freshmen with too much time on their hands?

The phone rang.

Well, why not? A phantom phone call was a perfect way to end a strange day.

Quickly I picked up the receiver, said "Hello" loudly, and prepared to talk to the air.

This time was different. The line was alive, bristling with static. I heard a voice or thought I did. Then it faded, along with the static, both of them swallowed up by a force I couldn't understand. I hadn't been able to make out actual words. Not *Hello*, or *Is this Linnet?* Or even *I think I dialed the wrong number.*

After waiting for several minutes, I finally hung up, but I wasn't as befuddled as I'd been previously. Somebody had placed the call and tried to communicate with me. The possibility of contact and an explanation existed now, even though the phone was still disconnected…

But… How could that be? I picked up the receiver again. The static was gone; the dead air back. The voice might have been a figment of my imagination.

For the love of God…

No. This was the devil's work.

The thunder rolled in, crashing directly over the roof. As lightning slashed the sky, I remembered that talking on a landline telephone in a storm could be dangerous.

Of course I wasn't really talking to anyone.

I slammed the receiver down in its cradle, not caring if it broke, frustrated that I had missed what might have been an important message and a chance to solve the mystery.

Suddenly I wanted above all to hear the shrill ringing again.

We had unfinished business, the phone and I. As with my fourth hour class, meeting it head on was the best strategy.

I FOUND MY DINNER in a plate of cold cuts and an evening's activity in the room where Violet Julaine had died. It was now crammed with boxes from the move, each one neatly labeled. I decided to start unpacking my college books, a tedious chore I'd postponed for weeks.

While the storm continued to rumble and electrify the sky, I dusted paperbacks and carried them into the smallest room in the house, the one I'd set aside as my study.

One of the boxes was labeled Discard. It wasn't mine.

Curiosity overcame tedium as I pulled it under the overhead light and pried open the top. Inside I found a red and pink jumble of small objects. A cursory examination revealed that they were all in some way flawed.

A tiny teapot without its lid. A three-dimensional picture of Cupid, with a chunk broken off from its gold leaf frame. A white china heart box on which perched one dove where formerly there'd been two. Miscellaneous Valentine figurines, all chipped. A wooden music box lying upside down.

This I turned right side up and gasped in delight at the illustration on the top. The Queen of Hearts stood over a table in the castle kitchen, spooning cherries into shells, while the Knave of Hearts peered through a window, his roguish eyes fixed on the delicacies. He looked a little like Ned.

Tiny valentine hearts bordered the picture. According to the faded writing on the bottom, the music box's tune was *Believe Me If All Those Endearing Young Charms*.

I turned the wind-up mechanism, eager to hear that haunting love song again, but it reached a certain point and would go no further. Its music days were over, but it could still hold small valuables.

I lifted the lid. Inside on the white velvet that lined the interior lay a small heart pin with dark red stones and a broken clasp.

This was exquisite.

I set the pin on my knee. Surely a jeweler could fix the clasp. Perhaps whoever had tossed the little heart into the Discard pile hadn't taken the time to examine it carefully. It looked valuable. Could those stones be garnets or rubies?

I lifted the pin to the light. No, they must be red glass. Besides, who throws away gems when they could be reset?

Idly I shifted through the rest of the objects. Most of them could be repaired or recycled, and the chips on the figurines were hardly noticeable.

As if responding to a silent lure, I came back to the music box. *The Queen of Hearts/She baked some tarts...* Cherry, of course. No other kind would do. As I pondered hearts and tarts and the Knave who resembled Ned, a strange idea slipped into my mind. Maybe it wasn't so strange.

Could this music box be a clue to Violet Julaine's murder, one overlooked by the police because to connect it to the murder required a modicum of imagination?

Suppose Violet's killer had given her two presents, the cherry tarts and a music box that played a sentimental love song, intending the second gift to foreshadow her death. And she would never suspect it.

That was fiendish, but then a person who could concoct such a murder was a fiend.

The next time I saw Lieutenant Gray, I'd show it to him. It was possible that the killer's fingerprints were still on the surface.

Yawning and out of the mood to dust books and sift through a dead woman's possessions, I slipped the pin into my pocket and set the music box aside. Clue or not, if Violet Julaine's heir had intended to discard these particular items, I could help myself to them with impunity.

In the meantime, the music box would add a unique, whimsical touch to my coffee table, and the little heart pin, repaired and cleaned, would brighten any one of my dresses or sweaters.

As for the rest, they were Violet Julaine's broken treasures. I planned to make sure they stayed in her house. She would be pleased about that.

"A VALENTINE MUSIC BOX," said Tansy Stewart the next afternoon as we sat on my front porch. Her gaze kept straying to the open door. "I'd love to see it."

"Let's go inside, then. It's on the coffee table."

She fidgeted with the pillow on the back of the wicker chair. "I don't think so, Linnet. I promised myself I wouldn't."

"Well you shouldn't have done that. Violet's gone. I live here now."

"But I remember everything so clearly. It was so—ghastly."

She was about to change her mind. I could tell by the hungry gleam in her dark eyes. I guessed that Tansy liked to know everything about everybody in the neighborhood. I was the newest neighbor. That I happened to live in the forbidden house had kept her away until now.

"I could bring it out here if you're afraid..."

"Maybe I'll just step into the living room," she said. "But not the kitchen and not the bedroom. I still have nightmares about finding poor Violet there."

"It isn't a bedroom anymore," I said. "It's filled with boxes."

"I guess it'd be okay. Just for a few minutes."

Everybody has hang-ups, I thought, understanding Tansy's reluctance to enter the house where she'd discovered her friend's body. But this one was unhealthy. Fortunately she appeared ready to move beyond it.

I opened the screen door and gestured for her to go inside first.

She did, slowly, and stood in the vestibule, gazing around in wonder. "Oh, my. This is so airy and cool. So simple."

"Well, I haven't finished decorating."

"I meant simple in a good way. When Violet lived here, every room was cluttered. She started collecting Valentine memorabilia years ago and never stopped. The house was bursting at the seams. It was almost claustrophobic. One or two distinctive pieces—that's the way to go."

We sat on the sofa, and I handed her the music box. She stared at the picture, frowned, and quickly set it back on the coffee table as if she was afraid it would grow teeth and bite her.

"Don't you like it?" I asked.

"It's a handsome piece, but… Well, cherry tarts. It reminds me of the murder."

"Me too. Everything will, if you let it."

"There's something else," Tansy said. "This is the first time I've seen it."

"When the music stopped playing, maybe Violet didn't want to keep it on display."

"Violet liked to fix broken things. She never threw anything away if she could help it. I meant that I never saw it here, and we were in and out of each other's houses all the time."

"There's no telling when it broke," I said, loath to latch on to another mystery. Still, didn't Tansy's insistence that she hadn't seen the music box before support my theory that it had been a gift?

"Cherry tarts! This is too much of a coincidence. It gives me the creeps. Oh, I'm not criticizing your taste, Linnet. Don't think that."

I smiled to let her know I wasn't offended. "I like it, and the little hearts complement the house."

"It's pretty enough, but there's something funny about it," Tansy said. "If you don't see it now, you will."

After Tansy went home to tend to her own baking—whole wheat loaves in a bread making machine—the Valentine music box kept drawing my attention to itself. Furthermore, it seemed to have acquired a soft pink glow, like an aura.

Sheer imagination, I told myself. *It's just a pretty trinket. The illusion of a halo comes from all the pinks and reds in the picture, combined with the light through the window.*

Tansy could be right. It was compelling. Maybe I should move it to a less visible place.

And what would that accomplish?

In truth, I was in a mood for wild imaginings. Fourth Hour had been too subdued today. Jimmy, Dale, and their cohorts had outdone themselves to be cooperative. The class was actually—almost—orderly. I was waiting for the ax to fall. Or was it the other shoe?

Something was going to happen soon. Either at my home or my school. I knew it and intended to be prepared.

SEVEN

CAN YOU EVER PREPARE for an irate parent who appears unannounced at your classroom door? One who claims that you are to blame because her son got into a scuffle with another boy and knocked you into the closet door when you attempted to separate them?

The incident happened in fifth hour, twenty-five minutes earlier. I'd recovered my equilibrium and sent both boys to the principal's office with disciplinary referrals. The boys arrived; the referrals didn't.

Now here was Tina Donnell, red-faced and breathing heavily in the heat like a dragon filling the air with fire. She must have run all the way from her house to Alcott.

"You should be keeping better order in your classes, Ms. Shellwin," she said. "My Oliver doesn't get into fights."

A plump middle-aged woman whose frizzy coppery red hair clashed with the ruddy blotches in her face, Mrs. Donnell paused to take a breath. Her Kelly green shorts, too tight for her massive hips, must have been cutting off her circulation. I glanced down at her sandals. No doubt intended to be fashionable with straps crisscrossing their way up to her knees, they resembled alligator feet.

"Did you check in at the front office, Mrs. Donnell?" I asked. "That's the procedure. After you do that, the secretary gives you a visitor's pass and an office aide escorts you to your destination."

That was the school's ironclad rule, designed to prevent angry persons from wandering freely through the halls of Alcott. It protected staff and students alike. Legitimate passes were bright blue plastic rectangles. If Mrs. Donnell had one, I couldn't see it.

"I'm a taxpayer, Ms. Shellwin," she said, "which means I'm part owner of this school. If it wasn't for me, you wouldn't be making the big bucks."

"I pay taxes, too," I felt compelled to add.

"And I don't expect to have my kid beaten up by a bully or suspended because of a teacher's incompetence."

Two years of teaching had given me experience in holding on to my temper. "Neither boy was beaten up," I said. "I'm the one who was pushed into the door."

She didn't react to that detail.

"That's my point, Ms. Shellwin. If you kept your students in their seats and busy, this wouldn't have happened. My Oliver never got in trouble with a teacher before."

I sensed that she wanted to say more, perhaps add a snide reminder that I'd allowed my students to get out of control before. That one of them had tried to kill me.

What was stopping her?

"Oliver needs to be challenged," she said. "He needs to be *taught*."

Keep cool. Be polite. Don't let her see that she's upsetting you. That's the only way to come out ahead in this scrimmage.

I glared at her but didn't say anything. She stopped to catch her breath, waited for her words to sink in.

I let them fly past me and out the window. It was futile to argue with a woman who could see only one side of an issue—that of her precious son.

In any verbal attack, such as this, a teacher could generally count on the physical and emotional support of the principal or his assistant. No doubt aware of that, Mrs. Donnell had panted her way up the staircase to my room alone. Even now, I could insist that we move this impromptu meeting to the front office, but I felt that she was about to end her tirade.

After all, what else could she say? Endless repetitions of the same grievances in different words?

"So it's my fault I got caught in the crossfire," I said, hoping she was capable of detecting sarcasm. "I'll try to keep Oliver and Terry on a shorter leash."

Oh no. Wrong choice of words.

She cast me a look of pure venom. "You do that, Ms. Shellwin. You try. Our district has always had an A#1 reputation. It only takes one rotten apple to spoil the barrel."

The rotten apple being me, I assumed, not young Oliver Donnell.

She stalked out of the room with a parting threat, or what sounded like one. "We'll see what the Board thinks of these shenanigans."

When all was quiet again, when the *clop clop clop* of her footsteps had faded, I closed the windows, gathered my grade book and purse, took one last look around the room and locked the door.

Another day down.

Suddenly I remembered Candace Ann. She had failed to appear for our private tutoring session after school yesterday and had been absent today. Chances were she wasn't coming, but if she showed up, she'd know where to find me. I walked downstairs to the first floor, feeling freer with every step.

And with every step, I thought of a snappy retort I might have made, while imagining Mrs. Donnell's kelly green shorts shrinking and shrinking until they squeezed the breath out of her.

I hadn't handled that confrontation as well as I might have.

Dealing diplomatically with parents was an essential part of a teacher's job, sometimes more difficult than dealing with their offspring. Would Tina Donnell really take her complaint about me to the Board of Education? If she did, I knew I could count on the principal as an ally. But any hint of trouble would revive memories of the Plot and lead to more unpleasantness.

I hated to have people talking about me, hated that my hip hurt when I moved, and hated the bruise that I hadn't seen yet.

I remembered then that I hadn't told Mrs. Donnell about the disciplinary referrals that had disappeared. It would be interesting to see how she reacted to the assistant principal's brand of discipline. He tended to be touchy about students tearing up official documents.

Desperately needing a respite from the school madness that surrounded me, I headed for the teachers' lounge.

Three fans, strategically placed in this spacious room, created a cool, restful sanctuary in the middle of the school. No students nor parents with grudges allowed. Only teachers and the custodians who kept it clean and neat.

Long glossy tables and soft leather couches with matching chairs invited teachers to socialize or work in an atmosphere of peace before going on to their next class. For those of us with sixth hour conference periods, the next stop was home. What I liked best, though, was the view of the hill that sloped gently down to little-traveled Quincy Road.

This afternoon, Marellen, who taught American history, sat reading Milla Schoenherr's romance, *Capture My Heart,* while Jody, a veteran math teacher, punched keys on a calculator. Mrs. Crumle, who also taught history—no one ever called her Eloise—corrected papers. Her red pen flew over the paragraphs leaving them sliced and diced. Conrad and Al, both in the Science Department, were drinking coffee and reading the *Free Press* sports section. Occasionally they exchanged heated opinions on the Tigers baseball team.

I had arrived unencumbered with books or folders. My review and final exams were finished, awaiting duplication in the office. Even if I had schoolwork to take home, I wouldn't have done it. I deserved a free evening after the encounter with Oliver's mother.

At the pop machine, I put my quarters in the change slot and selected root beer. I caught the bottle in mid-tumble and took it to a chair under the windows. One long sip of the icy drink revived me. Another made me feel that the day might still hold something good.

Jody looked up from her calculations. "You look upset, Linnet. Did you have more trouble with fourth hour?"

Since the Plot, my fellow teachers had adopted a mother hen attitude toward me. They responded to every sign of anxiety, however mild, with empathy and practical advice.

"No, but I just had a run-in with Oliver Donnell's mother," I said. "She's the most unpleasant person I've ever met."

"She's downright nasty. We call her Tina the Terrible."

"She didn't bother to get a visitors' pass," I added.

"You should report her," Marellen said. "Why aren't those hall monitors patrolling the doors?"

Conrad looked up from the paper. "They're taking an ice cream break at Dairy Land."

"That's how Mrs. Donnell operates," Jody said. "She throws all the blame back on you before she knows the full story and even when she does, her precious little Oliver is never wrong. What did he do this time?"

I told them, and Jody frowned. "Don't try to come between two fighting kids, Linnet. You could have fallen on that slippery floor."

I hadn't thought of that. How easy it would have been to break my arm or hip. Then how would I be able to care for my new puppy?

"No kid would dare make me fall," Mrs. Crumle announced, looking up from her papers. "Nor would they start a scuffle in my class."

She wasn't being critical of my classroom management skills, merely stating a fact. I believed her.

"Leave the rough stuff to us men," Al said.

A policeman before becoming a teacher and coach, Al had broken up more than his share of brawls at Alcott where fighting was strictly forbidden, although fights broke out all the time.

"There weren't any men around at the time, but don't worry. I learned my lesson."

"What was the fight about?" Al asked.

"They wouldn't say. I'm assuming it was about nothing in particular. Only a primitive male desire to scuffle."

Even though it was too hot and sticky for physical contact. But maybe teenaged boys didn't think about humidity and discomfort.

"I'm glad Mrs. Donnell didn't have a gun," I said. Then I remember her oversized striped tote. "Maybe she did."

Jody shook her head. "Two murder attempts on the same teacher in two months. It's unlikely."

"But not impossible."

"We need better security in this building," Marellen said.

She was our building's Michigan Education Association representative, always looking for ways to improve working conditions for teachers.

"The Donnell woman is always looking to stir up trouble," she added. "I tangled with her myself during Open House."

"She didn't come to see me at the last one," I said.

Marellen rolled her eyes. "Well, Oliver is an all 'A' student."

We had talked the incident quite literally to death. I leaned back on soft leather and thought about summer. Warm sunshine, a sandy beach, blue water, my puppy learning to swim. Quiet. Peace. And somewhere on the horizon, a man to share the liquid days and languid nights with me.

Which one? Since this was a daydream, I had three choices: A police lieutenant, a cowboy, and a knave.

Choose the knave, my heart whispered. *Ned the Knave.*

Sitting here, doing nothing, had a marvelous restorative effect on me. I swallowed the last of the root beer and set the bottle aside for the custodians who were always happy to collect the deposit money.

Mrs. Crumle took her red pen and papers and left the room. Marellen closed Milla's book, marking her place with the day's attendance list. I didn't have to look at the clock to know the hour was winding down.

At last the bell rang, ending another school day and ushering in a student stampede to the lockers. Ten minutes later, the hall outside the lounge was quiet.

Cheer up, I told myself. *Only a few more days.*

Then *No more classes,/No more books,/No more students' dirty looks.*

The happy little rhyme accompanied me all the way home.

AFTER DINNER—a ham sandwich and doughnut tonight—I liked to stroll through my backyard and check the progress of the perennials that had reseeded themselves in past seasons. Then, if I was in the mood for solitude, I'd sit on the back porch or on the front porch if I wanted company.

This afternoon I craved solitude, but Bonita had come out to plant red impatiens around her shrubs. I always enjoyed talking to her. She never failed to inquire about my experiences at Alcott and always announced that she could never be a teacher. Not in a million years, not for a million dollars a year. She regarded me with awe.

I'd told her about Tina Donnell's attack and immediately the incident began to grow a little less devastating. With luck, I would never have to deal with Tina Donnell again, unless she had younger children. Or unless she took her complaint about me to the Board of Education. In the meantime, she didn't exist in my quiet green world with its rustling leaves and mixed floral scents.

"I'm going to have a slew of black-eyed Susans," I said, examining one of the tall hardy plants that reached up to my chest.

Bonita got up and peered over the fence. "They're pink coneflowers, Linnet, and those tall plants in front are balloon flowers. I remember when Violet planted them. They were small and there weren't so many."

"They should bloom soon," I said. "I'd like to plant a few flowers, but with a new puppy, that's asking for trouble."

"When are you getting her?" Bonita asked.

"This Friday. I didn't want to drive all the way up to Ludington alone, and the breeder, Sandra Weston, is attending a dog show in Ohio this weekend. She'll deliver the puppy right to my doorstep."

Bonita went back to her planting. She was a master at multitasking. "Haven't you seen her yet?" she asked.

"Only on the computer screen. She's a little doll. She has the sweetest face. Her coat is the color of butterscotch or caramel with more white on one side of her collar than the other. She has a swirl on her shoulder. Sandra says she's smart and has loads of personality."

I stopped, realizing that I was bombarding Bonita with information in response to her simple question, but she seemed to be interested.

"Are you going to name her Butterscotch?" she asked.

"No, that's too long a name for a baby."

"Buttercup then?"

"Too cute. Her name is Caramel."

Bonita kindly refrained from pointing out that butterscotch and caramel were similar in color and each had three syllables.

"That's wonderful, Linnet," she said. "You'll have all summer with her."

While I'd been extolling the virtues of the puppy, Bonita had planted half a flat of impatiens. They were scarlet. The deep, rich color contrasted beautifully with the various shades of green in her yard.

Next year Caramel would be old enough to respect flowerbed boundaries. I could plant an old-fashioned garden then.

Inside the house, the phone began to ring. Imperious rings blasted through the open windows, demanding immediate attention. The sound had never seemed so loud; it was as if someone had turned the volume to high.

I'd been hoping the mysterious caller would try to contact me again, and here I was in the middle of the yard.

"I guess I'll let it ring," I said.

Bonita looked up from her plantings. "Let what ring?"

"That's my phone. Why does it always wait till I'm outside or away to ring?"

"I don't hear a phone," she said.

Her words dropped into the silence like stones raining on concrete.

Three additional loud, impossible-not-to-hear rings, and they stopped.

"It rang," I said, my tone ragged. "Six or eight times at least. You must have heard it."

"Sorry. I didn't." She mounded fresh dirt around three impatiens plants and reached for her watering can. "But if it's important, they'll call back."

"Yes. Probably."

There was no point in going inside now. I walked around to the front porch and flopped down in the wicker chair, feeling oddly drained. This was a time for company, but no one was strolling by on the sidewalk eager for an idle chat.

My thoughts were a jumble, impossible to untangle. All I knew for certain was that Bonita hadn't heard the phone ring, and I had. How could that be?

EIGHT

I SAT ON THE FRONT PORCH until the light began to fade, taking with it the oppressive heat. In the hours before dusk, the strollers appeared, singly and in pairs, walking dogs or pushing baby carriages, sometimes doing both at the same time. No one appeared to be in a hurry.

Although the phone didn't ring again, I could think of little else. If Bonita, separated from me by a mere picket fence, hadn't heard it, that could only mean I'd imagined everything—phone, static, and voice.

Well, if there was no mysterious caller on the other end of the line—if there wasn't even a line—then I didn't have anything to worry about. Except my mental health.

How many teachers had been driven over the proverbial edge by packs of wild freshmen?

I called up my mental calendar, which offered a mix of good and bad. Tomorrow and Friday were set aside for review in all of my classes. Monday and Tuesday were exam days when the classroom atmosphere would shift slightly, for better or worse. Longer sessions meant more blocks of time to keep my groups in control.

Next Wednesday and Thursday were teacher work days. Quiet days. Along with correcting exams and figuring out grades, we could count on departmental meetings, long restaurant lunches, and a festive air. Then Friday was a half day of last-minute work and short meetings, after which we were free to begin our summer vacations.

Four more days with students. I could deal with that—and with Jimmy and Dale and even Tina the Terrible if she made a return appearance. But that hunk of black plastic on my kitchen wall, that shrill-voiced, capricious harbinger of good or ill that apparently rang only for me… How could anyone be expected to cope with the unfathomable?

At the moment I didn't know.

Take it apart? Dissect it? See what makes it tick?

I amused myself with thoughts of the phone lying on the kitchen table thoroughly disabled, its wires cut, its constantly twisting cord stuffed in the trash can.

Could my landline problem be so easily solved?

Probably not. Suppose I dismantled the phone and it still rang?

That was a tired thought, a nightmare scenario, not the best kind to have before retiring. I'd better get ready for bed so I could be up early and bright—I hoped—to face my classes and be on the alert for signs of the mean plan.

I got up slowly, wanting nothing more than to sink back down again into the puffy pillow that made the wicker seat so soft.

"Hey, Linnet."

I recognized Milla Schoenherr's voice before I saw her, although we'd only met one time. She was in front of Bonita's house, rapidly closing the distance to mine. Even in aqua Capri pants and a ruffled white top, she managed to look elegant. As soon as she came to a stop, her silvery blond hair fell obligingly into place.

"Are you going in?" she asked.

"I'm thinking about it."

"On such a gorgeous evening? I like to enjoy every second of light and warmth."

So did I, now that company had arrived. "Won't you sit down for a while?" I asked.

"Thanks. I was running, or rather walking fast. Young women run. Not so young women amble or stroll. Violet and I used to walk together every morning in the summer from six to seven. Then we'd reward ourselves with tea and doughnuts."

I smiled. "That's my idea of exercise."

Milla settled herself comfortably in the matching wicker chair. She glanced at the basket where *Capture My Heart* lay on top of *Michigan Home*. I wished I'd read a little of it, at least the beginning.

"I love the grand old Victorians on this street," she said. "Violet's house—sorry, *your* house—is one is one of the most attractive."

"Do you live near here?" I asked.

"Over on Park Street. I have a small brick ranch. It's very ordinary. No pretty embellishments. You'll have to come visit me when school's out. We'll have a tea party."

That reminded me of Milla's fortune telling.

"I met a dark and handsome stranger the other day," I said. "He was in my driveway, admiring the Valentine window, but I didn't get his name."

"You will the next time you see him." Milla's blue eyes sparkled as if the upcoming meeting were her own. "We'll definitely have to consult the tea leaves again. What else have you been up to?"

I told her about the boys' scuffle, my collision with the closet door, and Tina Donnell's veiled threat to report me to the Board of Education.

"Don't give her a second thought," Milla said. "She's all blather. Tina Donnell likes to think she's an asset to the district because she headed a few successful fundraisers. The lady's a liability, always ready to stir up trouble for somebody."

"I'm so tired of discipline problems and overly protective parents."

"That's why we teachers have summers off. To relax and unwind. It takes until the end of August to be completely rejuvenated, and remember, the troublemakers all grow up. If you happen to meet them in later years, they might recall those pranks fondly. As an added bonus, they might look older than you."

Milla smiled, as if remembering a highlight from her past. "I had a class in rebellion once. English Literature. All seniors.

One day they walked out of the room and went to the cafeteria to sit and drink pop. All thirty of them. There I was at my desk all alone."

"How embarrassing for you," I said. "How did it turn out?"

"They were as organized as any union. Unfortunately for them, they didn't have a union's clout. The assistant principal marched them back. He suspended six who refused to move."

"What did you do when they were all in class again?"

"I went on with the day's lesson, the last act of *Macbeth*. This happened in October, and they never did settle down, but we managed to form a truce of sorts. Then there was another time with a wild sophomore class…"

Milla halted her reminiscences in mid-sentence. All the rosy exercise-induced color seemed to drain from her face at once.

A burly, dark-bearded man and a young woman with long black hair were coming down the street. The man gripped the leash of a black Belgian shepherd in one hand. The other rested possessively on the shoulder of his companion.

The bearded man nodded to us, his expression unreadable. The dog tugged on the lead, tail held straight, eyes blazing. He was a step away from lunging at us.

"Tac!" the bearded man said in a gruff, no-nonsense voice, and the dog fell back in step with his master. To us, the woman murmured, "Nice evening, isn't it?" But she didn't wait for a response, and the trio walked on toward Main Street.

"I'm getting my new puppy in a few days," I said. "I'll have to watch out for that hairy monster. The dog I mean."

Milla, who had fallen silent, fumbled with the ruffle on her neckline.

"Do you know them?" I asked.

"I've seen the woman walking in the neighborhood. The man's her boyfriend, I guess. He looks rather rough and ready. It must be the beard."

None of this explained Milla's sudden discomfiture. The color still hadn't returned to her face.

"It's almost dark," she said. "I'd better head on home."

"Thanks for the pep talk. I feel better about those wretched boys and even Mrs. Donnell."

"Any time," she said. "Most school upheavals aren't the end of the world."

I watched Milla walk down the street, back in the direction from which she'd come, until she was a blue-green blur in the distance.

I really *did* feel better. If only I could have told Milla about my other concern, the whacked-out landline.

But no one could ever know about that.

THE NEXT DAY DAWNED with a burning sun in a cloudless sky. The weather forecasters sounded the alarm with frightening solemnity. Heat wave! Hazy, hot, and humid. Ozone action day. Their advice was predictable and grounded in common sense. Drink plenty of liquids. Keep pets indoors or in the shade and provide them with fresh water. A cooling center was open twenty-four hours in the basement of St. Perpetua's Church.

In musty old school buildings without air-conditioning, do your best.

Because the authors of the Alcott dress code had forbidden students to wear tank tops, I needed to set a good example. After a breakfast of cinnamon rolls and orange juice, I slipped into one of my favorite dresses. Sleeveless with tiny bouquets on a peach background, it felt like silk. I brushed my hair back, secured it on either side with pearl barrettes and decided I could survive seven hours in a stuffy classroom.

Until I stepped inside Alcott, that is. The still, hot air smelled of bubblegum, chocolate, lemon furniture polish, and inexpensive perfume. It seemed to push back at me as I waded through wave after wave of heat. Even climbing the stairs to the second floor required an extra burst of energy.

It was much warmer up here on this level. Farther from the wide-open front doors and closer to the sun.

I unlocked my classroom door, dropped my purse in a desk drawer, and began opening windows. My room shared the teachers' lounge view of the downward-sloping hill with Quincy Road at its foot. Quincy led to Golden Lake, thirty miles to the west, a popular summer hangout for Maple Creek teens.

Oh to be going somewhere today! Not just anywhere. Up north to the lakeside cottage I didn't have yet. With a picnic basket of fruit and bottled water. With my new puppy sitting demurely in the passenger seat gazing out the window with wonder…

That was a fantasy for another day. Today I had work to do and only fifteen minutes before the official start of class.

Dust motes stirred lazily in the beams of sunlight as I moved from the front of the room to the back. The desk tops were as clean and shiny as if the custodian had just swept through the room with polish and cloth, and the floor had a new coat of wax.

The last window refused to open all the way. As I gave it a tug, a screw flew out and rolled across the floor. Carefully I pushed the window back in place. I'd better tape a note to it before someone, in a desperate quest for more air, pulled it out of its frame.

I knew that an oral warning would be soon forgotten.

A note on the window and another to the custodian to repair it. The day's announcements. Attendance slips. Where was my pen? I was always losing it.

The bell rang, the day began.

My first hour class, the smallest one with eighteen energetic young scholars, streamed into the room, most complaining bitterly about the heat, as I knew they would. The second and third hour students did the same. I had no major problems except for the ongoing dialogue about the cheap school district that couldn't even distribute fans to the sweltering children of Maple Creek.

Problems were more apt to break out in the afternoon classes, especially during fourth hour. Still, I fielded endless pleas to go to the drinking fountain. *(It's just right outside the door, Ms. Shellwin. You can watch me.)* I confiscated a forbidden water pistol. In third hour, two girls asked for passes to the office, claiming they felt ill.

I could sympathize with them. My thick dark hair lay heavily on my neck, and the peach dress, usually so cool and comfortable, seemed to draw the heat happily into its silky folds. I found myself wishing that, just for this week, the administration would lift the ban on pop in the classroom. I'd love a cold root beer or Vernors myself.

By lunchtime, the temperature must have climbed several degrees. I felt thoroughly wilted and was grateful for the maple trees that shaded the redwood benches.

Annabelle had taken a personal business day. I ate with Marellen and Jody, all of us lunching on cold salads and talking about the heat, wondering if today's temperature would break a record. We weren't so different from our students, after all.

Back in my room, I waited for the arrival of fourth hour, as always trying to ignore the apprehension that tied knots in my stomach at this time of day.

I shouldn't be a teacher, I thought. *I need a job with less tension. One with only a modicum of danger.*

Candace Ann slipped quietly into the room and set her books and notebooks down on her desk. "That's a pretty dress you have on, Ms. Shellwin."

"Why thank you, Candace Ann," I said. One sincere compliment should hold me until the last bell rang.

"I didn't hear anything more about the... You know," she said softly.

"Don't worry about it. I can handle anything."

If I said it aloud and often enough, maybe I'd believe it.

"I'm sorry I couldn't come after school the other day," she added.

She didn't offer an excuse. I didn't ask what had prevented her.

"Well, here's a crash course for you," I said. "Make sure every sentence you write has a subject and a verb. If either one is missing, you have a fragment. And those run-on's can be corrected by writing two separate sentences or using a semi-colon or connector like 'and' or 'but'."

She scribbled madly in her notebook as I talked.

"You know all this," I said. "You just have to proofread your work before handing it in."

"Can you give me an example of a run-on sentence?" she asked.

"Sure. *It's hot today we need a fan in the room.* Where would a new sentence start?"

"After today?"

"Right. Good."

"Yuk. Grammar." That was Jimmy stamping into the room with unnecessary noise. "It makes me want to barf."

"Naah." Dale followed him in. "It's that chicken goop they made us eat for lunch."

"Chicken à la king," said Candace Ann.

"It's too hot for English." Jimmy eyed the tall stack of packets intended for fourth hour. "Are those for us?" he asked.

"They're the review."

"Why is it so long?"

There was only one answer to that question. "Because the exam is long."

Basically, it revolved around *Great Expectations* with grammar and writing seamlessly and insidiously woven in: *Miss Haversham's wedding cake was old nobody wanted to eat it. Rewrite the sentence, correcting the error.*

I was proud of my creativity. My students, I was sure, didn't appreciate it. I should have presented the review questions to them as a game. Unfortunately, I wasn't a game person.

The rest of the class swarmed in, the noise level rose to the boiling point, and I braced myself for endless variations of the same lament: *It's hot in here.* Every student was a weather forecaster today.

As we made our way through the review, I watched carefully for the first signs of an uprising. For spells of unusual quiet or whispered instructions to "Pass it on." For any deviation from the norm, however insignificant it might seem.

What did fourteen-year-olds consider "mean"?

Milla's seniors had walked out of her classroom. Surely my freshmen would never be so daring. But if they did stage a similar protest, wouldn't that give Tina Donnell more ammunition to take to the Board?

Relax, I ordered myself. This wasn't the last day of school when, according to Candace Ann, the mean plan was scheduled for launch. There was still tomorrow and exam day.

Okay. On which day would it happen?

As the minutes ticked by, I *did* relax a little. I regarded the screamed-out responses to my questions as wild enthusiasm, stopped worrying about disorder and annoying Murielle across the hall, and waited for the bell to ring. Eventually it did, and when Bill, the bully, chased Azalea out the door, I let him go with an admonishment so mild it was lost in the general clamor.

NINE

THE STREAM OF COLD WATER hit my neck and trickled down my left arm. An angry exclamation died in my throat as I looked up. My assailant was Ned Glint, fellow teacher and longtime crush. He stood nonchalantly in the doorway of my classroom, armed with a water pistol. His gray eyes sparkled.

The last bell had rung five minutes ago, and everyone with the exception of Ned and myself had vanished from the hall, or so the silence suggested.

"That's mean, Ned," I said, opening my middle drawer. "I should report you to Dwight Dunlap."

"I couldn't resist. You looked so warm and uncomfortable sitting there shuffling your papers."

I patted at my arm and decided that the water felt good. "I'm entitled to look warm. It must be at least ninety degrees."

"Ninety-three. Boston cooler weather."

I whipped out my confiscated water gun, aimed it at Ned's face, and pulled the trigger. A few drops dripped down on my desk blotter. The original owner, Johnny Bartlett, had nearly emptied it.

"Always check to see that your weapon is loaded before you fire it," Ned said.

"Did you want something or are you roaming the halls in search of helpless victims to drown?" I asked.

"You helpless, Linnet? Ha! Seriously, we're having a meeting after school tomorrow. It'll be short. Fifteen minutes, tops. Can you make it?"

"I'll be there."

"That's two of us confirmed," he said with a grin. "My room.

Five after three. Bring the refreshments. I'd like chocolate-iced brownies."

I smiled at his audacity. "I'll bring myself."

Ned, I knew, was an excellent group leader, better by far than dour, dry Principal Dunlap whose meetings seemed to last forever. Ned would raid the pop machine in the teachers' lounge and haul out his private store of bottled water. We'd sit around his conference table, trade school anecdotes, and laugh. As fifteen minutes stretched to an hour, someone would remember that we had gathered in Ned's room to discuss the new course.

I stashed the reviews in the top drawer. "If you're leaving now, I'll walk out with you. Just wait a second." I closed the window nearest my desk.

"Here, I'll do that for you." He shoved the water pistol in his belt and closed the others. "You're not still concerned about Carl and Adam coming back, are you?"

I avoided giving him a direct answer. "Sometimes I feel isolated up here on the second floor."

"People tend to clear out pretty quickly," he said. "Except for Mrs. Crumle. She's taking apart her bulletin board."

"Already?"

"She likes to keep a dozen steps ahead of the rest of us. I'll bet she has her autumn leaves already cut out. No one would dare pull a gun on a teacher with Eloise Crumle in shouting distance. And don't forget. My room is just down the hall."

I knew that; still I worried when I was working alone in the room during my conference hour. On the other hand, I refused to let fear drive me down to the teachers' lounge every day.

"If something else was going to happen, it would have by now," Ned said.

"There's still the last day," I reminded him.

"The cops will patrol the lot as a precaution. Usually they focus on the high school, but our kids are getting livelier every year."

"And not necessarily in a good way."

I took my shoulder bag and grade book out of the top drawer, made sure the closet was locked, and walked with Ned out into the hall and down the stairs.

"Shouldn't you turn that water pistol over to Dunlap?" I asked.

"Shouldn't you turn in yours?"

"Darn. I left it in the room."

"I'm holding on to this one until the bitter end," he said.

At the foot of the stairs, Ned turned toward the front office. With a quick pat on my arm, he said, "See you tomorrow—with the brownies."

Brenda Carroll, the afternoon hall monitor, was sitting on a bench near the doorway reading *Capture My Heart*. "It's hot outside, Linnet," she said. "Be careful."

"I will," I said with a smile. "Is the book good?"

She grinned. "Good and steamy."

Since my Honda had air-conditioning, I would be cool for the short drive home. I checked to make sure no students were loitering in the parking lot, then opened the door and let the air circulate before getting inside.

The lighthearted encounter with Ned had been a rare and pleasant occurrence. Until we'd both volunteered to develop a new English-Business course for Alcott, whole weeks would pass with only occasional greetings in the hall. I'd admired Ned's blond good looks and quick wit from afar—at teachers' meetings and in passing. But I could have sworn that he hardly knew who I was.

Suddenly it seemed as if we were on our way to becoming friends, as if Ned had finally noticed me as a woman rather than the harried ninth grade English teacher. Who knew where that friendship would lead in the coming weeks?

There were six of us in the group, I reminded myself. One was Rae Allister, a vivacious single mother who brightened dangerously in the presence of a male.

Well I could be bright, too, if I tried. I thanked the Fates that had inspired me to volunteer for the project. Developing a relationship required time and proximity which the regular sessions would provide.

After all, I wasn't too old for a high school romance, although I suspected that my students would disagree with me. I could almost see them convulsed with laughter at the thought of Ms. Shellwin and Mr. Glint out on a date.

THE POLICE CRUISER PARKED in front of my house set off alarm bells. What had happened now?

Then I realized that the officer inside the car was Lieutenant Dalton Gray. The cruiser's windows were open. Nothing about Dalton's posture seemed official or suggested urgency.

He waved as I walked over to him. "Hi, Linnet. You gave me a rain check a few days back," he said. "How does tonight sound?"

"For a cup of coffee? I've been dreaming about something more in keeping with the season. Like ice-cold lemonade or a Coke."

"I can make that happen. How about a soft drink with dinner and a sundae after—to celebrate the end of school?"

"Well…" My hair felt like a damp mop; so did the rest of me. But I could easily change that, and the banter with Ned Glint had energized me. "It's not exactly the end of school yet, but that doesn't matter. What time?"

"Say a couple of hours? Six?"

That would give me time to wash away chalkboard dust and ink stains and select a dress appropriate for an evening with Maple Creek's illustrious woman-loving lawman.

"It's a date," I said.

"I'll see you at six then—in the convertible." He winked; his cornflower eyes sparkled. Why did all men with a streak of deviltry have eyes that sparkled?

He pulled away, and I hurried inside, eager to begin my transformation from a drooping school teacher to a summer glamour queen.

As soon as I opened the front door, the house wrapped its

arms around me. Strange how a mere wood structure did that. Rather, strange that I felt as if it did.

Its arms were made of heat and silence, the deep all-encompassing silence I'd yearned for throughout the day while freshmen came and went, polluting the air with screams and fragments of inane conversation.

Here the silence was absolute except for familiar household sounds and…I listened. Something else, barely discernible. The walls seemed to pulsate with whispers. With only myself in residence, the pink Victorian was downright spooky.

I turned on the ceiling fan and its soft whir added to the ghostly atmosphere.

If I concentrated I could almost see Violet Julaine, a woman I'd never set eyes on in life, smiling with delight as she accepted a Valentine gift from a shadowy visitor. I could almost hear her say, "I never eat any food unless I've prepared it myself, but these look so good. Thank you."

For my death.

Tansy Stewart had found the empty plate and fork and teacup on the kitchen table. Only one of each. Naturally the gift giver would have made some excuse not to stay to sample the tarts.

In the kitchen, I drank a glass of iced tea and waited for some unbidden noise to intrude on the delicious quiet. This was the phone's cue to ring.

But it didn't.

If I was going to be ready at six, I'd better move. I drained the glass, poured myself another, and took it upstairs to my bedroom.

By six o'clock when Dalton knocked on the door, I felt like a new woman, cool and willowy in pale lavender. This woman would never be intimidated by her own house or an old landline phone.

My reward was instant, telegraphed in Dalton's sparkling eyes.

"Wow! You look terrific, Linnet. So does the place."

"Thank you."

I wondered if I should be flattered, sharing the spotlight with my decor.

"This room looks larger now," he said. "I didn't like all that Valentine clutter that was in here before. You could hardly move or breathe."

His remark surprised me. "Were you a friend of Violet Julaine's?"

"No. I just answered the call the day we found her body. And I investigated the murder."

"I'm going to keep these rooms spacious," I said. "Stuff lying around gathers dust."

"The whole house looked like a souvenir shop when I first saw it. Ms. Julaine had dozens of collections. Like this..."

He indicated the music box, the lone ornament on my vintage coffee table.

It looked perfectly ordinary to me today. Just a plain wood box with a pretty top. No rosy aura hovered over it. No secret significance cried out to be recognized.

Dalton turned the wind-up mechanism and discovered, as I had, that it was broken. He read the label and frowned. "*Believe Me If All Those Endearing Young Charms?* What kind of song is that?"

"It's about love lasting on into old age."

"I never heard of it, but that's a nice idea."

"Did you notice anything unusual about the picture on top?"

"It has a Valentine border. That's typical for this house."

"Anything else?"

"Here's a lady baking and a man watching her from outside through the window. It looks like an illustration from a little kid's storybook."

"The lady is the Queen of Hearts," I said. "That's the Knave of Hearts spying on her. She's baking cherry tarts, and he's plotting to steal them."

"Interesting. A fairy tale crime in the making. He should just ask her for one."

"I found it in a box labeled Discard. Someone forgot to throw it away."

"The estate sale people, probably. Too bad. I'll bet someone would have bought it, broken or not.'"

He studied the illustration as intently as if the red hearts that framed the picture were drops of blood. "Cherry tarts, you say."

"That's what they look like to me. That's how the rhyme goes." I paused and added what was really on my mind. "It's like a forewarning of how Violet would die. Do you think it could be a clue to the murder?"

"What makes you say that?"

"It was just a thought."

"Well..." Dalton set the box down carefully. "I don't believe in forewarnings, Linnet. Ms. Julaine had hundreds—make that thousands—of Valentine figures and pictures, all kinds of red stuff, scattered throughout the house. I remember seeing a couple of prints of cherries in a bowl. But, if you like, I can have it examined for fingerprints."

"Any number of people might have handled it," I said. "Maybe someone at the sale broke it. That happens."

He tapped it and looked up at me, grinning. "I can tell you one thing now. There's no secret compartment."

"I found a heart pin inside," I said. "It was broken, like the music box."

"Did you think that could be a clue too?" he asked.

"Not offhand. I'm going to have it repaired."

Since we seemed to have exhausted the music box topic, I saw no harm in initiating a quick conversation about the phone.

"Do you know anything about landlines?" I asked.

"Just what the average person does. Why?"

"I have a question. A theoretical one. Could a disconnected phone ever ring?"

"You're sure it's disconnected?"

"The line is usually dead. Not always though. There's static on it sometimes."

"Then it can't be disconnected," he said.

"And someone could call me on it?"

"If it was operational, sure they could. Where are you going with this theoretical phone, Linnet?"

"Into Stephen King country." I smiled, hoping he wouldn't guess I was serious. I wasn't ready to reveal more about the phone.

"You'd have fit right in with Ms. Julaine's writing group," Dalton said. "They called themselves the Gothic Writers and wrote weird stories about ghosts and vampires, and for all I know, disconnected phones that ring in the night."

"Vampires make me queasy," I said, thinking again that the Valentines on the music box reminded me of blood.

"I always believed that one of those writer ladies poisoned Violet Julaine. I still do. But which one? No one had a clear-cut motive. To hear them talk, they were all best friends. But every single one of those gals could bake up a storm."

"But who had arsenic in the cupboard?" I asked.

"If I knew the answer to that, I'd have my killer," Dalton said. "All this talk about cherry tarts is making me hungry."

I picked up my evening bag and smiled up at him. "I'm hungry, too."

He hadn't really answered my question about the phone, but, to be fair, I'd given him only a piece of the background. In turn, he'd given me something new to think about. A group of female writers with a flair for creating horror stories. Werewolves and vampires and maybe haunted phones.

One of them might have had a secret reason for wanting Violet Julaine dead. Now, I needed to find out their names. Dalton would know.

"If you're ready, let's go." Dalton took my arm and looked

around the room as if he were seeing it as it had been in Violet Julaine's day.

"Violet's killer must think she committed the perfect crime," he said. "But someday I'll find her."

TEN

WE DIDN'T GO FAR.

Dalton drove the convertible a few blocks, turned on Main Street, and parked in front of the Blue Lion.

Blue car, purple pansies spilling out of twin window boxes, and an escort with cornflower-colored eyes. I felt as if I were awash in blue. It made the sultry evening air feel almost balmy.

Dalton raised the top and turned off the CD player in the middle of the same sixties tune I'd heard when he'd stopped the car on Beechnut Street.

It seemed like ages ago, but it was only last week.

"They have the best banana splits in Maple Creek here," Dalton said.

"Don't you mean the *only* banana splits?"

"You may be right except for those gooey wannabes at Dairy Land. After dinner, we can go cruising out to one of the lakes—if you're game."

"Oh, I'm game, but which lake did you have in mind?" I asked.

"Huron." The devil's sparkle appeared in his eyes again, making them even bluer.

I smiled, thinking of the many miles to that particular body of water. It was in another county, practically a day trip. Surely Dalton was only teasing.

"Tomorrow is a school day," I said. "I can't mix late nights with rowdy freshmen. How about going to Marble Lake instead?"

"It's your choice, ma'am," he said.

Marble Lake was one of our local tourist attractions, often

mistakenly called Maple Lake. Dinner, a short moonlight drive, home again. That was a respectable agenda for a first date.

I wasn't ready for more—not yet. With a quick glance at my handsome companion, I thought, *Later I might be. Oh, yes. Later.*

Dalton walked around the car and opened the door for me. "We could go to another restaurant, if you'd rather."

"When we're at the Blue Lion's door? This is fine. I like to eat here on Fridays to celebrate the end of the work week."

"And I like the steaks and the pictures on the walls."

We, or rather Dalton's vintage Cadillac, attracted admiring glances from the two elderly couples who were leaving the Blue Lion. Dalton's lovingly restored automobile was a one-of-a-kind treasure from another era. I thought we ourselves made an interesting pair. Dalton in a gray suit and blue shirt, instead of his policeman's uniform, and his date, the lady in lavender.

People were familiar with Lieutenant Gray, as he was practically a public figure. And no doubt they knew me as the teacher whose student had waylaid her in her own classroom, even though neither my name nor picture had ever appeared in a paper. Dalton was illustrious; I was infamous.

Dalton took my hand and helped me over an uneven section of curb to the sidewalk. "If you have to count down the days to Friday, I'd say you didn't enjoy teaching very much."

"Well, it has its moments."

"Some good, some bad. I know. It's the same in law enforcement." He held open the heavy restaurant door. "I've been meaning to tell you, Linnet. I'm very impressed with the way you bounced back after that gun incident. Other teachers might have taken a leave of absence or even resigned. You're still standing in front of your class, teaching and counting days."

"Perseverance is my motto," I said.

"Mine too. We have a lot in common."

I didn't tell Dalton that for a brief time, I'd considered changing professions. However, my pride and an innate stubborn streak would never allow me to walk away from the one I'd chosen. Besides, when Carl had burst into my room with a gun, I'd only recently become a homeowner. I had a new mortgage. Times were hard and growing harder every year. These days, a teaching contract was a ticket to financial security. But most important of all, I loved Maple Creek and Alcott Middle School, too.

Difficult classes aside, how often did a disturbed teenager resort to violence?

Too often, I thought. *And sometimes people die.*

Abruptly Dalton changed the subject. "I like those golden streaks in your hair, Linnet. They shine like sunlight. What do you call them?"

"I call them natural," I said. "And thank you."

And I like everything about you, Lieutenant Gray, I thought. *Everything that I know, that is.*

His unexpected compliment sent my spirits soaring and a warm glow to my face.

When was the last time anyone had noticed my hair? I couldn't remember. It was long and dark brown, cut with layers, but otherwise unremarkable except for the light strands.

I thought for a moment that Dalton was going to touch my hair, but then we were taking our places at the end of the short line and being heartily welcomed by the suave, bespectacled owner, Phillip Lyon, who had never noticed me before.

"I eat here all the time," Dalton said. "Steak one night, fish the next, pie for dessert."

The hostess greeted us with exuberant warmth and led the way to what must be the best table in the Blue Lion. It was an ideal setting for a date, a small alcove, next to a window with a view of a water pond.

Dalton studied the medieval wall border where knights in armor and hounds with jeweled collars guarded their highborn ladies from herds of lions and unicorns. Smiling, he pointed to a tiny yellow lion that seemed to hide itself behind the scarlet skirts of a golden-haired maiden.

"We're in luck tonight, Linnet," he said. "This is the only

lion in the house that's yellow, not blue. If you're close enough to touch it, you can make a wish and it'll come true. That's what they say, anyway," he added with a sheepish grin.

Remembering the wish I'd made over Milla Schoenherr's teacup, I said, "This is a wishing town."

I reached across the table and traced the little yellow face with my fingers. "You can't very well find it unless you happen to be seated here."

"And you don't sit here unless you're a V.I.P."

"Like Maple Creek's premier policeman?"

"And the town's Most Valorous English Teacher. Make a wish, Linnet," Dalton said.

"Did you make yours already?"

"Just now."

He smiled at me in a new way, I thought. In a significant way? Perhaps it was the candlelight. Or my imagination. Or a heady combination of both. Or simply the man sitting across from me.

Remember his reputation, I told myself. *And remember Ned.*

"Okay. I will."

I looked straight at the yellow lion and wished for a long and happy life with the perfect mate, whoever he might be. It didn't seem like too much to ask for.

AFTER A DINNER OF broiled whitefish and rice followed by the most sumptuous banana split ever assembled, I asked Dalton a question that had puzzled me. "You seem convinced that Violet Julaine's killer is a woman. I've been wondering why."

He had an answer ready. "Because the Gothic Writers were all women except for a retired police chief who lives on frozen dinners. The closest he ever came to a cherry tart was in an Awrey's box."

"You once said those women could bake up a storm. I see. So that makes them suspects, but the police chief, who doesn't know his way around a cookbook, is innocent?"

Dalton countered that with a smile. "There's more to it, Linnet. Rob Leaver is an old friend of mine, a sort of mentor. I know him as well as I know my own brother."

"What about some other man in Violet's life then? One with a talent for whipping up pastries?"

"If there was one, none of her friends knew anything about him. Except Captain Franklin—maybe."

"Who's he?"

"A retired navy man who recently split from his wife. They say all the older ladies in town are crazy about him. Turns out he's taken three of the Gothic Writers out on dinner and movie dates."

"Including Violet?"

"One time. Yes."

"Was he a suspect in the murder?"

"No. Franklin was at a reunion in Florida the week Violet was killed. He has plenty of buddies who will vouch for him."

I turned back to the scoop of rocky road ice cream topped with fresh strawberry sauce. It seemed that the more of the elaborate concoction I ate, the larger it grew.

Dalton said, "The killer had to be a friend or acquaintance of Violet's. No one invites a stranger in and eats something she brings, no matter now nicely it's presented."

"I had the same thought. Do you remember who's in the writing group?"

"Sure—I talked to each one at the time of the murder. In case you didn't know, they disbanded after Violet was killed. They were all local people, and they're still around."

"Who were they?"

"You probably know two of them already. Tansy Stewart lives across the street from you and Milla Schoenherr teaches at Maple Creek High."

I couldn't have been more surprised. Tansy? And Milla?

"But Milla writes romances," I said. "She just had one published."

"Isn't there such a thing as Gothic romance?" he asked.

"You're right. They're hot today."

In more ways than one. Tales of romantic encounters between mortals and supernatural beings were indeed popular, but I didn't care for them—with the exception of Matthew Arnold's Victorian jewel, *The Forsaken Merman.* Fresh from my college literature classes and more than a little naive, I had tried to teach the poem in my first year at Alcott, only to be taunted by "Chicken of the Sea" chants.

I was under the impression that Milla had written about human lovers in an earlier time period. I'd have to read her book.

"Who else was in the group?" I asked.

"There's Ellen Trehearne. She works part-time at the Tea Room. Annette Coffman lives a few miles north of Maple Creek and has a cottage industry with her sister. They grow herbs and fruits for jams, I think. Loretta McDermott quit her job last year to attend college full time. Josie Smith is a stay-at-home mom with five teenaged boys to take care of. She claims that the group was a good excuse for a night out."

"She wasn't a serious writer then?"

"I doubt if any of them were—except for Milla. There's one more, the youngest, Doreen Snow. She spends weekends boating with her boyfriend on Lake St. Clair. Those were the folks who attended every meeting. Four others showed up a few times, then dropped out. Milla is the only one who's been published."

"They sound pretty tame to me," I said.

"On the surface, yes. But let's look deeper. Take Tansy Stewart. Tansy and Violet were longtime neighbors, friendly but not especially close. There's no history of trouble between them except for an altercation over a pair of old sycamore trees Tansy had cut down. They were in Tansy's front yard, and she didn't want to have so many leaves to rake every fall. Violet thought destroying healthy trees was an outrage and said so to whoever would listen. That blew over in time."

"It's hardly a motive for murder," I said. "What else do you know about these shady ladies?"

"Milla and Violet graduated from high school in the same class. They were friends for a long time, but you never know. Throw a stolen boyfriend into the mix, and you might have a serious grudge."

"From their high school days? That's so unlikely."

"Pure speculation. I agree. But how about a year or two ago? They both went out with Captain Franklin."

"If he's a man to kill for, I want to see him."

"No you don't," Dalton said. "Let's move on to Ellen," he said. "She came under suspicion because of her prize-winning Traverse Cherry Cake. Every summer she drives up to the Traverse Cherry Festival and brings back cherries for her friends. They call her the Cherry Lady."

I couldn't keep from laughing. "And last year she froze a spare quart so that she could bake a batch of lethal tarts to poison Violet? Unlikely again and plain silly. Why would she want to murder Violet?"

Dalton smiled. "I haven't a clue. Ellen is one of the gentlest, most self-effacing women I've ever met. She hates to offend people and goes out of her way to accommodate them. She's afraid of her own shadow."

"Ah ha! That's the kind of woman most likely to kill," I said. "All we need is a motive for Ellen."

"I can't think of any. Motives were non-existent in this case."

"Who else?" I asked.

"Loretta was always at odds with the other writers. She used to bring rough drafts to the meetings, full of mistakes. One of the ironclad rules was that manuscripts had to be polished before they were read. Loretta cheerfully ignored it."

"She should have been asked to revise her work or leave," I said.

Dalton looked up, obviously surprised at my vehemence. "You English teachers have no mercy."

"Not when it comes to fracturing the English language."

"I'll remember that. Josie used to miss meetings regularly. That didn't go down well with the others. Also, the members were all pretty health conscious except when it came to sweets. Josie used to bring fried chicken and potato chips—stuff like that—as her potluck contributions.

"That brings me to Doreen. She was too harsh in her critiques. Doreen and Violet clashed several times over her approach."

"They sound like an ordinary group to me," I said. "You don't really think one of the Gothic Writers killed Violet, do you?"

"Those were our only suspects."

"They weren't good ones."

"Agreed. No one had a credible motive to kill."

"I notice you let Chief Rob off the hook. Lawman turns killer. Isn't he worth considering?"

"Don't even joke about that," Dalton said. "Rob Leaver is above reproach."

"What a sexist comment! My money is on the chief."

"Give me one good reason to back that statement up."

"Well..." I knew that he wouldn't accept just any reason. "I've never seen a picture of Violet, but they say that she was a beautiful woman. Suppose she rejected Leaver's advances and he killed her?"

Dalton scooped up the last bit of his banana split—a spoonful of marshmallow and nuts. "Unrequited love. I'll buy that. About twenty years ago, a Maple Creek man killed his girlfriend because she found someone she liked better. That's another story. But Rob? No way. Besides, if a woman turns him down, he just finds another one who's willing. And he doesn't even own a cookbook."

"Anyone can doctor tarts from the Bakery on Main."

Dalton laughed. "Like I said before, Linnet, you would have been a natural for the Gothic Writers group."

"I intend to write a book one day, but it's going to be a

mystery for teenaged girls. No murders or blood. When I was in high school, I thought about police work. If I ever decide to leave teaching, do you think I'd make a good detective?"

"You might—with training."

He was serious. This was the second compliment of the evening. Could I hope for a third? Maybe one for my sexy lavender dress that had apparently gone unappreciated?

While we were reviewing the Julaine case, I'd eaten my way through almost an entire banana split. Now I couldn't eat another bite. I left the last scoop of ice cream melting in the bottom of the glass boat.

"Everything was perfect, Dalton," I said.

"The best is yet to be." He smiled, as if pleased with a task well accomplished. "That's a quote from Browning—just to show you that I read."

"I never doubted that."

"Let's go take a spin around Marble Lake now," he said. "There's a full moon tonight."

The invitation sounded like poetry.

MARBLE LAKE LAY IN AN embrace of leafy hardwoods and fir trees, her water still and luminous, her sand soaking up the moonlight. A woodland scent wafted from a nearby wood that bordered the lake's eastern side. Incredibly, Dalton and I were the only people on the beach.

We left the convertible, and strolled, hand in hand, along the shore.

"Back there where we parked there used to be a lovers' lane," Dalton said. "We'd sweep the area three, four times a night. Finally the kids found another place."

"Did you drive them off so you police could have the beach to yourself?" I asked.

His soft laughter might have been the only sound in the world. "Not so loud. That's a secret."

"There's no one around to hear."

"No one at all."

"But somebody was here earlier."

A sand castle lay directly in our path. It was a charming little structure with towers and turrets, a miniature American flag, and even a moat, every inch of it still intact. "I hope it doesn't wash away," I said.

"It will eventually, but there'll always be another one."

We walked slowly toward a stand of weeping willow trees that grew almost to the water's edge, their graceful fronds brushing its surface.

Dalton stopped and looked down at me for what seemed like a long time. "Linnet..." He drew me into a deep kiss, crushing my lips and my half-formed plan to be a little circumspect, a little aloof with him.

My plans and my thoughts melted in the heat of another kiss and another... My arms found their way around his neck. I felt as if my body were engulfed in fire, melting. As if Dalton belonged to me, had always been mine, would always be mine.

Remember... His reputation... You're one of many...

A razor-sharp retort cut through the still night air.

My thoughts died. My reflexes froze.

"What the hell!" Dalton pushed me roughly to the ground. Around us, gunfire shattered the night into millions of pieces.

ELEVEN

BULLETS. COMING MY WAY. AGAIN.

I clung to Dalton, inhaled the damp earth under my face, and felt a rock grazing the side of my leg.

Then the gunfire stopped. For a fragment of a second, it was quiet. Sound came back all at once, as if an invisible hand had turned a switch. Wind stirred the lake. Willow fronds sighed. Beyond the water, a bird cried out a strange, eerie lament.

Dalton's voice had a ragged edge. "Are you all right, Linnet?" he demanded.

"I think so." My own voice was a hoarse whisper. I raised myself and took a quick inventory. No blood gushed out from a wound. There was no pain, only an all-over iciness. Shock, I imagined. If one of the bullets had hit me, wouldn't there be blood and pain?

"Thanks to you, I'm just shaken," I said. "How about you?"

"There's not a scratch on me. I think he's gone or we'd have heard more shots."

Dalton pulled me to my feet. We stood close together, well hidden in the dark shelter of the willow. Slowly I regained my equilibrium.

"Lucky for us, our shooter is a poor marksman," Dalton said.

"The shots came from over there…" I struggled to keep my voice steady. "On the road."

"You're right. We'd better move."

Dalton held me close for a moment, released me too soon.

He said, "Listen, Linnet. I'm taking you back to the car." A jingle of metal punctuated his words. I felt keys being pressed into my hand. "Drive out to Maple Road. Wait for me at the turn-off."

As he spoke, he began walking briskly along the beach, practically dragging me with him, away from the willows.

"Dalton… Not so fast!…" I caught my breath. "What about you?"

"I'm going to look around."

"But you can't," I said. "It's dark… Dangerous…"

"I can. Don't argue, Linnet."

Several feet ahead of us, the light blue Cadillac shimmered in the moonlight. Dalton flung open the door and pushed me inside. As he raised the top, he barked orders. "Start the engine. Don't turn the lights on. You don't want to make yourself a target."

I did as he said, while he fumbled in the backseat. Moments later, he moved into the light, armed with a gun and flashlight.

"Lock the door," he said. "I'll meet you at the turn-off. Go!"

He headed back toward the stand of willows. I wished I could have waited for him here on the beach, but it was best to follow instructions. So I turned the car around. It seemed like a great blue dragon. Too long in the back, too long in the front, different from the vehicles I was used to. And the soft material of the convertible top made me feel vulnerable.

But the old restored engine had a dragon's power. The Cadillac took me out to the road, over a twisting rock-strewn surface. No monstrous shape rose up from the lake in pursuit. No other vehicle materialized in the darkness to cut off my exit.

On Maple Road, I parked in the shadows and waited for Dalton, listening to the purr of the engine and the cry of the night bird.

Why was I trembling now, so many minutes after the shooting?

It hasn't been that long, I thought. *And I'm afraid for Dalton. Please let him be okay.*

A BEAM OF LIGHT snaked out of the woods. I gripped the wheel and stepped lightly on the accelerator. Just in case. But it was all right. Dalton emerged from the underbrush as tall and powerful as ever, apparently unscathed.

I unlocked the door and slid over to the passenger's seat. Dalton was in charge again. I could go back to reacting.

"Did you see anyone?" he asked.

"No one. Nothing at all."

He made a U-turn on Maple Road and headed back to town.

"Did you find anything?"

"No. I'll come back in the morning."

"If he shot at us from a car, from the road, then he didn't leave anything behind. Just the bullets."

"Right. I'm going to look anyway. Finding bullets is the same as finding clues. They can be matched to a particular gun."

"Do you think it was random?" I asked. "One of those drive-by shootings?"

"It could be, but that'd be a first for Maple Creek."

He swerved to avoid a branch in the road. The movement flung me against the side door.

"Put your seat belt on," he said.

We'd both forgotten them.

"I think those shots were meant for me," I said, as I buckled myself in.

"You do?" The slightest hint of amusement slipped into his voice. "What have you been up to lately, Linnet?"

"Glaring at troublemakers in the hope that a look will stop them. They call it stalking."

"Anything else?"

"I've been boring. I made my classes stop talking during a

quiz." This litany of failings felt uncomfortably like a confession. "I won't let them make up old assignments that they didn't bother doing. No exceptions. Yesterday I refused to change a grade from a 'B' to an 'A'. Typical teacher stuff."

"I can top all of that," he said. "Someone is always out to get me."

"How do you ever relax?"

"You get used to it. You stay on guard."

"I never will."

I glanced at the speedometer and was immediately sorry. Dalton was speeding—with impunity, I knew. A crime had been committed, and I was a part of it. Once again.

"Are you going to report what happened?" I asked.

"Of course." There was the slightest hint of condescension in his tone—as there had been the slightest hint of amusement a moment ago.

"I'm sorry, Linnet," he added. "My dates don't usually end up running for their lives."

"Because you normally don't go out with wicked English teachers?"

"I never said that."

If his eyes weren't fixed on the road, I knew I'd see the blue sparkle again.

We turned onto Main Street, passed the Blue Lion—closed for the night—and drove down Beechnut Street. Everything was quiet in Maple Creek, everyone bedded down for the night. Or they were keeping out of sight.

"I wonder how they—he—whoever—knew where we were," I said.

"We were visible enough. In the restaurant. On the road—on the beach. Everybody knows this car."

"I thought we were alone."

Highlights of the evening replayed themselves in my mind. A series of Technicolor scenes ranging from flirtatious to erotic. My face grew warm; I was glad for the darkness. It never occurred to me that someone could have been watching us, waiting for the moment to strike.

"On our next date, we'll leave the outskirts of Maple Creek in the dust," Dalton said.

"Our next date."

"Sure, if you'll risk it. You will, won't you?"

"I will. This one was interrupted."

And the mood had been irrevocably broken. That was what I thought until Dalton drove the Cadillac into my driveway and walked me up to my door. The light of the porch lamp bathed the pink surface of my house and the Valentine window in a rosy romantic glow.

My sanctuary, I thought. *This is the one place where evil can't touch me. Only love.*

In the distance, the night bird cried again. But it couldn't be the same bird, flying over our heads all the way from Marble Lake. There must be more of its kind making their home in Maple Creek, all with that plaintive call that sounded like grieving.

Suddenly I felt cold; my flesh touched with icicles, ice water running unchecked through my veins. The night air was cool, but I hadn't thought about the weather since Dalton arrived at my door.

"Let's go in," Dalton said.

We stood inside the vestibule as the clock in the living room chimed eleven. I was going to be tired in the morning. Tonight, I didn't care about time.

Dalton took me in his arms. His kisses brought back the passion of our evening—before the gunshots.

"Once again you came through in a crisis, Linnet," he said. "I wouldn't mind having you for a partner. That's after you graduate from the Police Academy."

Well, that wasn't the kind of compliment I'd hoped for, but I decided to accept it.

"Would you like a nightcap?" I asked. "Something to drink? A cup of coffee?"

"What I'd like is another rain check," he said. "Usually I have good luck with them."

"You've got it. Will you let me know what you find out?"

"As soon as I can."

"And find out where Carl is. Maybe he's free again."

He promised he would, gave me one last good-night kiss and left, taking my sense of safety with him.

But how safe had I been this evening in the company of Lieutenant Dalton Gray, a man I'd been thinking of as virtually invincible, simply because he wore a badge and carried a gun? Dalton and I had lived through this night, but life offered no guarantees for the future. No one could ever be certain of safety in this mad, mixed-up world we lived in.

The coldness within me grew.

No matter what Dalton and logic told me, I suspected that the gunfire had been meant for me. And I feared that the next bullet would find its mark.

THE LAST DAY WITH MY fourth hour class! Would it happen today or on exam day? By three o'clock, I would know.

How ironic that I could face gunfire and still be apprehensive about a mean plan concocted by a band of yammering fourteen-year-old malcontents.

I wasn't, not really; and I wasn't a bit tired after my harrowing evening with Dalton. To prove this to myself, I'd donned a silky red dress with a square neckline and floral pattern. I looked and felt bright and well able to cope with anything fourth hour could hurl at me.

The idea rolled out of left field. What could be meaner than shots in the night, interrupting a romantic tryst between a teacher and her policeman date?

Surely that surpassed mean.

I closed my grade book, set the yellow attendance slip on the corner of the desk, and picked up my copy of the *Great Expectations* review on which I'd made copious notes.

"Settle down," I said, my voice louder than theirs. "The bell rang."

I stared at the packet in my hand. It was hot-off-the-press fresh, not a single word written on it.

Was this the mean plan?

Hardly. It wasn't mean enough.

Still, I heard a girl's giggle coming from the back row. All at once that whole section of the room erupted in laughter.

Don't let them know that anything is wrong.

"Quiet! We've got a lot of work to do and not much time."

I didn't need written notes. They were alive and well in my head. But someone had them.

Jimmy? Dale? Azalea? Debbie? Brandy who looked unusually smug this morning? Somebody I didn't suspect?

Whoever had apprehended my copy would try to use it for the exam. Tomorrow I'd patrol the rows, watching for the thief to incriminate himself.

"Turn to Page 10," I said. "We're halfway through. We should be able to finish today."

I surveyed the faces of my students, recalling my recent dream about the advance of Farmer Jones' barnyard animals. Why were so many of them laughing? Smiling? Smirking? Roaring with merriment? Didn't anyone feel sullen or sad or queasy from the heat?

"Here are some characters you'll have to identify on the exam. Azalea, who was Biddy?"

Instead of answering my question, Azalea asked one of her own. "It's too hot in here, Ms. Shellwin. Can't you bring a fan in for tomorrow?"

"I would if I had one."

"Rich teachers," muttered an unseen male. "She probably has an air conditioner at home."

"Buy one," Azalea said. "North-Mart has them."

You buy one, I thought. *I'm comfortable.*

I wasn't, of course. It was another steamy morning with only seven windows open. The custodian had repaired the eighth one by nailing it shut. Not that it mattered, as the air that streamed in was hot and dusty.

I was amazed that all thirty-two of my students had found their way back to class after lunch and no one had tried to sneak a forbidden pop can in.

"Azalea, do you know who Biddy was?"

"The dog!"

I frowned. "There's no dog in *Great Expectations*."

That simple statement set off a new round of giggling.

Was there a dog in Dickens' novel that I'd overlooked? I must have read that book a dozen times.

"Look, Ms. Shellwin, it's your sister."

A medium-sized reddish and white dog with freckles on her muzzle stood in the doorway, eagerly wagging her tail. Undaunted by the noise, she took a few tentative steps into the room. I noticed that she wasn't wearing a collar.

I longed to pet her, to give her something to eat, which were my first impulses when encountering a dog. There was my slice of angel food cake left over from lunch and... Just in time, I recalled another school rule—besides the "no food in class" rule. "No dogs allowed in the building."

"She'd better go to the office," I said, scanning the room for someone I could trust with the errand.

Sherry screamed. "No! They'll call the pound. They'll kill her."

"Maple Creek doesn't kill dogs," I said.

"Here, girl!" Dale held out his pencil, and the dog bounded happily up to him, licking her chops.

"She's thirsty, Ms. Shellwin," Candace Ann informed me. "Can I get her a drink from the fountain?"

"She can have this." Dale produced a can of Coke from his pocket and reached for the dog's ruff. With a menacing growl and show of white teeth, she backed up.

Sherry screamed again.

"Uh oh," said Jimmy. "Here comes another dog."

Murielle Evans had poked her head into the room. Pinning

Dale and the puppy with a frigid glare, she said, "Is everything all right in here, Ms. Shellwin?"

"It's fine," I said.

"Dogs aren't allowed in school. I'll notify the principal."

"Boo!"

That was Brandy, no fan of Murielle's, always ready to support her twin.

"Thank you," I said. "Just close the door please."

"No! Leave it open!"

I couldn't tell who dared to give me that order.

Sherry wailed. "Do you want us all to die?"

Not on my watch.

Immediately ashamed of the flippant thought, I turned to the dog. "Here, pooch. Come here."

Whining, she ran to the back of the room.

"Biddy was Miss Haversham's dog," Azalea said. "Biddy died when she ate a piece of that moldy old wedding cake."

I couldn't see the dog. I said, "Wrong. Someone else? Anyone?"

Dwight Dunlap rapped on the door, pushed it open. His face filled the small rectangular glass; his expression was disapproving.

I opened the door.

"I hear you have a problem, Ms. Shellwin."

"No problem. Just a stray who wandered in."

Where had she gone? I looked for her, saw her crouched behind Candace Ann's desk, trying to make herself look small.

Dwight said, "Come along, sir."

"It's a girl, Mr. Dunlap," Candace Ann told him, and Azalea giggled.

Seeing the door to freedom open, the dog streaked out to the hall, almost knocking Dwight off balance as he grabbed the air in the general direction of her neck.

"What a jerk!"

Fortunately I was the only one to hear that.

"Carry on, Ms. Shellwin," the principal said with a bracing look. He closed the door again to a chorus of groans.

"Now," I said, "someone tell me. Who was Biddy?"

The silence was as thick as the heat in the room.

At last, Stacy Conrad said, "The bell's gonna ring."

Her announcement drowned in a cacophony of books slamming shut, feet shuffling, and shouting that didn't have anything to do with English.

How could the hour have gone by already? It seemed that we'd just started class. Or had someone tinkered with the clock again?

Impossible. I'd never taken my eyes off the class. The clock hung on the wall behind me.

"Finish the review for homework," I said quickly. "Hand it in tomorrow before the exam. Here's a bit of advice. Look up 'Biddy'."

The bell rang. Papers and colored binders, torn into miniscule bits and pieces, flew up into the air, creating an instant shower as they returned to the floor. The room was thick with confetti. The air filled with cheers. My room resembled a carnival fun house.

Surely *this* wasn't the planned prank?

If so, I had expended a great deal of time and energy worrying about nothing.

TWELVE

SHREDDED BALLOONS AND PAPERS carpeted the floor of Ned Glint's classroom, and wishes for a happy summer covered the blackboard. This disorder was a stunning departure from Ned's usual surroundings. He was a fanatic about neatness in his domain.

"You have glitter in your bangs, Linnet," he said, as I took the last seat at the conference table.

I brushed lightly at my hair. A shower of multi-colored paper bits fluttered down to the shiny wood surface. From the top of a high bookcase, Ned's table fan blew them out the door.

"Rough day with the ninth graders?" asked Beverly.

"Typical," I said. "Sorry I'm late."

With my mind lost in a remembered rain of bullets and, recently, in confetti, I'd only remembered the after-school meeting at the last minute.

We were seven, wilted from the humidity but trying to summon up that last dollop of energy all of us have. Beverly, Rae and I represented the English Department, while Ned, Arthur Roman and Lou Cornwall were the business half of the group.

Rae removed the plastic wrap from a paper plate heaped high with cookies. Besides Ned's papers, the table held an assortment of pop, including my favorite, vanilla cola. Ned had borrowed paper napkins from the cafeteria and provided bottled water for the health conscious among us, meaning himself and Lou.

"Everyone—have some cookies," Rae said. "I got up an hour early to bake them."

How dedicated, I thought.

"I'm sorry about the brownies, Ned," I said. "I *didn't* get up early."

He cast me a sympathetic smile. "You can make it up to us, Linnet."

Now that I didn't have to be bright and alert to guard against nebulous mean plans, I felt exhaustion closing in on me. I helped myself to a vanilla cola, hoping a light dose of caffeine would wake me up. But all I could think of were soft white sheets and fluffy pillows. An early night. Dreamless sleep.

"I promised this wouldn't be a long meeting," Ned began as he passed out his agenda.

Rae seized it and waved the sheet languidly in front of her face. "That's good news, Ned. It's too hot for intensity."

She looked and sounded like one of my fourth hour students, except none of them would use a word like "intensity." And what did intense have to do with our meeting?

"Well, it *is* summer," Beverly reminded us. As if anyone needed reminding.

"I read that July is supposed to have more than an average number of storms," I added.

Ned said, "We have to work out a schedule and a place to meet."

"Aren't we meeting in the building?" I asked.

"We could, but no one says we have to. I thought it would be more comfortable to take turns hosting the group. Some of us have pools and outdoor grills. I have a cottage on the lake."

"We'd get more accomplished in the school," Arthur said. "Say we work in the library. If we have to do research, the materials will be right on hand."

Rae scoffed. "And we can bring lunch in a paper bag or go to Dairy Land. I, for one, prefer Ned's idea. Maybe, after we finish for the day, he'll let us swim in his lake."

Ever agreeable, Ned nodded. "How about the rest of you?"

"I'd like us to take turns playing host," I said.

So did everybody else. Arthur gave in to the majority's preferences gracefully.

Ned beamed. "It's settled then. Linnet will bake her brownies, and we'll all have a chance to see the inside of her Victorian house."

I wondered why Ned kept talking about me and brownies. He certainly liked to hold on to ideas. I hadn't baked or eaten a brownie since my own high school days, had never even mentioned them to anyone in my two years at Alcott. I supposed I'd have to provide them when I hosted the group.

Rae passed around the plate of cookies. "I created this recipe myself in my own kitchen," she said.

Lou discreetly set his cookie on his napkin.

"What's in them?" Beverly asked.

"Mostly marshmallow, fudge chips, and almonds. They're fat free and sugar free."

I took a bite and quickly ate the entire cookie. It was one of those melt-in-your-mouth treasures, far too good to be "heart smart" as well.

"They're wonderful, Rae," I said, taking another one.

"I don't know about the marshmallow and fudge chips," Rae added. "But a little fat and sugar shouldn't hurt anybody, and nuts are good for you."

"They're like s'mores," Arthur said.

"No. You make s'mores with graham crackers, chocolate bars and marshmallows."

Ned fixed his runaway group with a stern look, bringing us back on track. "We're contracted to meet three times a week, four hours each session. It might as well be Monday, Wednesday, and Friday. That'll be easy to remember. Any objections?"

Except for crunching and the overhead whir of the fan, the room was silent until Beverly said, "None, I guess."

"Good." Ned sent two papers on their way around the table. One was a sign-up for the meeting hosts, the other a hand-drawn map to his cottage. "It's a twenty-minute drive from Maple Creek to Lime Lake. My place is the only green house on the beach. I'll provide the hot dogs and buns."

"I'll bring the chips and beverages," Beverly said.

"And I'll make my famous potato salad," Rae said. "This is going to be fun."

Lou took his usual business-only view. "Creating a new course from scratch is going to be work, not fun, Rae."

"Spoil sport!" she countered.

"We can have fun doing it," said Ned. "Ten o'clock at Lime Lake then. We'll work for two hours, take an hour for lunch, and be done at three."

"If you all like these cookies, I'll bring some more," Rae said.

Ned glanced at me, his mind no doubt on brownies. "That'd be great, Rae. Now, if everyone has signed the sheet, we'll adjourn. Thank you all for coming."

He gathered his papers into a neat brown folder and put the folder in his briefcase. "Be careful," he warned. "Those floors are slippery."

Rae, Beverly, and I walked out to the parking lot while the men trailed after us, deep in an impromptu discussion of the latest baseball trade. Out here balloons, discarded pop cans, and heaps of confetti littered the blacktop. A whole semester's worth of assignments and notes, destined for the trash.

What a waste! But apparently, for our students, grade point averages were more important than knowledge.

The red and white dog was snoozing in the shade of Dwight Dunlap's camper. Good! She'd eluded kids with grasping hands, the principal, and the dogcatcher.

At our approach she looked up and eyed us warily.

"That's the mutt who was running in and out of classrooms all day," Rae said. "I wonder who owns her?"

"Probably no one." I thought of my collie puppy, due to arrive on Friday. She would never roam free and look so scrawny and desperate.

On an impulse, I unwrapped the slice of cake I'd saved from lunch and tossed it to her. She pounced on it and dashed into the wooded area that adjoined the school, her treasure held fast in her mouth.

A police cruiser was just pulling out of the lot. From a distance, the form of the officer inside reminded me of Dalton, but I had no way of knowing if he was the school's one-man patrol force.

Whoever it was had done well. My tires still had their air, and no unflattering names defaced the windows. A mess in the lot could be cleared up in no time.

I bid my companions goodbye, got into my car, and locked the door, even though I didn't see anyone else in the area. Even though the men were still standing on the walk, presumably talking baseball.

The woods were filled with hiding places. A shooter could be kneeling behind a car. A hundred men couldn't protect me from a determined assassin.

I wasn't being paranoid, only a cautious teacher who'd recently come under fire. After fourth hour's exam, scheduled for tomorrow morning, I could relax—or maybe not. I didn't think the demons that pursued me adhered to the school's schedule.

LATER THAT AFTERNOON, Milla Schoenherr sat with me on my front porch again. A pitcher of pink lemonade and ginger wafers, my hastily-assembled refreshment tray, combined with the spacious awning to stave off the evening's heat.

Milla had come strolling down Beechnut Street with a parasol and an elegant straw hat trailing green ribbons. Very classy and ladylike. Very Scarlett O'Hara. Her mint green sundress and nostalgic accessories suited a romance novelist.

She offered a vague apology for leaving so abruptly last night. So much had happened to me in the meantime that I'd forgotten about it.

"I felt suddenly ill and wanted to be home," she said. "It's this beastly weather. I'm not at my best when the temperature passes eighty."

So apparently the appearance of the bearded man, his

black-haired girlfriend, and the menacing Belgian shepherd had nothing to do with her flight.

I didn't ask Milla why she was out walking in the heat if she disliked it so much. It seemed rude. But I had to admit I was curious.

"We're going to have severe thunderstorms tonight," she said.

"A little rain would be nice. I love stormy weather. When I'm inside, that is."

"Well, I'm afraid of lightning." She paused and poured more lemonade in our glasses. "Did anyone tell you that your house was struck by lightning? It brought down an old maple tree and started a fire."

The unexpected information knocked me off balance.

"There was a fire here? No one said anything about it."

Not Tansy Stewart, not Bonita White, not the Realtor. Someone should have mentioned it.

That familiar iciness stole back into my bloodstream. It seemed that Milla was telling me more than a hitherto unmentioned detail about the pink Victorian.

"Did this happen when Violet lived here?" I asked.

"No. After she was killed. Almost a year ago, last July, while the house was on the market. Lightning set off a blaze in the kitchen. Tansy Stewart called the Fire Department before it caused more extensive damage."

"I'd never have known it," I said.

"The agency hired a good restoration company from out of town."

I recalled that the kitchen was the only room in the house with freshly-painted walls—those ghastly bright yellow walls that I meant to paint over someday.

"You look upset, Linnet," Milla said. "I'm sorry I brought it up. Anyway, don't they say that lightning never strikes twice in the same place?"

"I don't think that's true."

"Maybe not. When Mother Nature goes on a rampage, we all take our chances."

She segued smoothly into a discussion of her own last day at the high school. Her juniors had given her a surprise gift. "Perfume! Can you imagine? *Sultry Night.* They said it's compensation—for giving me such a hard time all semester."

I only half listened to Milla's last-day reminiscences. Something tugged at me. It slipped out of my grasp and came back—almost—a detail that danced just beyond my awareness. I sensed that it was important.

What was bothering me?

Nothing that Milla had said. Not directly, anyway. Something about lightning and a fire at the pink Victorian and…

The phone! Could the lightning strike have altered the landline in some way, rendering it capable of ringing when disconnected? Could this interference have allowed a caller to contact me?

It seemed possible. It could explain everything.

It's the answer! It has to be!

Somehow, in a way I didn't understand, the rogue lightning bolt had changed the landline into a rogue phone.

Dalton had only a layman's knowledge of telephones. I should ask a science teacher. Annabelle. And I'd better ask her soon before we went our separate ways for the summer.

I sat back in the chair, drank my lemonade, and felt confident that at least one of the ripples in my summer was about to be smoothed out.

But, wait! A lightning strike couldn't explain why Bonita White hadn't heard the phone ringing.

Nor had I for a few days, come to think of it.

"My sister, Lisa, used to teach at Teasdale Elementary," Milla was saying. "Her kids gave her all kinds of presents at the end of the year. Candles. Books. Plants. Candy. You name it. In high school, it isn't cool to give your teacher a present. That's why I was so surprised… Oh, I'm boring you, rambling on like this."

"No," I said quickly. "No, you're not, Milla. I'm just a little tired."

"How did the year end at Alcott?" she asked.

"With a bang and a whimper and endless confetti. But nothing deadly."

Milla laid a reassuring hand on my arm. "You had a terrible experience, Linnet. Nothing like that will ever happen again."

No one could guarantee that, but it sounded good.

"Teenagers can be a little like Mother Nature," I said. "They're capricious. They don't give a warning. One strike, and you're dead."

Milla frowned. "Oh, my, Linnet. You can't be that cynical."

"I guess I'm overly dramatic."

That would satisfy her. I couldn't tell Milla about last night's gunfire because then I'd have to mention Dalton. He was my secret for now.

Some secret.

Anyone in Maple Creek could have seen us together last night. Milla herself might have been in the Blue Lion having dinner not far from our alcove.

But wouldn't she have mentioned it? Asked a few questions. Tried to find out if our relationship was a serious one? She was, after all, a romance writer.

Now she said, "Let's go out to lunch sometime, Linnet. Maybe this weekend, when it's really all over."

"I'd like that. I should be able to finish *Capture My Heart* by then."

She smiled and opened her parasol. "Be warned. I'm going to ask for a critique."

"I'm sure I'll love it." I tried to hide a yawn and failed.

"I'll go home now and let you get some rest," Milla said.

She started to rise and quickly sat down again.

About eight houses away, a man and woman were walking a large black dog on Beechnut Street. I couldn't see their features clearly, but there was no mistaking the breed of the canine.

"Here comes that Belgian shepherd who was so unfriendly yesterday," I said. "Maybe you'd better wait."

"Could we go inside for a minute?" she asked.

"Sure."

She picked up the empty lemonade pitcher, and I opened the screen door. From the living room window we watched the trio walk by. The man with the dark beard held tightly to the leash. He said something to his companion. She laughed and hooked her arm through his. The shepherd cast a baleful glance at the house but didn't try to detour into the front yard.

"I wonder who they are," I said.

Milla shrugged. "They must live nearby. People like to walk on this street because of the beautiful houses."

You know them, I thought. *Or you know of them. Only yesterday you said the woman lived on Beechnut Street.*

But I couldn't challenge Milla. Especially when she seemed a little nervous.

Here was one more mystery. Someone thought I didn't have enough to occupy my mind.

THIRTEEN

AND NOW TO BED.

Well, not quite. It was only eight-thirty. I was finally alone, and as soon as I neatened the kitchen, I could lose myself in any activity that appealed to me.

Like reading *Capture My Heart.*

I rinsed the lemonade pitcher and tumblers and set them in the sink to air dry. The old Victorian didn't have a dishwasher; nor was there room for one. A medium-sized microwave swallowed up half the counter. My canister set and spoon rest occupied the other half, leaving a free section roughly the size of a dinner tray.

I wondered if Violet Julaine or the house's previous mistresses had ever decried the lack of work space in the tiny kitchen.

Thunder rolled across the sky, reminding me of the coming storm. I closed the windows, knowing I couldn't entirely shut out danger. Damaging winds, downed trees and power lines, flooding, lightning… Any one of these calamities could find me as easily as a bullet.

Unlike Milla, I'd never been afraid of electrical storms. Now I added a lightning strike to my growing list of concerns. Although I wanted to know the house's history, I could have lived happily without Milla's account of the fire at the pink Victorian.

But perhaps lightning wouldn't strike twice in the same place.

Looking at the walls, I would never have known that smoke and flames had once filled the room, choking the life out of appliances and devouring furniture. A hasty call to the Maple

Creek Fire Department and the restoration company had saved the rest of the house and returned the kitchen to its previous state. But how strange that the fire had left the phone intact.

Suppose—on a night for wild imaginings—another lightning bolt were to draw the strange power out from the phone.

On an impulse, I crossed the room, took the receiver off the hook, and held it in my hand. It was cold and silent. Decidedly dead.

"Hello?" I said, and, smiling at my foolishness, added, "Who are you and what do you want with me?"

My answer came in the form of three soft raps at the side door.

I turned on the outside lamp and peered through the curtained window. Dalton stood under the awning in a misty sheen. The lamplight turned his eyes to blue jewels and his badge to gold.

I opened the door, content to let Fate decide my evening's activity.

"I saw your light," Dalton said. "Otherwise, I wouldn't stop by so late."

"It's not late. The sky's just dark. Come in."

"You're looking good." His gaze swept over my face and came to rest on my hair that I'd twisted into a long ponytail. "After last night, I was worried about you."

"You'd never know we survived a shoot-out."

"For me, it's all in a day's work. For you… Let me just say, I'm proud of you, Linnet. You're a very courageous lady."

I felt my face grow warm at the unanticipated praise. For weeks, I'd been thinking of myself as a coward. Apparently Dalton didn't think so—or so he said. Perhaps that was part of his game plan. To ply me with sugar-tongued flattery, then move in for the kill.

Dope, I chided myself. *Milla was right. You are cynical. And you don't need to be won over. A man like Dalton knows when he's made a conquest.*

"You make it sound like you get shot at every day," I said.

He grinned. "Every other day."

"Are you still on duty?"

"Not anymore," he said.

"Then I can offer you a drink. What would you like? A beer? Wine cooler? Something stronger?"

"Just ice water," he said. "Thanks."

I poured a glass for each of us from the tap, added ice cubes, and looked around for something to go with water. The ginger wafers from the grocery store were still on the dessert plate. Milla and I had eaten half of them—for they were indeed wafers, very thin.

As we sat down at the kitchen table, I said, "Did you find anything on the beach?"

"Two bullets and miscellaneous junk."

"There were more than two shots," I said. "Or did it just seem like more?"

"I counted eight. The other six bullets could be anywhere."

I nodded. "Buried in the sand or at the bottom of the lake. How about Carl Hogan?"

"He and Adam are still in custody."

I absorbed this news, realizing that it didn't make me feel any better. "Then someone else out there wants to kill me."

"Or me. Or it was random."

I took one of the wafers and broke it in two, had to restrain myself from crumbling it into tiny pieces. That would only make a mess and betray my agitation to this man who thought me brave.

The shadowy enemy bent on my destruction seemed to move a little closer, like the thunder, almost overhead. I could almost feel his hot breath on my neck.

And he was no longer contained in my fourth hour class.

But for the moment, just the moment, I was safe.

Deciding to change the subject, I said, "Have you ever seen a bearded man who owns a black Belgian shepherd?"

"Many times. You've just described Garth MacKay. He has a title business on Main Street—Sky and MacKay Title. It's in an old purple house. You must have passed it hundreds of times."

I had and even thought how striking it looked with contrasting shades of lavender in a surround of green shrubbery.

Encouraged by his response, I continued. "I've seen him walking with a woman, his girlfriend, I guess. She has long, black hair."

"That's Katherine Kale." Dalton's tone was cool and clipped, police-department official.

I broke another wafer in two. Dalton knew more about Garth MacKay and his girlfriend but didn't intend to talk about them, leaving me to speculate on my own, which was always risky.

Was it Garth, Katherine, or the black dog who had elicited that jittery reaction from Milla? The strange desire to remove herself quickly from their presence?

Garth, I decided. With his burly shape and dark beard, the man looked like danger personified. But he also looked intriguing. Was he a man from Milla's past? An old lover who had scorned her? Someone she feared?

"What's your interest in MacKay and Katherine?" Dalton asked.

I hesitated, not sure myself, except for Milla's odd response to them which I didn't intend to share with Dalton.

"They have a beautiful dog," I said. "You don't see many Belgian shepherds in this area."

"Tac is the only one in town. I agree. He's a handsome animal."

I suspected that Dalton knew I had another reason for being curious about Garth and his entourage, just as I knew he could have told me more about them. But I didn't intend to pursue the matter with him. Not now.

"If you're free next Tuesday, how about we continue our date?" Dalton said.

"I'd love that."

"We'll go to a restaurant miles from Maple Creek. No one will find us. If they do, I'll be ready for them."

"That sounds more like a stake-out," I said.

"It'll be a date. A right and proper one. Starting at six when I pick you up."

His lazy smile promised immeasurable pleasures. Firecrackers but no gunfire. That was exactly what I wanted.

I remembered those golden minutes before the shooter ruined our romantic evening. Kisses on a moonlit beach. A new awareness of the man who held me close. A sudden longing to stay in his arms… Well, not forever, but for a long, glorious time.

"I'll be looking forward to it," I said.

"I'm going to be at Alcott tomorrow during lunch and after school. I want to know how you managed with the killer class."

That all-too-accurate description of my fourth hour freshmen dragged me from the rosy clouds down to earth. Before I could enjoy Dalton's kisses, before he jump-started my summer with fireworks, I'd have to live through an hour and a half of ninth grade madness and possibly more.

TOMORROW'S WATCHWORD was survival.

At Alcott Middle School, traditions were sacred—except for the one governing the exam day schedule. Dwight Dunlap liked to play with it, loved to throw everyone into a state of confusion. "Keep them guessing" was his motto. That applied to staff as well as student body.

Last year, over the two-day testing period, we'd begun with first hour and ended with sixth. That made sense.

So did variety. At the semester change, Dunlap had reversed the order. This June, he'd decided that we would give fourth, fifth, and sixth period exams on Wednesday, with tests for third, second and first hour classes on Thursday. It was a combination with built-in confusion. No one could be sure he was in the right place at the right time without checking the posted schedule.

For me and other teachers with sixth hour conference periods, Wednesday was an easy day; and having my most challenging class first when my energy level was at its highest point made it easier still. Heaven knows, I needed every dollop of strength I could muster.

I'd been in my classroom a half hour early, moving desks farther apart, leaving more space between aisles. In other words, making it more difficult for would-be copiers.

Last night's storm hadn't brought the hoped-for cooling in its wake. The morning's steamy air stole through seven windows, providing enough heat to keep a cup of hot chocolate warm. The eighth window was still nailed shut, but it was so hot inside and out, that hardly mattered.

My freshmen looked tamer than usual and even quieter. Complaints about the stuffy room persisted, but they were a little less abrasive. If this class had always met first hour in the morning instead of after lunch, the dynamics of our relationship might have been different.

Jimmy had brought his own fan, a miniature model run by a battery. Predictably, everyone wanted to sit next to him. I frowned, noting several seat changes that had already taken place.

Was *this* the mean plan? To trash my carefully thought-out seating chart?

They weren't going to do that. Not on this all-important test day.

"Let's have everybody back in their assigned seats," I said. And waited.

Nobody moved.

"Don't you know our names by now?" Debbie asked, not bothering to disguise the sneer in her voice.

"That isn't the point. You have assigned desks. Sit in them."

I didn't intend to waffle or grant exceptions as that would amount to a slight relinquishing of control. This was their last chance to even that vague score. They were, after all, the class that had planned my death.

Rephrase that, Linnet, I ordered myself. *It's the class with two students who tried to kill you and thirty others, some of them collaborators who had cleverly eluded detection.*

No one looked particularly murderous today. Only whiny, lethargic, revved up, disagreeable, bored. In other words, I had a typical mixture of moods to cope with.

"Geez, Ms. Shellwin," Jimmy said. "It's our last day."

"I know that."

"Why can't we sit where we want?" demanded Brandy. "After today, you'll never have to see us again."

"That's true—as long as you pass the class. If you don't, you'll be here next fall in ninth grade English, doing it all over again."

I hated to sound so harsh, but a teacher had to use every weapon at her disposal.

"You'd like that."

Like three stones, the accusation sailed through the hot air. I felt as if all three of them had struck me.

There was always a certain male voice I couldn't identify. His tone was invariably derisive, the words distinct. They oozed dislike for me and disrespect.

That voice, I thought. *Catch it and your troubles may be over.*

But I simply couldn't tell who had spoken other than that it was a boy sitting somewhere in the back.

In any event, soon it wouldn't matter. I glanced at the time, promising myself that I would do this only once. Clock watching was a guaranteed way to make a ninety-minute session twice as long.

"Let's *start*," Sherry said. "What are you waiting for?"

I glared at her. "For the class to be totally quiet."

The unidentified voice spoke again. "You're the one talking, Shellwin."

In the sudden silence that followed this rude observation, I heard the grating of metal desk legs being dragged across tile. Dennis Hargraves was sliding closer to Candace Ann.

"Move your desk back in the row, Dennis!" I said.

He didn't budge but stared back at me, eyes ablaze with defiance.

I held on to the stack of tests and waited. Stood still and hoped for a quick end to this nonsensical confrontation.

"Oh, for Pete's sake, Dennis, just do what she wants," Sherr said. "I wanna get out of here early."

"A reminder," I said. "Nobody leaves until the bell rings. Principal's orders."

The short-lived silence erupted in a volley of objections.

"But that's so dumb," Azalea said. "What if we have fifth hour Study Hall?"

"Then report to the cafeteria and study for your sixth hou test."

"What if we just go out the back door quietly?" Dale asked.

"You're not going to do that," I said. "So don't rush through the test. Take your time. Write thoughtful answers."

"You can't keep us here like prisoners," Dennis said.

I didn't answer. I held on to the tests and didn't move. Here was a classic battle of the wills. Hold your ground. To the bitte end. No surrender.

Give me one more cliché. No, give me a line of pure, lofty poetry, one applicable to this ridiculous stand-off.

This is the way the world ends…

The exams in my arms grew heavier. The temperature in the room soared. I longed to dab at the dampness between my breasts. The small blades in Jimmy's fan did their best to move the stagnant air. It wasn't good enough. I felt the first throbbings of a tension headache.

This is the way the world ends…

The noise slowly faded, rose again, and died. In the blessed lull, Dennis moved his desk back, a respectable distance from Candace Ann.

One small victory for Linnet Shellwin.

I counted out seven tests for the first row and moved on to the second. Six tests here. Seven for the third row…

Soon everybody was writing. An occasional cough or shuffle of feet were the only sounds in the room. Finally, on the last day, I had the order and quiet I'd yearned for all semester.

I wasn't naive enough to think it could last.

BY TWENTY MINUTES PAST NINE, the untidy mound of completed tests on my desk had grown high, and the class had become understandably restless. First whispers. Then slightly audible exchanges, followed by louder ones. Then pandemonium. For the few students still working, I had to maintain order.

To the bitter end.

"Quiet down—everybody," I said. "The test is still going on."

"Yeah, for the slowpokes," Brandy said. "Hurry up so we can talk."

Nine more minutes. Eight.

"My pen died!" Debbie wailed.

Dale laughed. "Then stop writing."

"Drop dead, Dale. Ms. Shellwin. What am I going to do?"

This is the way the world ends/ Not with a bang but a whimper.

Except Debbie's annoying whine could never be described as a whimper.

As I gave her another pen, I saw that she had a half page of short essays to write in six minutes.

She scribbled a line or two under each item and gave the test and pen to me without a word of thanks.

Well surely I hadn't expected one.

The bell rang. Test packets landed on my desk in no particular order. I straightened them, noticing that my copy of the review had come back. Naturally I hadn't seen who turned it in. At this point, I didn't care. The class managed to exit without the screeching and confetti showers of yesterday.

Oh, thank God. Thank you, God. It's over and nothing terrible happened.

Candace Ann, as usual the last to leave, stopped at my desk. Like most of the other girls, she was casually dressed for exam day in shorts and a fussy ruffled top that could have doubled as a dress. Both were bright pink, and her face was flushed either from the heat or the stress of test taking. She looked, I thought, a little desperate.

"When will you have our exams corrected?" she asked.

"Soon."

"Because I have to know my grade. Not just for the test. For the course."

"You will. I'm not a grading machine, Candace Ann. There are a lot of essays to read, and I have five classes…"

I sounded a bit whiny myself. I should have stopped with "You will."

"Can I come back after lunch?" she asked.

I sighed. "Sure. If you don't have a sixth hour exam."

"I have Study Hall. Do you think you'll have mine done by then?"

"I'll do my best."

She reached for my snow globe paperweight, the object that had always fascinated her, and turned it slowly, her gaze on the make-believe snow shower falling on Bambi. Without looking up, she said, "I wanted to tell you they changed their minds, kind of."

"Who?" I asked.

She shrugged.

But I knew who. Euphoria at Alcott Middle School was short-lived. How could I have thought that because the course was over, the plotting would end too?

"The kids," she said. "You know. They're going to do something in the summer when school's out so they won't get in trouble like Carl and Adam."

I spoke calmly, determined not to let Candace Ann know that her remark had upset me. "Well that depends on what they do. The principal has a long arm. So does the law."

"All I know is it's something mean," she said. "I just want you to be careful, Ms. Shellwin. I really like you. You're cool."

I smiled, aware that my lips were trembling. "And you're a thoughtful girl, Candace Ann."

The principal had given us an extra ten minutes for passing from one class to another today and for general unwinding between exams. My fifth hour students were beginning to trickle in. Candace Ann set the snow globe down beside the tests.

"You'd better run on, now, or the hall monitor will get you."

"See you for my grade this afternoon," she said.

I couldn't remember promising her that it would be ready by then, but Candace Ann was one of the few likeable students in fourth hour. I shuffled through the stack, found her test, and moved it to the top.

She was one of the rare girls I would remember and miss.

FOURTEEN

In a dream I sat at my kitchen table eating a cinnamon roll and reading the Maple Creek Tribune:

At the height of the storm, a lightning bolt started a fire in a vacant house on 147 Beechnut Street, damaging the kitchen. Only the telephone on the east wall was left untouched.

That happened at my house! Before it was my house.

There was more, but as I attempted to finish the story, the letters blurred. Smoke billowed out from the walls. To my horror, I discovered that my lungs wouldn't fill with air. Only with vile smoke. I began to cough. I knew that I should run from the flames, but I couldn't move.

The phone rang, its familiar strident screech lost in the roar of fire. A barrier of thick smoke hid its form from view, but I knew where it was. Throwing off the covers, gasping for breath…

I shuddered into a waking state, dream fragments breaking over me. Full awareness came quickly.

Exhausted from the day's heat and turmoil, I had fallen asleep at the kitchen table over iced tea and Milla's torrid romance novel. There was no cinnamon roll, the glass felt warm, and the phone was actually ringing. The same phone that only last night had been dead.

It needs to be buried, I thought. *Ripped off the wall, silenced forever. Because when I answer it, no one will be on the other end of the line.*

Expecting nothing, I held the receiver to my ear. The line was alive, crackling and bristling with static. Positively electric.

"Hello?" I said. "Who is it?"

This time, I heard a woman's voice, soft and lightly accented. "Linnet Shellwin."

"I'm Linnet Shellwin. Who are you?"

"At last! I thought I'd never get through. I have something to tell you. Listen carefully..."

Static overrode the woman's voice. Then she was back, speaking raggedly, leaving gaps between words. It was as if she too struggled for breath.

"There isn't much time. Linnet? Are you still there?"

"Yes. What did you want to tell me?"

"You have to..."

The voice fell into dead air.

No! Not after finally making contact!

"What? What is it?" I pushed the receiver closer to my ear, willing the voice or even the static to come back, knowing they wouldn't.

The phone had snatched the connection away. I was holding on to a mere hunk of plastic. It had no power to connect one person to another or transmit conversations.

Discouraged, I slammed the receiver back into its cradle and sat down again. I looked for the cinnamon roll, found only the glass of tea. By now it was lukewarm and unappealing, the ice cubes melted. I drank it anyway, mulling over what the unknown woman had said.

Something I had to... Do? Know? Stop?

And why the urgency?

I wanted to slam something else, and the empty glass was handy. It almost shattered as it banged on the table.

That phone had toyed with me as a suspense writer would, stopping at a point of high drama to make sure the reader turned to the next page. I felt manipulated and more than a little odd to be thinking of an inanimate object as if it were a human.

As I recalled what little there'd been of the woman's message, something struck me as significant. The caller had pronounced my name correctly. Most people on first meeting me called me Lynette. So she knew me, or knew of me.

I stared at the phone, hoping it would ring again but suspected that it wouldn't. Not tonight anyway. The phone was in charge of the situation. I was an unwilling pawn in some demented game.

Since my move to Maple Creek, frustration had been a constant in my life. It seemed that something always came along to bedevil me. With the killer class disbanded, their mean plan still hovered over my life. A disembodied voice on a haunted phone had just issued a cryptic, albeit incomplete, warning. My precious collie puppy might be coming to a dangerous home.

Did I miss anything?

Oh, yes. The Violet Julaine case. I lived in a house that had once belonged to a murder victim. The evil vibes were out to get me.

EVEN THOUGH THE HEAT WAVE continued, the next day at Alcott was more pleasant. The atmosphere in the halls was practically festive. I was giving three tests instead of two, but my classes were more cooperative

For me, yesterday had ended on an anti-climactic note. I had seen Dalton's patrol car in the lot, but not Dalton. I wasn't inclined to wait in a hot parking lot for him to appear. He would find me, sooner or later. Danger had forged a bond between us.

That was good. The bond, that is; not the danger.

Then there was Candace Ann. I didn't see her. For some reason, she had apparently lost interest in knowing her course grade ahead of time. And finally, Annabelle. When I'd looked for her to ask about the possible effect of lightning on telephones, I learned that she had left school early for a meeting and wouldn't be in the building until Friday.

No wonder I'd gone home to fall asleep and have that strange dream.

But today was better in every way, and lunch was its high point.

Louise, our cafeteria lady, had a surplus of chicken pies that she didn't want to keep frozen over the summer. She distributed them, free of charge and warm from the microwave, to those teachers who were staying at school during the noon hour.

Ned made a quick trip to Dairy Land and returned with chocolate sodas for everybody, and Marellen provided a large basket of fruit. They'd known about the chicken pies yesterday.

This last lunch on the shady Alcott grounds had the look and feel of a picnic. Ned's usual partners had gone to the Blue Lion for a meal of meat and potatoes in an air-conditioned environment. Consequently, Ned joined Marellen, Mrs. Crumle, Jody, and me on a bench beneath the school's leafiest maple tree.

"I'd rather have you lovely ladies to myself than a filet and French fries," he said.

"How gallant!" Marellen said.

I slipped a long plastic spoon into my soda. "These look wonderful, Ned. You're so generous."

"And that's only one of my virtues," he said with a wink.

"Yes, thanks." Jody raised her glass high. "It's been a wild year. Let's toast the end with sodas."

"I'll drink to that," I said.

"So will I." Mrs. Crumle looked up the hill, toward the school's front entrance. "Who's that? He looks familiar."

The Levi's clad man was heading in our direction, sure of his destination, apparently certain of his welcome.

"He must be one of the subs," Marellen said. "Who isn't here today?"

As the newcomer drew near, I realized that he was the man I'd seen last week looking up at my stained glass heart window. I'd been suspicious of his interest in my house until he mentioned his connection to it. We hadn't introduced ourselves, and he'd walked off into the rain. I'd forgotten about him until now.

Ned turned around, a broad grin spreading over his face. "That's one of our illustrious graduates, Marellen. Don't you ladies remember Randy Galloway? Ten years ago?"

I didn't, of course. Marellen said, "He was such a nice boy. I don't remember him being so attractive, though."

I looked at him more closely, this man I'd thought of briefly as Milla Schoenherr's teacup stranger. With his burly build and dark good looks, he was indeed handsome. He reminded me of someone I'd seen recently. A younger version of that man.

But who? I hadn't been anywhere to meet new men in months.

Randy reached our bench and smiled at everyone, although he addressed his first remark to Ned. "Mr. Glint? Do you remember me?"

Ned shook his hand enthusiastically. "Randy Galloway! I never forget one of our bright stars. Won't you join us?"

"Just for a second. I'm on my way to the high school."

Randy nodded to Mrs. Crumle, Marellen, and Jody and let his eyes rest on me with no sign of recognition.

"I'm Linnet Shellwin," I said.

"Oh—I remember now. You live in the old Julaine house."

"That's my claim to fame."

"Linnet is our ninth grade English teacher," Ned said. "She can actually make literature interesting."

I could?

"She even makes those dry old Dickens characters come to life," he added.

I hoped I wasn't blushing—not over an undeserved professional compliment. Hadn't Ned heard that I was boring? That I'd driven my students to murder? Well, let him enjoy his delusions.

"What are you doing now, Randy?" Mrs. Crumle asked.

"I'm in town for my high school reunion and thought I'd see if any of my old teachers were still around."

Mrs. Crumle hadn't been specific, and Randy had neatly dodged her question. Why? I studied his expression but saw nothing but delight at reconnecting with old teachers. No sign of dissembling. But something about Randy Galloway wasn't quite right.

"You came back just in time," Ned said. "After tomorrow, we'll be scattered all over the globe."

"Not all of us," Mrs. Crumle said. "I'm going to spend the summer working in my garden."

"I remember those bouquets you used to bring in, Mrs. Crumle. We always thought you bought them in a flower shop."

She laughed. "Sometimes I did. When my garden turned green."

"Turned green?" Ned said.

"Stopped producing flowers."

Randy's gaze swept over the old brick building on the hill and the white farmhouse-cafeteria that already had a "closed for the season" look.

"I loved this old school," he said. "There's not another one like it in the county."

"Nothing has changed," Ned said.

"I heard they were tearing it down," he added.

"Not this year or next."

"When is your class having its reunion, Randy?" Jody asked.

"This Saturday—at Loosestrife Inn."

"It's always fun to meet with old friends," I said, remembering my own first reunion and the odd sense of falling back into time. Newly married girls on the arms of their husbands. Ginger and Heather, still single, not a bit changed since our last get together.

"Well it's interesting," Randy said. "I hope our old teachers can make it. We invited all of them."

The sound of the bell drifted down the hill, calling staff and students back to their rooms for the last exam of the school year.

"Well that's it." Jody scooped up the last of her ice cream.

"What do you say we take up a collection to buy Louise something? A plant or roses."

"What a good idea!" I reached for a five dollar bill and promptly found myself in charge of the project.

In the general rush to gather up dishes and tidy the bench, Ned said, "Remember we have an extra ten minutes."

Randy rose. "It was nice seeing you guys again."

"Stop by the next time you're out this way," Ned said. "We'll still be here."

"What a dismal thought," Jody murmured. "I hope I'll be some place more exotic."

"I always liked that young man," Mrs. Crumle said when he was out of ear shot. "Why didn't he tell us what he's doing now, I wonder?"

I stared after Randy's departing figure, wondering that myself. "Because it's illegal?"

I'd managed to shock her and the other three as well.

"Linnet!" Mrs. Crumle said. "Randy was a model student. He was captain of the football team. Class president. Popular with the girls. Every teacher's dream."

"All that? What a reputation to maintain."

"I'm sure he's doing something important," she said. "Maybe he works for the government."

"Didn't he want to be an archaeologist?" Marellen asked.

Ned laughed. "What boy didn't? I remember something about the Naval Academy. I wrote a letter of recommendation for him."

"We should have asked him," I said.

"I *did*," Mrs. Crumle reminded us.

All I knew about Randy Galloway was what his former teachers said about him and what he'd told me about delivering papers to Violet Julaine. Also, the news of her untimely death had angered him.

Because I was wired to look for hidden agendas these days, I felt that there was more to the Randy Galloway story. Unfortunately I was unlikely to see him again.

"How did it go with that killer class, Linnet?"

Dalton strode into my classroom, looking grand and powerful in his uniform. He sidestepped a widening pool of water. Phil and Chet, two third hour students who had never given me a second of trouble, had started a water pistol war in the last minutes of class.

They'd surrendered their weapons readily but not before drenching several of their classmates, all of them squealing girls.

""'Not too bad," I said. "Did anyone else have trouble?"

"Nothing serious. I confiscated illegal fireworks on the first floor and emptied a bottle of Jack Daniels. There was a fight at the high school. It's been brewing for weeks. One kid ended up with a broken arm."

"To spend the summer in a cast. Boys!"

I gathered the day's exams, my grade book and purse. This was my last homework of the year. Tomorrow I'd only have to record grades. Our final staff meeting would be a formality with cake and ice cream and a gift for Jody who was getting married in August.

Dalton sat on one of the students' desks in the front row, looking like a giant in a doll house. "Looks like your killer class was all talk," he said.

"I don't think so." I told him about their new time table, according to Candace Ann.

He shook his head. "I wouldn't worry about it if I were you, Linnet."

"Well, Dalton, I'm not a mighty police lieutenant with brawn to spare and guns at his disposal."

He grinned. "That's good for us men. Seriously, you must know that kids rarely think about getting even with teachers in the summertime. There's too much else to do."

"For a while. Then boredom sets in. Mischief is born. I'm in trouble again."

"I have confidence in you," he said.

I warmed at the unabashed admiration in his eyes. It was

strange how other people's opinions of me differed from my own. Ned thought I could make Dickens' characters interesting. Dalton believed I was a match for the killer class. To Candace Ann, I was cool.

Maybe I was underestimating myself.

FIFTEEN

ON FRIDAY MORNING, AFTER marking my cards, I stripped the classroom to its veritable bones for the summer vacation. The contents of my desktop and teachers' editions of textbooks went into the closet, and faded construction paper from the bulletin boards into the overflowing wastebasket.

One corner of my desk was stacked high with corrected tests and various forms I had to turn into the office as my passport to freedom. Everything was complete and in order.

I closed the seven windows and taped another note to the one with the broken lock, hoping that MacGregor or one of his crew would fix it before September. This done, I stood for a moment in the front of the room, breathing hot, dry, air. On this last day I wore jeans and a top with a low neckline but was still too warmly dressed.

Harsh sunlight magnified every crack in the faded beige paint, every chip in the floor tile, and every scratch on the furniture. Dust motes floated through the air, eager to reclaim their territory. The old room had never been so quiet or empty or… I searched for the best adjective to describe what I felt and settled on sinister.

That was the word. Filled with echoes and memories, the classroom was haunted by the legions of freshmen who had come together here over the years and most recently by the spirits of the killer class.

But my fourth hour freshmen would never be a group again. I had to stop dwelling on past insults and fears.

Still the images came. Carl hunched over textbook, giving no warning of his murderous intent. Sherry's snide remarks. Jimmy's smirk. Azalea's insistence on writing notes in class.

Paper airplanes flying through the air. Whiny demands to leave the room for any one of a hundred flimsy reasons. Smiling faces hiding deadly plots. Whispered voices. "Pass it on!"

Stop! I shut them out of my mind, finished my bottle of lemon-flavored water and tossed it into the basket.

It was almost ten-thirty. The staff meeting was scheduled for eleven in the library. I had worked hard, finished early, and delivered a dish garden to a delighted Louise as a thank-you gift for our special lunches. Now what? Find someone to visit or help? Read more of *Capture My Heart,* which I'd tucked into my purse? Go for a hot morning stroll on the grounds?

Do something, Linnet, I told myself. *Don't just stand here in a silent, airless room. You'll melt or have a meltdown.*

Silent? When had it gotten so quiet? Earlier, Murielle and Mrs. Crumle had carried on a shouted conversation from their rooms. Someone had been playing a radio, blaring country music to end the school year with. Now there wasn't a sound. Could I possibly be alone up here?

If so, I'd better hurry downstairs and join the others.

I took one last look around the denuded classroom, gathered my materials for the office and my purse, and walked to the door, puzzled by my irrational reluctance to move on.

Hadn't I been waiting for this day since the semester change brought me that dangerous never-in-control band of miscreants?

Go, I ordered myself. *Lock the door. Give the key to Dunlap. It's over.*

Footsteps in the hall jarred me into high alert. I froze and listened as they came closer.

I wasn't alone on the second floor after all, but that in itself was no cause for alarm. Dalton might be in the building again. Or Candace Ann coming for her grade. Or Ned.

Or anyone.

An unbidden memory of Carl and his confederate rushed out of the blackness, forcing me to relive the incident. A door slamming. Being pushed open again. A gun pointed at me. Hurtful, mocking words. A trap that I'd never foreseen.

Quickly I assessed the present situation. The hall monitors had been released from their duties for the summer. No students were allowed in the building today; but when did school rules ever keep them away? If trouble developed, there were plenty of able bodied men on the staff to head it off. They weren't here now. I couldn't count on anyone except myself.

The teachers' scissors, with a broken blade, lay buried in the basket under construction paper, but my snow globe and letter opener, both potential weapons, were in my purse.

Hurry! Get out of here!

As I formed the thought, the footprints came to a stop. Out in the hall, a door creaked open. The one to the room next to mine, I thought. Annabelle's science lab. Annabelle might be inside, and I wanted to talk to her… But I could do that at the meeting.

Don't speculate. Don't linger. It could be fatal.

I glanced quickly up and down the hall. No one was there. Ned's and Annabelle's doors were open. Both offered plenty of hiding places. But I had no intention of investigating. I locked my door, then, moving faster than usual, headed toward the stairs.

Whose footsteps had I just heard? And where was the person now?

Behind me. Closing the distance on me in steady determined strides.

They were too heavy for Candace Ann. Not her then. A man but not Ned or one of my fellow teachers. The Alcott staff was famous for its camaraderie. If the mysterious walker were a teacher or custodian, he would have called out a greeting to me and said something predictable.

"All done, Linnet?" "Hot as Hades up here, isn't it?" "When does the meeting start?"

No one who knew about my brush with death in this very school would follow me stealthily down the hall. Therefore he was a stranger, one who didn't speak; therefore he was up to no good.

Just turn around, for heavens' sake, I told myself. *See who it is. Say hello.*

I imagined a long shadow catching up to me, looming over me. A ruthless hand gripping my arm. An assailant dragging me back into one of the empty rooms and leaving me there to die. *A frightful fiend doth close behind me tread...*

Thanks for that one, Coleridge.

Would anyone think of looking for me in a locked room on the second floor? How soon would MacGregor start cleaning? I could almost hear Dwight Dunlap say in the exasperated tone he reserved for those who annoyed him, "Where's Linnet Shellwin? Does she know that attendance at my meetings is mandatory?"

I broke into a run. The distance to the stairs seemed interminable.

What would happen to my puppy if I wasn't there to welcome her to her new home?

I turned around, just as the footsteps ceased. The hall was empty and filled with sunshine and, in places, with dark shadows. The open doors were far behind. How could a person have vanished? I reached the stairs and all but slid down to the first floor.

I can't wait to get out of this building, I thought. I don't want to come back. Ever.

ONE BY ONE, THE STAFF drifted into the library, today decorated with ribbons and paper bells by the secretaries, Sara and Donna. An enormous chocolate sheet cake and a wedding present occupied the largest table toward the front. Secure in the midst of my fellow teachers, surrounded by happy chatter and normalcy, my heartbeat slowed to a respectable rate.

This was a safe place.

I handed my farewell packet of materials to Donna, and marveled at how much lighter I felt. Ned and Marellen sat at a table toward the back of the room. Ned was studying a map, Marellen sorting through coupons. I joined them.

"Did you leave your room unlocked, Ned?" I asked.

"No. Why?"

"I noticed the door was open."

"That's strange," he said.

"Someone was up there, walking around." I marveled that I could speak in a steady voice.

"In the hall or in my room?" he asked.

"The hall."

"It must be a straggler or maybe a janitor. They hired a couple of new ones to paint the rooms this summer. Everything's locked up, but I'll check it out after the meeting."

And he wouldn't find anyone. I knew that as surely as I knew that I hadn't imagined the footsteps.

Dwight Dunlap moved to the place of honor behind the librarian's desk. "Let's get started. First, thank you for the extraordinarily successful year. I hope you all have a good summer and come back in September refreshed and ready to make next year even better."

A canned speech. The real school business had already been taken care of. This was a brief social occasion. The floor fan was blowing toasty air on me. Beginning to feel drowsy, I hid a yawn.

"I don't want to think about September now," Marellen said in a whisper.

As Sara began to unwrap paper plates and plastic forks, Dunlap continued. "Jody, I know you didn't want any fuss made over your coming nuptials, but we outvoted you."

To the accompaniment of lazy applause, Donna handed Jody the present. "Getting married is a once-in-a-lifetime event," he added.

In an ideal world, I thought.

Jody blushed and looked wistfully at the door, no doubt uncomfortable at being the center of attention.

"What did we get her?" Ned asked, also in a whisper.

Marellen, who was in charge of the Hospitality Fund, said, "An electric griddle."

"How romantic," I said.

"It *is*," Ned countered. "Just think of the great breakfasts Jody can make for her husband."

Marellen glared at him. "Chauvinist."

"Whose idea was it to eat cake before lunch?" I asked.

"Dunlap's. But this way we'll get out of here earlier," Marellen pointed out.

And indeed, as soon as Jody opened her present, thanked everyone, and told us we were all invited to her August 15th wedding, Dwight Dunlap adjourned the meeting, and people began to disperse with impressive speed.

I wrapped my cake in a napkin and reached for my purse. Annabelle had stopped to chat with Jody, and I wanted to make sure she didn't leave before I had a chance to talk to her.

"Would you like to go to the wedding with me, Linnet?" Ned asked.

"What?" My mind focusing on Annabelle and the phone mystery, I couldn't quite believe what Ned had said. "To Jody's wedding?" I said. "With you?"

"If you're free." His eyes sparkled. "There's no district policy against faculty members dating. None that I know of."

"August 15th. I think I'll be free. I'd love to go—with you."

You sound like an idiot, I scolded myself. *Any minute Ned will rescind his invitation, pulling some forgotten prior engagement out of the air.*

But he didn't. "Good," he said. "It'll be fun. See you at the cottage on Monday."

"On Monday," I repeated, realizing I'd almost forgotten about our new course.

Leaving Ned with a quick smile, I threaded my way through small groups exchanging goodbyes and caught up with Annabelle as she was about to go through the door.

"Are you leaving now?" I asked.

"Oh, hi, Linnet. Not yet. I have some tidying up to do in the lab."

"Do you need any help?"

"Not really, but I wouldn't mind company. Empty buildings depress me."

"They scare me," I admitted.

"It's no wonder. You must be thinking about that awful Hogan boy. I hope he pays for what he did. Attempted murder is a serious crime."

"I just hope he isn't back next year," I said.

As we climbed the stairs, I wondered if the unseen person in the hall, the intruder, was still in the building. He might be more dangerous than Carl and Adam combined.

I should have told Dunlap, I thought. *I will, on the way out.*

But that might be overkill. There were no footsteps now, no conversations in progress, no radio music. Most likely Annabelle and I were the only two people on the floor.

Annabelle frowned. "That's funny. I thought I locked the lab. I know I closed the door."

Ned's door was open too, both of them just as I'd last seen them.

"I think somebody's lurking around," I said.

"Somebody like who? It must be the janitors getting a head start on summer cleaning."

"Maybe we should wait before going inside," I said.

"Why?"

"To be on the safe side."

Annabelle shrugged. "There are two of us. I'll go in first—if you're jittery."

I didn't even try to deny that I was.

I was sure that Annabelle had locked her door, and she'd closed the windows. The lab was as stuffy as my room. It looked fairly neat to me and even spookier with Almond, the class skeleton, keeping a lonely watch over no one.

"I want to put these final projects in the closet," Annabelle said. "Nobody claimed them, and they're too nice to throw away."

They certainly were. Stacks of poster board with colorful, detailed material, incomprehensible to a science-challenged English teacher, clay dinosaurs, a contraption that resembled a trap.

I should have assigned projects to add variety to my classes, should have noted what other teachers were doing and adapted their methods to English. To my knowledge, no one had ever accused Annabelle of being boring.

"We make dinosaurs in her class!"

One excited youngster bringing a project home, and a teacher's reputation would begin to grow.

Well, next fall my classes would be different.

While we dismantled Almond and settled him in the closet for a long dark rest, I said, "I wanted to ask you about lightning, Annabelle."

As I set my theory before her, a look of unabashed amusement crossed her face.

"You're not serious."

"I am. What do you think? Could a lightning strike have that effect on a landline phone?"

She smiled and shook her head. "Only in a science-fiction story. Why do you ask?"

Because I disliked deceiving a friend, the answer I'd prepared had a dash of truth in it. "I might write a children's book over the summer and want to be accurate."

"I see. Well if your story is serious science-fiction, ax the magic phone. If it's for little kids, go ahead and have fun with it. For older readers, there's always the willing suspension of disbelief. A clever writer can make us believe anything is possible."

"Like Milla Schoenherr's plain, shy heroine being pursued by a sexy Texas sheriff?"

Annabelle laughed. "Exactly. That would never happen in real life, but we believe it. I'm surprised Milla published her book under her own name. Being a high school teacher, that is. Some passages are pretty explicit."

"I won't use a pen name for mine," I said.

"I think..." Annabelle surveyed the room, wiped white powder from her hands, and nodded "...we're done." Without a moment's hesitation or a neat transition, she said, "I noticed you were flirting with Ned at the meeting. Are you doing anything interesting this summer?"

I let her sly observation slip by. "Very interesting. Ned and I are working on the new ninth grade English course, and I'm getting a puppy."

SIXTEEN

THAT AFTERNOON A HIGH WIND blew out of the north, cooling the stifling air and stirring the wind chimes into motion. The sun dipped in and out of rapidly darkening clouds, and a smell of rain drifted down through the treetops.

Bonita was on vacation, and my neighbors on the left were seldom home; I hadn't even met them yet. The house with the willow-shaded pond that adjoined the back of my property was in foreclosure. According to the Realtor, the owners had moved out in March.

It seemed as if I were alone on Beechnut Street. I liked the illusion of solitude. For a while. Then I would begin to see danger in every shadow and crave company. I'd never been so skittish before, and it troubled me.

It's that school, I thought. *The constant need to be on guard. The danger that's as real as the blackboards and books.*

After leaving Annabelle, I'd come home to a discouraging voice mail. Caramel's breeder, Sandra, had set out for Lapeer County this morning with the puppy. A few miles south of the kennel, she'd driven into a thunderstorm and collided with another car that had skidded on a slippery stretch of freeway. No one was hurt, but her truck had sustained serious damage

That meant at least a week's delay in Caramel's arrival unless I drove up north to get her, which I might decide to do.

In the meantime, the crate I had bought for Caramel waited for its little owner. I filled it with two soft beach blankets and a plush collie toy and tried not to be too unhappy.

It was going to be a stormy summer.

Now I sat on my back porch, close to the kitchen, listening to the delicate music of the wind chimes and waiting for the phone to ring. Although I respected Annabelle's scientific knowledge, I couldn't accept her casual dismissal of my lightning bolt theory. Nothing else made sense. Nothing in this world, that is.

Of course, if I'd told her about a haunted landline and a phantom voice, she might have come up with a theory of her own. I didn't want to confide in her, though, lest she think my experiences at Alcott had unhinged me.

Maybe they had. But I didn't believe that either. Except… Why hadn't Bonita heard the phone ringing? I had no answer to that question.

The caller's urgency tugged at me. I needed to hear her fragmented message in its entirety as soon as possible. With luck, the next time she contacted me, we'd be able to carry on a conversation. Then I'd know what action to take, especially if that message proved to be a warning.

You have to… Do something? Know something? Stop something?

I sighed, looking out over my quiet green backyard, wishing I could find the tranquility I longed for.

Why did people always feel it was their duty to alert me to impending doom? Now that the school year had officially ended, I should be anticipating a season of golden days, but the disturbances at Alcott had followed me home where I was already dealing with the rogue telephone.

Cheer up, Linnet, I told myself. *You have two dates and a puppy to look forward to. That should balance the angst nicely.*

"Linnet?"

Milla Schoenherr stepped off the patio stone path that wound through overgrown grasses to the backyard. In a short cream colored dress with wavy tiger stripes, she looked like a different woman. Younger, sophisticated, ready for an adventure. She wore an agitated expression and a small ivory pendant shaped like a tulip.

Milla was obviously going somewhere special this evening.

I wondered where but, not wanting to appear nosy, decided not to ask. Instead I said, "That's an amazing dress!"

"Thanks. In the summer I like to break out of the traditional schoolmarm mold."

She had on a pair of brown sandals with high heels, but if she had brought a house key or wallet, they were well hidden. Surely she hadn't walked to my house in that uncomfortable footwear?

"I saw your car in the driveway," she said. "Are you busy?"

"Just unwinding. Come on up."

The tiny porch contained only a wicker rocker and a child-sized table. "I'll bring out another chair from the kitchen," I said.

"No, don't bother. I can't stay." She leaned on the railing and rubbed her ankle absently. "I would have called you on your cell, but I misplaced the number. I have to cancel our lunch next week."

"Oh, that's too bad." I waited, wondering if she'd offer an explanation. After all, our getting together for lunch had been her idea.

After a pause, she said, "My friend invited me to her cottage for the week. It's one of those offers that's too good to pass up."

"You should go, then," I said. "We can have lunch another time."

"Yes, as soon as I come home. Good luck with the new puppy, Linnet. You deserve a little fun."

"So do we all. Have a safe trip."

"I will. Now I have to rush."

She said a quick goodbye and walked out to the front, heels tapping on the patio stones. Her allusion to the puppy rekindled my disappointment at the delay in Caramel's arrival. Would I ever have her? If I were a superstitious person, I'd interpret this glitch as a sign that she wasn't meant to be my dog.

And I needed her.

Just be glad Sandra and the puppy are all right, I admonished myself.

Suddenly solitude wasn't what I wanted. Neither was company. Then what?

In the kitchen I made a turkey sandwich but was too restless to eat more than a few bites of it. I felt as I were frittering away the first precious hours of my summer vacation. I should work in the yard or take a long walk through the neighborhood. Neither activity appealed to me. Besides, it was going to rain soon.

I threw the rest of the sandwich outside for the birds, noting the gray-black streaks in the sky, and picked up the telephone. As I had expected, the line was dead.

A watched phone doesn't ring. Still, I held on to the receiver listening to nothing, waiting for static. *That's a pot, silly. And it's "a watched pot doesn't boil."*

Thunder crashed into the afternoon silence, and a series of unrelated images flashed on and off in my mind. Milla safe in her home, slipping off her high heeled sandals and brushing raindrops from her slinky dress. Dalton's vintage convertible passing Ned's Jeep, both on their way to my house. A frightened collie puppy, looking for a dark place to hide.

Violet Julaine stepping lightly out of the otherworldly mists into the kitchen.

Dear Lord! My imagination could take me to the strangest places.

I replaced the receiver and stood at the kitchen window, watching the wild sway of the trees in the wind.

Lightning never strikes twice in the same place. Was there any truth in that old adage.

LOVE, LOVE, TENDER LOVE,/Where are you tonight?/Moon and stars shine up above,/ But...

The plaintive lyrics of the song slipped in through the kitchen window and died in mid-refrain. *Dalton's old-time tape,* I thought, and looked out to see his blue Cadillac parked in my driveway. As the rain began to fall, he hastily raised the convertible top and rushed to the side door.

I opened it and breathed the scent of peppermint that came in with the wind and rain.

"Weren't we going out next Tuesday?" I asked, glad that I'd showered and changed clothes after school—just in case I'd mistaken the date.

"That's the day," he said. "I thought you might like to have a cup of coffee with me tonight. Or dinner, if you haven't eaten already."

"Coffee sounds good. Should I break in my new stove-top percolator?"

"I don't invite myself to a lady's house for food or drink," he said sternly. "We'll go out."

In the rain? If Dalton was oblivious of inclement weather, I could be too.

I found an umbrella but decided against a jacket, although it was raining harder now. Large drops struck with the force of hail as we hurried to the car. Dalton started the engine and pressed the CD button, allowing the song to resume…

…without you there is no light./Love, love, tender love,/ Hear my lonely cry…

The brush of windshield wipers against glass reinforced the sadness inherent in the lyrics, but Dalton's congenial mood dispelled the melancholy.

"We're going all the way around the corner to the Inn for Barbecued Ribs Night," he said with a grin. "Unless you have another favorite place."

"I love the Blue Lion," I said.

"Me too. Over dinner, I want to hear about your last day of school."

"And I've been wanting somebody to talk to," I said.

But I didn't introduce the subject of mysterious footsteps and unlocked classrooms until we were seated in the same alcove we'd occupied on our last visit, our chairs within touching distance of the yellow lion.

"It may be my imagination," I said when I'd told him about my fright on the second floor. "That hall holds bad memories for me. They're still hanging around, even with the kids gone."

"That's normal. Are you going to be in the building for that summer project you told me about?"

"No, we're taking turns meeting in one another's houses. I need a long vacation from Alcott."

"You do." He frowned. "A public school is far from a secured fortress. Anyone can wander in and out. What's important is that you're safe. We want to keep it that way."

"It was probably just ordinary business-as-usual," I said.

"After what happened the other night, maybe not."

I studied his expression. He was serious. This wasn't the reaction I'd hoped for.

"Then you'd be concerned—if you were me?" I asked.

"It pays to keep your eyes open and be ready for anything. Wherever you are."

I would have been happier if Dalton had dismissed my experience as nerves or imagination or an unfriendly new custodian. He was always going to tell me the truth, I realized. And that was what I wanted, even if the truth was worrisome to hear.

A waitress handed us our menus, and Dalton quickly scanned the day's specials, nodding when he found the one he wanted. "Did the kids give you any trouble on the last day?" he asked.

"Just run-of-the-mill nonsense."

I didn't mention Candace Ann's new timetable for the mean prank, as I'd already told Dalton about it. With a mental show of spirit, I tossed it aside. Those freshmen tormentors weren't going to cast a shadow on my summer. Not if I could help it.

They were tenth graders now, on their way to the high school over the hill. Moving on, growing older every day, out of my life, and, I hope, taking their mean spirits with them.

"That sounds like a teacher's lot—unfortunately," Dalton

said. "Would you like to try Northwoods Style Barbecued Spare Ribs?"

"I would. Coffee dates with you tend to get pretty elaborate."

"Wait till you see the dessert menu."

I smiled up at him, remembering our sumptuous banana splits. As I did, I noticed three newcomers being seated at a nearby table. Garth MacKay, his girlfriend, Katherine, and Randy Galloway appeared to be in a merry mood in spite of rain-soaked hair and clothing.

Now I knew why Randy had looked familiar to me. Except for his clean-shaven face, he resembled Garth closely enough to be his younger brother.

Dalton followed my gaze and nodded coolly to Katherine. "Who's that with them, I wonder," he said.

"That's Randy Galloway. He's in town for his high school reunion."

"Do you know him well?" Dalton asked.

"Not at all. He stopped by Alcott to visit his old teachers. Do you see the resemblance to Garth?"

"It's there, all right," he said, frowning, falling silent.

"Is something wrong?" I asked.

"No. Nothing. Galloway is probably a nice young man, which is more than I can say for MacKay."

DALTON REFUSED TO EXPOUND on his comment. In fact, he gave me the impression that he had spoken without thinking, which didn't happen often, and that he regretted it.

His reticence allowed me to form my own conclusion. I suspected that Dalton had once been fond of Katherine who had preferred Garth MacKay. But what woman with an appreciation for outstanding male splendor would choose Garth over Dalton?

You don't know either man, I chided myself, *and you certainly don't know Katherine Kale. It's just that Dalton looks so true blue all-American. Garth is danger personified. That dark beard, the arrogant stance, the way he seems to dominate his companions—and they let him do it.*

It's never wise to speculate on a person's character based on appearances alone. I knew that and made up my mind to forget about Garth who had no relevance to my life. As for Dalton, I wanted to know him better. It seemed that was going to happen.

And where would that leave my crush on Ned Glint?

Crushes are for schoolgirls, I told myself.

"You're distracted, Linnet," Dalton said. "Are you sure you told me everything that's been going on?"

"Everything that matters."

His smug grin made me feel uneasy. "It can't be the company."

"I'm just hungry. I didn't think I was."

"Then let's order and eat—and find something interesting to do."

A WATCHED PHONE DOESN'T RING. It waits until you're in the bathtub or in bed, until you're not thinking about phones or warnings, only about a man whose idea of something interesting is an evening of wine and kisses.

Minutes after I found a comfortable position under my light summer quilt, I heard the familiar shrilling notes of the landline phone.

It's about time!

I hurried down the stairs, trusting the banister to keep me from tumbling forward. In the kitchen I turned on the light and picked up the receiver. The line was alive, crackling with static as it had been before. Between gasps, I managed a breathless "Hello?"

"Linnet..."

It was the same soft, lightly accented voice. The same woman.

"Yes, this is Linnet."

"I'm sorry. We were cut off before. Sort of."

"Who are you?" I demanded.

"That's not important," she said. "I need to tell you something. Listen carefully. We're almost out of time."

"Then tell me before we get cut off again." I raised my voice above the static, praying that the caller would stay on the line.

"It's about your death," she said. "There's a slight chance I can help you prevent it."

SEVENTEEN

"My *what?*"

"You're going to die two weeks from tonight unless you do as I say."

"Who are you?" I demanded.

"That doesn't matter."

"Of course it does! Tell me your name this minute or I'm going to hang up."

I could hear the anger in my voice—red hot, boiling over, spilling into the fear. This was nothing more than a crank call, probably the freshmen's mean prank, postponed until after the end of the school year.

And I'd fallen into their trap, waiting anxiously for the phone to ring, willing to believe the impossible. Somehow, they had enlisted the aid of an unscrupulous adult to scare me with this ridiculous forewarning of my death.

But that easy explanation had serious flaws. How had a group of middle school students managed to breathe life into my disconnected phone? Equally puzzling, how had they found a dead woman's unlisted number? My anger gave way to a creeping coldness.

Could this be something more than a macabre ruse? I gripped the receiver tightly, pressing it closer to my ear. Of course I had no intention of hanging up. The caller must know that. "Well?" I said. "Who are you?"

"I can't tell you that, Linnet."

"Then I can't believe you."

"That would be a mistake. Not everyone gets a chance to outwit death."

I took a deep breath and decided to humor her. "All right. For the sake of argument, what should I do?"

"A couple of things. First, can you let a friendship die? Cut someone off without a word of explanation? Do it and never look back?"

"I suppose so—if I had to."

"It's the only way."

"You have to be more specific," I said.

"Of course. You've made a dangerous friend, Linnet, and in three days, you're going to make a fatal mistake..."

As if responding to an invisible cue, the rest of the sentence drowned in a burst of static. The connection died.

What dangerous friend? What fatal mistake?

"Are you there?" I shouted into the silence, knowing that she wasn't.

I should have anticipated this development. The phone enjoyed taunting me. Rather, the caller did, letting a little information seep through, stopping at a crucial point.

I held on to the receiver a little longer waiting for the line to come alive again. The minute hand on my kitchen clock ticked by. *No use,* it seemed to say. *No use no use no use.*

Was that breathing on the line? A faint squeaking in the background?

I couldn't tell.

Hang up so she can dial again.

Reluctantly I did, but I stayed in the kitchen, listening to the rain, telling myself that I wasn't afraid, still waiting. The more I thought about the message, the easier it was to believe in the woman's warning. I'd be foolish not to take it seriously, even though she couldn't possibly have been vaguer.

Maybe my would-be murderer had already tried to kill me that night at Marble Lake. If that were the case, then the dangerous friend couldn't be Dalton because we had been together at the time. Thank heavens for that. I didn't think I could end my friendship with him on the basis of an anonymous warning.

Who was she? And how could anyone know what was going

o happen in the future and what I was going to do before I did t? One more question. Why did this woman care what hap- ened to me?

My rational self felt that the calls were an elaborate hoax. The woman's message sounded like the gloom-and-doom abble of a fortune teller. But I couldn't afford to dismiss it ummarily.

The time had come to tell Dalton the entire truth. However lamaging the personal fallout, I needed his help.

JNABLE TO GO BACK TO SLEEP after the call, I lay in bed and ondered Violet Julaine's murder. The mysterious Queen of Hearts and her poisoned cherry tarts. Friends. My friends, Violet's friends, counterfeit friends.

I hadn't realized how many friends I'd made in Maple Creek intil I started making a mental list of their names. Except for Bonita, Tansy, and Milla, I'd met most of them at Alcott Middle School.

How could I know which one intended to harm me?

The caller hadn't made a connection between Violet Julaine's murder and my own danger, but instinct told me there was one.

Getting to know Violet's writer friends was by far the easier way to approach the mystery. After our first date, when Dalton and I had discussed suspects in the Julaine case, I'd jotted their names down in a spiral notebook and later added addresses. Now, in the hours before dawn, with rain still pounding on the oof, I lay in bed, leafing through the pages.

Dalton was convinced that Violet Julaine's killer belonged o her Gothic Writers group. An unofficial low-key investiga- ion might net relevant information. If I chose to believe the loomsday message, I had two weeks to learn the identity of that langerous friend, with or without the caller's help and three lays to avoid making a fatal mistake, whatever that proved to be.

And then?

I'd have to wait and see, but because this person might wel be a murderer, I'd better be careful.

Rather than waiting for the woman on the phone to contac me again, I decided to visit each member of Violet's group o her home turf and initiate a conversation about writing, publica tion, the critique group, my own mystery book—anything tha might lead to Violet and connect to the mystery of her murder In other words, hold open a door and see what, if anything flew in.

Milla Schoenherr's name topped my list, but she was tem porarily unavailable. Besides, I thought I knew her fairly well Curiously, she'd only talked about Violet at our initial meetin and never even mentioned the Gothic Writers.

Tansy Stewart, who had clashed with Violet over trees an perhaps other matters, lived across the street. It should be fairl easy to waylay her one morning when she was watering he flowerbed. Ellen Trehearne worked part-time at the Tea Roon within walking distance of my house and a pleasant destinatio for a June morning. Doreen lived in the opposite direction.

With a great deal of luck, I could avert a grim future withou additional help from the mysterious woman on the phone.

I WOKE UP EARLY THE NEXT morning, still drowsy from a lac of sleep but eager to begin my sleuthing. The storm had passed leaving a deep blue sky and glistening green landscape tha smelled of grass and flowers. The knowledge that this was m first full day of summer vacation filled me with euphoria.

I stood on my front porch and surveyed the fragrant pep permint plants on either side of the fence that separated m yard from Bonita's. They were winning their battle for survival although the dandelions threatened to choke them out. Soon this weekend definitely, I'd have to do some weeding.

Across the street, Tansy Stewart backed slowly out of he driveway. She waved to me. No matter; I could talk to he another time. In the early hours of the morning, I'd mapped ou my itinerary, loosely based on geographical location. Today' venture involved lunch in the Tea Room where I hoped to find novice horror writer Ellen Trehearne waiting on tables and afterwards, a walk to Park Street where I'd try to make contact with Doreen.

"Ms. Shellwin! Wait up!"

Candace Ann, summery and sunny in shorts and an orange top, steered her bicycle out of the street and brought it to a stop at my side. She stared at my house, her eyes riveted on the Valentine window with its rosy sunlit shimmer.

"Wow!" she said. "Do you live *here*?"

Quelling a ripple of unease, I smiled. "Yes."

I wasn't happy that one of my former students had discovered my address, but Maple Creek was a small town. Most of its school-age population probably lived in nearby neighborhoods. In any event, Candace Ann was harmless.

"All by yourself?" she asked.

"Yes, again."

"It's a palace."

"I like it," I said. "Are you going anywhere special this summer?"

"Just to the beach and Cedar Point. I'm supposed to visit my Grandma down south in August." Abruptly she changed the subject. "Do you remember my grade in English, Ms. Shellwin?"

"Not offhand, but I'm sure it's good."

It was an A or A minus, but I couldn't recall which.

"Can't you go inside and look it up?" she asked.

"Unfortunately, no. The principal has the exams and my grade book, but the office should mail out report cards in a few weeks."

"I guess I'll have to wait then."

"Weren't you going to stop by for your grade yesterday?"

"Yeah, but I had to babysit." She pulled a coffee mug with a red bow tied to its handle out of her pocket. "This is for you. I didn't wrap it or anything."

I turned the mug around, exclaiming over its delicate pattern.

Tiny red and pink Valentine hearts danced across its surface, spelling out *For My Favorite Teacher.* "No matter what anyone says, you're the best," she said.

"Why thank you. It's beautiful."

I'd have to take Candace Ann's present inside or leave it in my car. For some reason, I didn't want to do either until she rode on. While I hesitated, she said, "I heard something else—about the plan."

I sighed. Would it never end?

"Those kids from our class…" She glanced around nervously, but we were alone on the street. "Those guys… They're going to complain about you to the Board of Education. They're going to say you never taught us anything, that you just let us sit in class and fool around all hour."

"Well…" I shrugged. "Let them. We know better. By the way, who are they?"

"Dale is one, and some of his friends." She lowered her voice. "If that doesn't work, they're going to make up a story about you. Something bad."

It was a struggle to keep my emotions in check. How had I managed to instill such deep hatred in my students? The thought of lies passing blithely from one school board member to another was almost as chilling as a voice on a disconnected phone prophesying my death.

The next board meeting was rapidly approaching, and Tina the Terrible, mother of Oliver, had already muttered similar threats. If the caller's prophecy was correct, I'd be dead by then.

Untenable thought.

I couldn't let Candace Ann know that her words had shaken my composure. Summoning a bright smile, I said, "Here's a lesson for you, Candace Ann. No matter how hard you try, you'll never please everyone. So just do the best you can and please yourself."

"But aren't you going to do anything about it?" she demanded.

"I don't know what I can do," I said. "Thanks for the pretty mug. I'll use it every morning at breakfast."

SITTING INSIDE THE TEA ROOM over a pot of Orange Pekoe and fresh strawberry muffins, I let the morning's trauma and tension slide temporarily into the past. I'd have to deal with all of it soon enough—the danger, a false friend, and a besmirched reputation. But none of the above had followed me to this small elegant restaurant across from the park.

I was in luck. The lone waitress on duty wore a nametag identifying her as Ellen. She was an attractive blond woman, possibly in her forties, with a short, bouncy hair style. I considered. Waitress, Gothic writer—poisoner of critique partner. That last sounded far-fetched. Maybe it wasn't.

I had brought along an old Gothic novel to serve as a lure. As Ellen passed by my table with a carafe of hot water, she saw it, as I hoped she would. Her eyes, the color of soft gray flannel, literally lit up.

"*The Wailing Winds of Cranberry Hall,*" she said. "My! That's an antique."

"It's very suspenseful and spooky."

"I wish there were more Gothics being written today. Once that's all you could see on the book racks—blue and green covers with ladies running away from castles or abbeys or whatever."

"That was before my time." I caressed the fragile, well-worn paperback. "I found this in a library sale for fifty cents."

Ellen filled my teapot with steaming water and gazed down at the book. "I'd love to write a Gothic novel of my own, but it's taking me a long time to get the hang of it. In the meantime, they've gone out of style."

Here was the opening I'd hoped for. "How did you learn to write in that particular genre? Did you take a course?"

"I read every Gothic I could find and took an online class," she said. "Then I belonged to a writers' club for a while."

"I'm working on a mystery for girls. Do you think I could join this group?"

"Oh, no," she said quickly. "I mean, it isn't exclusive, but our founder died last year. That is, she was murdered."

"How terrible!"

"Her name was Violet Julaine. Violet was a remarkable lady. She kept us all on track. After she passed, the group just fell apart."

"That's too bad."

"It's just as well. The police thought one of us killed her. We couldn't really trust one another after that, so..." She shrugged. "They may have been right."

"Why do you say that?" I asked.

"It looked like the killer knew Violet well, and there we were. Nice and handy. The usual suspects."

Her eyes swept over the room and its scattering of customers. No one appeared to need any service, but she started to move away, toward the counter, empty carafe in her hand.

I had to say something quickly. "Do you really think one of your friends committed the murder?"

Ellen stopped and paused, as if thinking through her response thoroughly. "I never said they were my friends," she said. "I have to get back to work."

Leaving me with a sense of a conversation cut off at the midpoint, Ellen stationed herself behind the counter, transferring muffins from their tins to showcase platters. She didn't look my way again.

Who associates by choice with people she doesn't consider friends? I could believe this if Ellen was only looking for feedback about her writing and didn't care who provided it. But I suspected that she might have said more.

I recalled the hints of dissention Dalton had mentioned. Rivalries, resentment over harsh criticism, professional jealousy, and the irresistible Captain Franklin who had dated both Violet and Milla.

Yes, the killer might well be one of the Gothic Writers. But the only way I could learn more from Ellen Trehearne would be to visit the Tea Room again, which would be no hardship.

I drank the rest of my tea slowly, ate every crumb of the last muffin, and left the restaurant, vowing to make this my favorite place in Maple Creek and to initiate another conversation with Ellen as soon as I could.

EIGHTEEN

AS I LEFT THE TEA ROOM, warm air washed over me in gentle waves. The splash of falling water from the park's unseen fountains beckoned. But at the end of the block, the Jewelry Chest also beckoned. As I was practically at its doorstep, I might as well see if Violet Julaine's pin was ready to be picked up.

My pin now, I corrected myself.

The only other customers in the little store were a young couple browsing in the wedding ring aisle. I headed for the Repairs sign at the back and produced my receipt. Moments later, I was looking at a dainty floating heart made of rubies and pearls, perfect for Valentine's Day, or any day.

Aside from its new gold clasp, the pin seemed slightly different to me, but I couldn't say in what way. A bit larger or smaller, fewer stones—I realized that I'd never looked at it that carefully.

"This is an exquisite piece," the clerk said. "Is it a family heirloom?"

"Possibly, but not mine. It was part of an estate sale."

"If you ever want to sell it, let me know. I'm Casper Landford," he added. "The owner."

"I'm sure I won't," I said.

I reached into my purse for a twenty-dollar bill. He started to slip the pin back into a small brown envelope.

"Wait," I said. "I'm going to wear it."

I pinned the heart to my sundress and glanced in the small mirror on the counter. The rubies gave me a touch of color, a quality often missing in my life. I tested the clasp to make sure it was secure and promised Casper that if I ever wanted to part with the pin, I would contact him.

Outside again, I crossed the street and entered the park. It seemed as if half the population of Maple Creek had come out this morning to enjoy the fair weather. I walked slowly under the maple trees, wending my way through plantings of late blooming tulips, past cool fountains and garden benches. At a small gazebo I bought a cup of pink lemonade and looked for a place to sit down.

Even with crowds milling around with their beverages and hot dogs, their children and pets, this woodsy oasis in the heart of town was beautiful and tranquil, a happy realization of heaven on earth.

But the illusion of peace shattered quickly in a chaotic melee of dogs barking and a male voice shouting, "Tac! Heel!" The noise was coming toward me.

A medium-sized brown puppy, all ears and wagging tail, ran out of a stand of cherry trees and jumped up on me, licking her chops as she caught a whiff of the lemonade in my hand.

In her wake bounded a familiar Belgian shepherd followed by an equally familiar trio: dark-bearded Garth MacKay, Katherine Kale with her long black hair loose and shining, and Randy Galloway wearing a fringed vest. The shepherd froze at the sound of his master's second command, while the puppy gave the cup a hard nudge with her nose. It tumbled to the ground.

I watched in dismay as a pool of pink lemonade widened in my lap. At my cry, the puppy dashed off around a fountain and sat surveying the damage unrepentantly, head tilted to one side.

As I mopped at the mess with a tissue, Garth MacKay said, "Sorry for the spill," and handed his now-leashed dog over to Katherine.

"Your pretty dress," Katherine lamented. "It's saturated."

"It'll dry in this heat," I said.

"White is hard to keep white in the summer," she added, and I noticed that she wore white herself, a silky sheath with a gold chain and matching bracelet, as unusual an outfit for a Saturday stroll in the park as my own.

I nodded, still mopping up lemonade. "Especially in a park."

She sat down beside me, and the subdued shepherd reeled in the empty cup with his paws and began to gnaw at it.

Garth said, "I'll get you another drink. What was it?"

"Pink lemonade from the gazebo. Don't bother. It wasn't your fault."

But he was gone.

Randy Galloway sat on my other side. "We met a few days ago, but I don't remember your name. You teach at Alcott, Miss...?"

"Linnet Shellwin." I cast about for an appropriate comment. "How was your class reunion?"

"It's tonight."

"I'm Katherine Kale," Katherine said, not knowing, of course, that I already knew her name. "The owner of this unmannerly beast is Garth MacKay, and I guess you know Garth's cousin, Randy."

"As he said, we met. I've seen you walking down Beechnut Street."

"Yes, I love to walk by those beautiful houses on Victorian Row. I've always loved your Valentine window," she added.

"Me too," I said. "That's what first attracted me to the house."

"Valentine Villa," Randy murmured. "When we were kids, we used to think it was a magic place."

In spite of Katherine's and Randy's attempt to start a friendly conversation, I felt increasingly uncomfortable, more so than wearing a wet dress warranted. Randy was staring at my pin, looking as if he wanted to ask me about it but couldn't quite summon the nerve.

Finally he did. "That's a nice brooch you're wearing, Ms. Shellwin. Are the stones real rubies?"

Katherine gasped. "Randy! A little discretion, please."

"It's all right. Yes, they are."

"It's gorgeous," Katherine said. "Do you collect Valentine memorabilia like… Like some people do?"

"No, I acquired this pin by chance. Did you know the woman who used to own my house?"

"Not personally, but one year, she opened her home and garden to the public for a spring tour. I saw all the hearts-and-flowers stuff she had. Individually the items were pretty, but the overall effect was suffocating."

"I had a pin just like that," Randy said. "I should say, my mother did. She's gone now."

His scrutiny was intense. I felt as if he were accusing me of stealing an item of great value from his family. In a sense, I *had* blithely helped myself to the pin, but Violet Julaine had abandoned it, tossed it into a box labeled Discard. No, I had nothing to feel guilty about.

I felt my hand travel up to the pin and rest on it.

Katherine said, "There must be billions of heart-shaped pins with ruby stones in the world, Randy. But I understand. It must remind you of your mom."

I was about to ask Randy what had happened to his mother's pin when Garth appeared with two cups of lemonade.

"Here you are. It's nice and cold." He gave one to me and one to Katherine. "This is for you, honey," he said to her. For some reason, she blushed.

I looked away, and my gaze fell on his large silver ring. It had an unusual setting, a lion's head with black stones and diamonds that gleamed in the sunlight. It definitely suited him.

"Thanks," I said. "You didn't have to do this."

But I was glad he had. I took a long drink, eager to sample the lemonade before this cup, too, met with a mishap.

"Sorry about Tac," Garth added. "He's usually better behaved. From now on, I'll keep him on his leash when we're walking."

"That's a good idea," Katherine said.

"He's forgiven." I offered Tac my hand to sniff. "That other dog was the real culprit. Even if you were chasing her."

Garth took possession of Tac's leash and Katherine's hand. Katherine said, "Nice meeting you, Linnet. We'll see you around the neighborhood."

Garth and Katherine were an obvious couple. And Randy, the cousin… Randy would attend the class reunion tonight and go back to his home in another state—wherever that was. I remembered Miss Crumle's little mystery about what he did for a living.

I should ask him, now that we were all together. Surely it wouldn't be considered rude. But they were all on their feet now, moving away, Tac with a longing last look at the shreds of paper cup, Randy with a puzzled backward glance at me.

My timing, as usual, was slightly off.

AFTER A QUICK STOP AT home to change clothes, I took off again in search of Doreen. I found her house easily. Built on a well-shaded double lot, it was a tidy gray brick ranch with stone trim and silvery shrubs smothered in russet-red mulch.

The driveway was empty. Belatedly I remembered that Doreen spent summer weekends boating on Lake St. Clare with her boyfriend. Deciding to come back one day next week, I headed home, disappointed in my first attempt at sleuthing.

What had I learned? Not much. Ellen Trehearne seemed to share Dalton's belief that the killer was a member of the Gothic Writers group and Randy Galloway, Garth's cousin, whom Dalton didn't appear to care for, was interested in Violet Julaine's pin.

Too interested?

Possibly, but he would be moving on, perhaps as soon as tomorrow.

I touched the pin, just to make sure it was still there. I'd wear it on Tuesday with another white dress for my date with Dalton.

"In three days," the caller had said. Tuesday was to be the day of my fatal mistake.

Please don't let it be Dalton, I prayed.

WAITING FOR A PHONE TO RING is perhaps the most pitiful of all activities. This is doubly true when by rights the phone shouldn't be capable of ringing. Still I waited and listened, desperate to hear the rest of the caller's message. My life might depend on what she intended to tell me.

Although I didn't understand what was going on, I no longer thought the phone calls were an elaborate hoax.

I found myself obsessing about the identity of my dangerous friend and the nature of the fatal mistake I was destined to make. How could I circumvent the perils that lay ahead without more information?

The woman simply had to contact me again. For the remainder of the day, I busied myself with a variety of mundane tasks, all of which required my presence in the kitchen close to the phone. Still, it didn't ring.

On Sunday morning, the temperature climbed to the high eighties, ushering us into a new heat wave, or continuing the previous one. At this point, it didn't matter. After lunch I sat on the back porch reading Sunday's *Tribune*. Nothing of earth shaking significance was happening in Maple Creek.

Our part of the state was overrun with ugly, dangerous wild boars that looked alarmingly like black bears and had no natural predators in the area. The Breadbasket, an organization dedicated to feeding the hungry, needed financial contributions and volunteers. Once again, Beechnut Street was preparing to celebrate the Fourth of July with a traditional block party.

Elsewhere in the nation… War, an assassination in a third world country, a plane crash, the recovery of a stolen painting valued at a million dollars… A headline caught my attention. "Teacher Sentenced For Sex Trysts With Student."

It had happened last year in Ohio. A science teacher at a rural high school had pleaded guilty to having an affair with her sixteen-year-old student. "I didn't mean for it to happen," she'd said tearfully. "It just did. I love him."

I shook my head in disbelief at the betrayal of trust, although the story was hardly unique. Here was more unnecessary tragedy. More ammunition in the hands of those malcontents for whom teachers were the scapegoats of choice. Some people, remembering a long past school incident of their own, would pounce on a story like this and keep it alive.

They make too much money for reading stories and drawing pictures—and playing games. I wish I could play games at work.

They get summers and holidays off. That's a year's pay for ten months' work.

Nobody knows what really goes on in a classroom unless you're there.

I recalled Candace Ann's latest warning. If the tales about my ineffectiveness as a teacher didn't work, Dale and his friends were going to make up a story about me. Something bad.

Tina the Terrible and people like her would believe them in a heartbeat. I didn't doubt that the Alcott staff would rally to my defense, but with the lie taking on a life of its own, the damage would be done.

I sat on my quiet porch, gazing at the expanse of green in front of me—at my own yard and the willow tree that shadowed the deserted pond. Although, for the moment I was safe from any such calamity, the scenario seemed all too real to me. It could happen. Maybe it was already happening.

I might be in the wrong profession, after all. For years, I had tried my best and been emotionally battered and even physically threatened for my efforts. How had Milla Schoenherr, who had taught successfully for several years, managed to survive?

I left the rest of the paper unread. My zest for news had evaporated.

NINETEEN

THE NEXT MORNING I WAS up before sunrise, drizzling vanilla icing over a dozen fudge-nut brownies. I'd baked them mainly for Ned, not to impress him with my culinary skills, which were negligible, but to surprise him. He didn't think I took him seriously; ordinarily I didn't.

Carefully I wrapped them in aluminum foil and glanced at my watch. It was already seven-twenty, and even though Ned's map couldn't have been easier to read, I planned to give myself an extra half hour for the drive to Lime Lake. You never knew when road work or a wrong turn would result in a delay.

As I stashed the brownies safely in the trunk of my car, the landline phone rang. It was the same strident sound I'd heard so often before, now slightly muted by the roar of a nearby power mower.

Now, of all times. But now was good. This was what I had prayed for.

I dashed back to the house, counting rings. Three…four… Up the steps to the porch. Through the door… Through the living room and dining rooms… Just as I reached the kitchen, the ringing stopped. I froze in the center of the room, my heart pounding, not believing that I'd missed this all-important call.

She'll try again.

Never before had the caller given up after only six rings. Something must have happened on the other end of the line. Another call? An accidental cut-off? The cat in the cream bowl?

I sank into the nearest chair, aghast that I was thinking of the landline phenomenon in real life terms. Still I sat in the kitchen and waited for fifteen minutes, tracking the progress of the clock's hour hand as my extra travel time ticked away.

Finally I realized that if I didn't leave now, I'd be late for the first meeting. I suspected that as soon as I was in my car, driving away, or at my destination, the phone would ring in an empty house. Once again, I'd failed to connect with my destiny.

"THAT WAS THE SHORTEST vacation on record," Rae said as she settled herself in a lawn chair on Ned's redwood deck. "Two whole days, and here we are back to work again."

"This is a vast improvement over a dusty old school building." Beverly stretched her long tanned legs out in a swath of sunshine. "Let's pretend we're still on vacation in someplace exotic like Hawaii?"

"Lime Lake is exotic enough for me," Rae said.

From the edge of Ned's property, we had a panoramic view of swimmers, boaters, kayakers, jet skiers, and sunbathers lying on colorful beach towels. The locale was infinitely more conducive to imaginative course planning than any classroom at Alcott Middle School. Not quite a tropical paradise, it was nicely removed from our customary work surroundings, and the many children in the vicinity were someone else's responsibility.

Ned's pretty gabled cottage had a fresh coat of light green paint, the color of seaweed. It created a fleeting illusion of undersea castles and jeweled caves. This was his family's summer place, he'd told us, dating from the early 1950s. Over the years, he had remodeled it several times. Eventually he planned to live at Lime Lake year around.

"It keeps me sane," he said. "You're all invited to stay and swim after we finish."

I gazed longingly at the sleek sailboat anchored to the dock. Also sporting a fresh coat of paint, she had the lonely look of one being kept away from the fun. Her name was *Jenny June*. From the deck where we sat with laptops, papers, and soft drinks, she seemed to issue an audible invitation.

Ned's lake siren.

Who, I wondered, was *Jenny June,* that Ned had named his boat after her?

"Who's *Jenny June?*" Beverly asked.

"My new boat." Pride resonated in Ned's voice as he sidestepped Beverly's question. "She's the most seaworthy craft in Michigan. We can take a spin around the lake later, if you'd like. Not all at the same time, though."

"Obviously," Lou said.

Beverly giggled. "I'm in."

Arthur made an elaborate production of consulting his watch. "It's five after nine. Are we ready to start?"

"We are," Ned said.

He had divided us into pairs, choosing Rae as his partner, which left Beverly with Lou and me with Arthur Rowan.

Arthur appeared uncomfortable in this ultra-informal setting. While the rest of us had donned shorts or slacks, Arthur wore a blue striped shirt and tie. I recalled that his plan to work in the building had been outvoted.

Unbidden, a thought drifted across my subconscious, denting a bit of my enthusiasm for the project. Would I have an opportunity to teach a section of the new course? Would I even be on the Alcott staff in the fall?

We would have our assignments two weeks before the start of the school year. No doubt I'd know my fate long before then.

Tearing my gaze away from the allurements of Lime Lake, I opened my notebook. Arthur had rolled up his sleeves but still looked overdressed for a lakeside meeting.

Based on our past interaction, I didn't think I'd enjoy working with him, but in the first fifteen minutes I realized that he was intelligent, imaginative, and had a buried-deep-down sense of humor. Between us, we'd brainstormed names for the new course, fine-tuned our goals, and were ready to go on to the next phase when Ned said, "Let's break for lunch."

It hardly seemed that two and a half hours had passed.

"I'll get the franks and buns," Beverly said, moving briskly to the kitchen door.

"I'll help." Rae was close behind her. She'd brought a large bowl of potato salad and a jar of homemade corn relish.

They were so obvious, those two, so ready to show off their domesticity. And I thought I was the only one who had a secret crush on the wondrous Ned.

Had, I realized. Past tense. Ned was as enticing as ever, but now Dalton had quietly entered the picture and given me another man to think about. Dalton, Ned… Two equally desirable men, one slightly more attainable than the other. How fortunate I was to have a choice.

And I'd choose… I had to think about that, had to look beyond the superficial attractiveness both men had in abundance.

Could I confide in Ned about Candace Ann's warnings or the more sinister ones that came to me on a disconnected phone? I didn't think so, but I could see myself sailing across Lime Lake with him at the helm of the *Jenny June*.

As for Dalton, I could hardly wait for our date tomorrow.

Who said I had to make any decisions about which male companion to welcome into my life? With disaster dogging my heels, romance should be the least of my concerns.

NED GRILLED HOT DOGS and bratwurst, Beverly manned the cooler, and Rae set her oatmeal cookies in front of my brownies, making a subtle statement. I smiled and agreed with her that today's mixes were every bit as good as real cakes.

With heaping plates, we gathered around Ned's redwood picnic table. It resembled the ones at Alcott, reminding us that we were officially at work, although the proximity of the water and happy noise that floated up from the lake suggested otherwise.

During a lull in the summer-plans conversation, I said, "I saw Randy Galloway in the park this weekend. He was with Garth MacKay. Did any of you know they were cousins?"

"No." Ned stopped eating his brownie—his second, I noted. "I'm surprised. They're so different. But now that I think of it, put a black beard on Randy and a swagger, and you have Garth."

"In what way are they different?" I asked.

"It's no secret that Garth makes his own rules. He has little if any regard for the law. Randy always conformed to authority. If you don't mind a cliché, Linnet, Randy Galloway was a golden boy. Probably still is."

"People change," Arthur said. "You knew Galloway ten years ago."

I remembered Garth's gentle way with Katherine—and Tac running free in a park with a posted leash ordinance. Also I recalled Garth's lion's head ring with its black stones and diamonds, although I wasn't sure how relevant that memory was.

"Are you saying that Garth MacKay is a criminal?" I asked.

"No. That is, not that I know of," Ned said. "He has a successful business here in town. It's Sky and MacKay Title on Main Street."

"Then what did you mean?"

"At one time MacKay was a member of the Michigan Militia."

In the stunned silence that followed, Beverly said, "Surely they've not active anymore."

"Don't count on it." That was Lou, who seemed about to say something more, then stopped.

"I talked to Randy at the class reunion on Saturday," Beverly added.

"I didn't realize we were invited," Ned said.

"Remember, I taught at the high school before I got demoted." At Arthur's disapproving frown, she added, "Just kidding, everybody. Anyway, I remember Randy well. He was a dream student then, and he hasn't changed at all, as far as I can tell."

"That's the kind of man who usually has at least one major flaw," I said. "Or one secret. Did Randy say what he's doing now?"

"He's between jobs. I got the impression that he wants to stay in Michigan. Maybe Mr. MacKay will help him."

"To get into the Militia?" Rae said, and Lou laughed softly.

"Why the sudden interest, Linnet?" Beverly's sly smile discomfited me. I had been a little too obvious.

"Just curious," I said. "He seems to be a man of mystery."

I couldn't tell her that I was concerned about Randy Galloway's interest in the ruby heart pin that had belonged to a murder victim. Let Beverly think whatever she liked. Nobody seemed to be paying attention to her, not the men who had launched a discussion of fishing, not even Rae who glanced surreptitiously at Ned from time to time.

Mentally I added Randy Galloway's name to my Interviews list, hoping that he would still be in town and accessible next week.

DAYLIGHT WAS WANING AS I parked the car in my driveway and stepped out into the thick hot air. My bare arms had turned a suspicious shade of pink, and they burned. Well, the ride in the *Jenny June* with Ned was well worth a little discomfort.

In spite of the heat, Bonita was planting a row of holly bushes along her side of the fence. Across the street Tansy came around to her front yard carrying a watering can.

I called out a greeting to Bonita and went inside, wishing I could have asked her if she'd heard my phone ringing during the day. Then I remembered the previous occasion when I'd heard ringing but she hadn't.

If only Violet Julaine had installed an answering machine with the same magical properties the old landline possessed. Then I'd know what I had to fear. I'd know everything.

But why waste time fantasizing?

I peered through the living room window. Apparently Tansy

had finished watering her hanging baskets. She was sitting on her porch with her wide straw hat tilted forward on her face and large sunglasses covering her eyes. I didn't need an excuse to cross the street and exchange a few pleasantries with her, although since I'd never done it before, one would be nice.

In the bathroom, I washed my hands and splashed water on my face, wincing as drops splashed down on my arms. They looked red in the double light of the vanity.

You should have worn a long-sleeved blouse, I scolded myself.

Tansy made a similar remark when she saw me up close. "The sun is a killer, Linnet. Bathe your arms with used tea bags tonight. They should help bring down the pain."

"Thanks for the tip. I will."

"I'll bet you were at the beach today," she said.

"You'd be right, but I was working." I told her about Alcott's innovative new course and described our attempts to make it both fun and relevant.

"Business and English," Tansy said with a grimace. "That wouldn't have been fun for me. When I was in school, I liked art and gym."

"We're hoping this new approach will help kids when they enter the work world." Seeing a credible segue, I plowed ahead. "So many of them like to write. I know I did. That's why I became an English teacher."

Tansy said. "I liked that too. Still do. You should have been in town a few years back."

I held my breath, suspecting what she was going to say next.

"We had a little writers' club going. Nothing fancy, but we had fun."

"What happened to it?" I asked.

"When poor Violet was killed, it fell apart."

"Why then?"

She shrugged. "It seemed fitting at the time. After she died, we only met once, for an informal memorial. Mostly people sharing their favorite memories about her." Tansy sighed. "I sure wish we had something like that again."

I said, "Why couldn't we? I'm writing a mystery book this summer. It would be great to get together with other writers."

"What a wonderful idea!"

Tansy's face took on a bright new light. It was as if somebody had plugged her in. "After all this time, there's no reason we can't start meeting again," she said.

"None that I can see."

"I still write my stories, but then I stack them on a closet shelf." She was flushed with excitement. "Let's do it. It'll be easy to round up the girls and—the Captain. I know they'll all be interested. We can take turns hosting the meetings, just like we did before, and have potluck dinners."

But without arsenic-laced tarts, I thought.

"If you have a minute, Linnet, I'll get my address book. You can copy down names and numbers and start calling people tomorrow."

"But… I have these meetings three times a week…"

"Most people are busy during the day too. Call in the evenings."

"But I don't know these people," I said. "They don't know me. You should call…"

"Just tell them that you bought Violet's house. You're a teacher, Linnet. You'll know what to do."

Before I could think of another objection, she said, "I'll be right back."

Left alone, I wondered how I had lost control of my plan. My idea had been for Tansy to talk about the members of the group. I wanted to be handed clues, not volunteered to resurrect a club.

On second thought, maybe this would work to my advantage. Having the usual suspects under one roof would be handier for me than trying to locate and question them at their individual homes.

Unfortunately, I anticipated a possible problem. Not everyone would be as excited about a Gothic Writers reunion as Tansy. Especially if one of the people in the group was Violet Julaine's killer.

TWENTY

THE VALENTINE PIN HAD an ethereal glow in the light of my dresser lamps. It was almost disturbing. I tapped the stones lightly, half expecting them to be warm, but they were like ice. Fiery ice, burning against the ruched bodice of my white dress.

Like my arms were burning. An hour's pleasure on Lime Lake had exacted a painful toll. I stepped back and surveyed my reflection in the mirror. Overnight, my face had acquired a red shine. I looked like a lobster dusted with Transparency #1. But I was more or less satisfied with my appearance, in spite of the sunburn.

Rubies were the perfect accent for a simple white dress. I touched the pin again, telling myself I was only testing the clasp. In truth, there was something strange about the little floating heart. I'd thought so on first seeing it again at the jeweler's; I thought so now.

Having just been taken from my jewelry case, the pin should be at least room temperature. Instead it was cold. Cold as an artifact lifted out of a grave.

Well, why not? The pin belonged to a woman who had been murdered in this house, and something of Violet Julaine, some essence, seemed to cling to it.

Which was as wild an explanation as anyone ever concocted.

For a moment, I considered taking the pin off and wearing a gold chain and bracelet, as Katherine Kale had done with her own white dress; and perhaps I'd look like a long-haired goddess too.

But I didn't change anything. I was Linnet Shellwin, not

Katherine Kale, and I was as ready as I'd ever be for a date with Lieutenant Dalton Gray. I turned off the lamps and went downstairs to wait for him.

Lest I make a fatal mistake, I had stayed in the house all day, drifting from one safe, unnecessary task to another, finally baking another batch of vanilla-iced brownies. I'd thought about making my calls to the Gothic Writers, but decided that was too hazardous a task for today.

All through the long hours, the landline phone had been silent. Now Dalton would arrive in a half hour. I'd done nothing out of the ordinary, and nothing unusual had happened.

There's still time. Don't let your guard down.

I vowed to be extra careful with Dalton, too. If I made it through the next several hours without stumbling unwittingly into danger, perhaps the caller's warnings would prove to be nothing more than a cruel hoax.

BY LATE AFTERNOON, THE weather deteriorated. Dark puffed-up clouds pressed low to the earth and thunder rumbled a warning in the east. With a storm approaching, the prospect of driving any distance for a dinner date seemed unwise.

That could be my fatal mistake.

The more I thought about it, the likelier it seemed that the pink Victorian was the safest place for me to be tonight. But we couldn't stay here for our date. I was dressed for an evening out, and Dalton had confided that he had special plans for us.

I knew he wanted to take me to a place far removed from Maple Creek where nobody would be likely to ambush us with a loaded weapon. Where, I wondered, would that be?

I was at the kitchen window when he pulled into the driveway with the convertible top up and the vintage music stilled. Moments later he wrapped me in a warm welcome hug. "There's a tornado watch until midnight. I'd just as soon stay in town if it's all right with you. How about checking out the menu at the Blue Lion?"

I didn't even try to hide my relief. "I'd love that, Dalton. Then if a twister turns in our direction, we'll be close to home."

"We won't go walking out in the open," he said. "We'll keep walls around us at all times."

"That should be safe enough. Did you find out anything new about the shooter?"

"Not yet. There haven't been any other attempts on my life. You've been okay, haven't you?"

"So far. No one's been lurking in the shadows, and I'm relatively unscathed except for a sunburn." I told him about my boat ride on the *Jenny June*.

"That looks painful," he said. "I guess I can't hold you."

"Maybe you can." I gave him an encouraging smile. "Carefully."

He put his arms around my waist and didn't say a word.

"After dinner, I'd like to talk to you," I said. "I need some professional advice."

"You said you were okay. Did anything happen?"

"Not yet, but it might."

"I don't understand. Are those freshmen still harassing you?"

"No. That is, they might be, but this is something else, something…"

A clap of thunder, louder and closer, cut off my sentence. The storm was traveling toward us with alarming speed.

"We'll hash it all out later," Dalton said. "Now, let's get going while the going's good."

INCREDIBLY THE BLUE LION was packed. Either people didn't take a tornado warning seriously or they didn't know about it. I could hardly fault my fellow diners. Instead of taking cover in a basement, I'd gone out into the threatening weather. But I felt safe with Dalton at my side. I always had, even when someone was shooting at us in the dark.

We had a short wait for a table and weren't fortunate enough to be seated in the lucky alcove, but soon, busy with selecting our entrées, I forgot about shadowy gunmen and lethal mistakes.

After dinner, I planned to give Dalton a slightly edited version of my experiences with the haunted landline, and, before the night was over, hoped to have the benefit of his official wisdom.

"You look fantastic tonight," he said when we'd placed our orders.

I smiled. "Even with my red face?"

"You look healthy. Speaking of red, isn't that the pin you found in Violet Julaine's old music box?"

"The same. I had it repaired."

"It's strange that a valuable piece like that got overlooked in the shuffle."

"Very strange. But I'm glad it did."

"Do you still think the music box is a clue?" he asked.

"I haven't thought about it lately. But here's something you might be interested in. Tansy Stewart manipulated me into getting the Gothic Writers together again. At least that's how it felt." I added my plans to write a mystery story as soon as the school sessions wrapped up.

"Be careful, Linnet," he said. "You don't know who you might be dealing with."

"I intend to be. I might put that music box in my book. Make up a history for it. Bring it to life."

"You're skating on thin ice. What if the real music box turns out to be a clue?"

"You didn't think it was."

"I don't know everything."

"No? I'm shocked." I gave him a flirtatious smile to let him know I was teasing. "No one's going to see it because I'm not inviting the group to my house. Since the founder was killed there, it would be too weird."

"I still want you to be careful."

"I will, but there can't be any danger in people reading stories to one another."

He didn't look convinced, but then the waiter set our meals in front of us and we let the subject drop. Prime rib for Dalton, broiled whitefish for me. Dalton turned to his dinner with enthusiasm. I frowned down at my steaming entrée, wondering if I should have ordered beef or almost anything besides fish. What if my deadly mistake involved choking on a fishbone?

Be careful, I told myself, echoing Dalton's earlier warning, and picked up my fork.

Outside, thunder crashed and rain pummeled the rooftop. The lights flickered out but came on again before the gasps of surprise died down. The whitefish was remarkably bone-free, and Dalton, in a high good humor, was more interesting and entertaining than I'd ever known him to be.

I'm having a wonderful time with this man, I thought. *If I'm doomed to make a mistake tonight, I can't imagine what it could be.*

As we were finishing our Devil's food cake, Milla Schoenherr stopped by our table. Raindrops glistened in her limp blond hair, and she looked pale and tired. "Good evening, Linnet." She glanced at Dalton. "Lieutenant. We meet again."

Dalton nodded curtly.

"I saw you two and thought I'd come over to say hello."

"How was your north woods vacation?" I asked.

"Nice. Quiet. I just got back to civilization, and I'm ravenous. I can only take so much tranquility."

Her gaze dropped to my pin and stayed there for what seemed like a long moment.

"That's a beautiful brooch, Linnet," she said. "Is it new?"

"Actually it's old." I repeated for what seemed like the hundredth time, "It was part of an estate sale."

"Well, it's exquisite. You'll be all set for Valentine's Day."

For some strange reason, Milla's remark made me feel as if I should have chosen a more seasonal accessory—a seashell necklace or colorful beads. But her smile was sincere. I was being too sensitive.

I thanked her for the compliment. "I'll call you soon about lunch."

When she went back to her table, I said, "Milla is the only member of the group who's published."

Dalton nodded. "I know. She wrote that racy paperback. Lacey down at the station has been reading it."

I'd heard that name at school when the teachers were gossiping about Dalton's dubious reputation with women. Lacey was one of his female conquests. "Isn't she the dispatcher?" I asked.

"Don't let her hear you say that. She's a lieutenant."

"Well..." Occasionally, I didn't know what to say to Dalton. "I bought a copy of Milla's book when she was having a signing at the Tea Room, but I haven't read it yet."

That was a genuine going-nowhere comment. We finished our cake, drank more coffee, and Dalton picked up the check. I began to feel a trifle uneasy. Next came the stressful part of the evening, telling Dalton about the phone. I could only hope that he'd look at me the same way after he heard my story.

"Let's head back to your house and you can tell me what's bothering you," he said.

WHILE THE RAIN CONTINUED, an unrelenting downpour that threatened to flood the streets of Maple Creek, Dalton and I sat at my kitchen table with a fresh pot of coffee and plate of brownies between us. In the dim overhead light, the cord of the landline phone cast a long shadow on my wall which added a slightly sinister touch to my tale.

Dalton had listened to my account quietly and dispassionately, giving no indication of his true feelings. But he *was* listening, even when I crossed over into impossible realms. That mattered to me.

"If this woman is threatening you, we can go after her," he said when I'd finished. "But the disconnected phone makes your situation complicated."

"They're not exactly threats. She says she wants to warn me."

"Why?"

"That I don't know. Out of the goodness of her heart? It's almost theatrical the way she says something, then we're cut off. It sounds planned."

"Maybe it is."

He got up and, before I could voice an objection, pulled the phone away from the wall with a few deft moves. Its wires were all in place, none of them cut and dangling.

"Why do you think your phone is disconnected?" he asked.

Instead of answering, I said, "Let's test it." I pulled my cell out of my evening bag and dialed Violet Julaine's old number. The landline didn't ring.

Dalton pushed the phone wires back into the wall. "Are you dialing the right number?"

"It's the one written on the card."

"I admit I'm stumped. You say you were supposed to make a fatal mistake today?"

"That's what she said."

"Think back. Did you do anything in the past twenty-four hours that could be considered a mistake?"

"Not a thing. I stayed inside the house. Then we went out for dinner."

"That's no mistake," he said with a half smile that set his cornflower eyes aglow.

"Just the opposite." I glanced at the kitchen clock. "There are two hours left until midnight."

"Mind if I stay till then?"

"I'd like that." I refilled our cups and pushed the plate of brownies close to him. "It looks like the tornado is going to miss us."

"The next time the woman calls, ask her what you did wrong today," he said.

"If there's a next time. Usually she calls when I can't get to the phone in time."

We were both quiet, sipping coffee. I transferred a brownie to my plate, imagining the caller spying on me through a window, timing her call so that I would almost reach the phone in time to pick up the receiver, but not quite. That would be part of the theatrics, of the plan to torment me.

What Dalton was thinking I couldn't guess. Then he said, "You wanted my official opinion, Linnet. Someone is trying to scare you. Maybe someone connected with your school. Maybe this ties in with the Gothic Writers and the Julaine case. But I'll be damned if I can figure out the mechanics of it."

On the calendar, I'd drawn a red question mark through the twenty-first of June. Dalton, who rarely missed a detail, had seen it but refrained from commenting.

"It's hard to go on with my life knowing exactly when I'm supposed to die," I said.

Dalton reached across the table and took my hand in his own. It was warm from holding the hot coffee mug, warm because he was warm and strong and reassuring. At that moment I felt as if I were going to live forever.

"I have no idea what's going on here, but you're going to get through it. I know that."

"And you don't think I imagined the phone calls?"

"No, I don't," he said.

Safe in my own house with a man who had just become more important to me than I could have guessed, I knew that too.

TWENTY-ONE

LAST NIGHT'S STORM HAD littered the streets of Maple Creek with fallen branches and left deep puddles of water at low-lying corners. Today, however, we had a twenty-four hour reprieve with hazy, warm blue-sky weather in the forecast.

On Wednesday night, severe storms were expected to return. In all seasons, Michigan was a state of variety. As a lifelong resident, I was used to her whims.

After the weather report, I switched to my favorite music station, surprised to find the song from Dalton's vintage tape playing. *Love, love, tender love, /Hear my lonely cry. /Moon and stars die up above/And without you then so do I.*

What strange, sad lyrics! Dying for love wasn't unusual in legend and song, but how often did it happen in real life? I couldn't recall a single instance.

Thoughts of death on this perfect June morning were counter-productive. Unfortunately, they were very much with me, thanks to the gloom-and-doom woman on the phone. Dalton's assurances had comforted me last night. This morning, I could hardly remember them. But working with the Alcott group on the new course would give me something to think about besides my imminent demise.

Objectives and goals and benchmarks—and whether Beverly and Rae would be subtle or blatant in their attempts to impress Ned.

Ned's image—blond, rugged, very handsome—rose up from the part of my mind that I reserved for fantasies. Did I want to go to Jody's wedding with him when my thoughts were centered exclusively on Dalton these days? I didn't know. August, that bittersweet end-of-summer month, was a long way off.

By August, Dalton, true to his reputation, might have moved on to another woman; I might have long since stopped caring. And all of the matters that plagued me now would surely be resolved by then.

In any event, I didn't regret accepting Ned's invitation. Variety, I reminded myself, gives life color—in the weather and in all other things.

Fifteen minutes later, I turned into Greenwood Estates, Maple Creek's new and only subdivision, and looked for Beverly's address. I'd always believed in leaving my personal problems behind when I went to work. I did that now.

GREENWOOD ESTATES CONSISTED OF cookie cutter brick ranch houses on streets that seemed to curve endlessly through the subdivision. Most of them were simply landscaped with shrubbery, young fruit trees, and traditional geraniums.

Beverly's house had one of the more creatively designed front yards. Blue flowering groundcover grew in place of grass, and an ornate birdbath holding a planter of snapdragons served as the sole lawn decoration.

I parked behind Ned's orange Mustang and lifted my English materials and my third batch of brownies out of the trunk. Balancing the load carefully, I made my way up a brick walkway to the open front door where Beverly waited to greet me. Dazzling in a shocking pink sundress, she eyed my baked offering with excessive enthusiasm.

"More brownies, Linnet? How nice." She took the plastic-wrapped plate. "We're having subs and fruit salad for lunch. Come around to the back. Everybody's here."

So they were. Arthur, dressed for the classroom in a white shirt and tie, Lou for leisure in a garish Hawaiian shirt, Rae in shorts and a frilly blouse, and Ned, magnificent even when wearing jeans and a plaid shirt.

Beverly's backyard arrangement was reminiscent of Ned's. I surveyed our work space appreciatively. Lawn chairs and a round table shaded by an orange striped umbrella occupied one half of a redwood deck. On a garden bench, no doubt brought up from the lawn for the occasion, doughnuts shared space with a coffee maker and bottled water in a cooler. Here was everything we could wish for except a lake, although Beverly had a trio of small water gardens.

"Grab a cup of coffee and help yourself to a doughnut," Beverly said.

Arthur looked pointedly at his watch. "Let's get an early start—if nobody minds."

Nobody did; rather, no one would voice an objection.

"That was quite a storm we had last night," Lou said. "I lost one of my birch trees."

"Birchwood is so fragile," Rae murmured. "We were lucky. They spotted a funnel cloud east of town."

Ned pulled out a chair for me. "The Board meeting adjourned early last night because of the tornado watch."

I looked up from my doughnut, apprehension warring with curiosity. How could I have forgotten that all-important date? "Did anything interesting happen?"

"Evie Erickson and Mrs. Crumle received silver watches for twenty-five years of service to the District. Mrs. Crumle got very emotional. I gave a report on our project. Everyone's enthusiastic about it. Oh, and a few of the mothers are pushing for a healthier lunch menu and uniforms for the high school."

Rae made a wry face. "Dark pleated skirts and white blouses. Lettuce and apples. The kids will love that."

"Some of the clothes the girls wear are positively obscene," Beverly added. "The boys aren't much better. They're all out of control."

"I thought that was our generation," Arthur said with a smile.

"Did any of the parents or students have anything to say?" I asked.

"The only kids there were Student Council volunteers, serving refreshments. The parents were quiet for a change, because of the storm, I'd say. People were on edge."

"That's all?"

"That's it."

I took a sip of coffee, now relaxed enough to enjoy my chocolate-iced doughnut. My enemies had stayed away from the meeting. There'd been no Dale to lodge a false complaint about his inept ninth grade English teacher. No Tina the Terrible to claim that I didn't have control over my class. I had no need to worry now because by the next Board meeting, in August, my classroom performance would be ancient history.

One major concern down, bringing the number to… Only about a dozen.

I smiled, and opened my notebook. Ned passed out the day's agenda, giving the session its official beginning. Even under the umbrella, the sun was hot on my burned arms, but it felt good.

THE LANDLINE PHONE RANG as I was coming through the front door later that afternoon. What perfect timing! I raced to the kitchen and picked up the receiver, managing to say "Hello" between breaths.

"Linnet. Finally. Don't you ever stay home?"

Ignoring her petulant tone and the question, which was no doubt rhetorical, I said, "Quick! Tell me everything I need to know before we get cut off again."

"That isn't quite what happens, though it's as good a way as any to explain it."

"And that's irrelevant." I made a great effort to keep my patience in check. "Tell me what I have to do."

I held the receiver in a death grip, so tightly I imagined it could easily dissolve in my hand. As if that would keep the line alive.

She said, "First, take that heart pin you found to the police. They'll know what to do with it."

"Violet Julaine's pin? How did you know…?" Realizing that my responses bordered on the irrelevant too, I said, "Why?"

"Just do it, and don't discuss it with anybody."

"But it's too late."

Tansy Stewart knew that I'd found the pin in the music box; I'd showed it to her. The jeweler knew, of course, as did Katherine, Garth, and his cousin, Randy, who had gazed at it with an intense interest that he hadn't adequately explained. Then there were Dalton, Milla, whoever had gone out to eat at the Blue Lion Inn last night… Thirty or forty people at least…

Glowing rubies in the shape of a floating heart on a white dress. They were practically a brand, difficult to miss.

"I've already worn it," I said. "People have seen me."

There was a brief pause. "That's unfortunate, but it isn't too late to hand it over to the authorities. You *have* to do that, Linnet."

At the first crackle of static, I held my breath, held on to the receiver.

"Just for the record," she said, "it wasn't Violet's pin."

Interesting but again irrelevant. "Who is this dangerous friend you warned me about?" I demanded.

"It's Milla Schoenherr. Stay away from her, and you should be okay. That's all I can say. What happens now will be up to you."

"Wait! What mistake did I make yesterday? What about my supposed death? Is it still going to happen? Who are you?"

"I'll say a prayer for you, Linnet," she said. "I'm hanging up now."

And she did, leaving me frustrated and angry. There was no use holding on to the receiver now or waiting by the phone for her to call back. She'd made it clear that our strange business was concluded.

I had no hope of arming myself with a weapon to outwit Death, but the long-anticipated call had given me one piece of information. The pin hadn't belonged to Violet Julaine, which didn't make any sense as it had been found among her belongings. The true ownership of the ruby heart only added to the mystery.

How could the caller know about a pin stashed in a broken music box and what I'd done after discovering it? More importantly, how could anyone in my disbanded fourth hour class know about it?

She couldn't. They couldn't. The implication of the realization dropped a layer of cold over me. The calls hadn't been arranged by a handful of young mischief makers, and the unknown woman with the lightly accented voice knew what went on in my house. I didn't even know her name.

As for Milla Schoenherr, she was one of the few friends I'd made a connection with since moving to Maple Creek. I'd promised to call her for lunch. She was a fellow teacher, a member of the Gothic Writers. I couldn't simply erase Milla from my life.

Dalton was right. Someone was trying to frighten me, and in a way I couldn't fathom, Milla Schoenherr was mixed up in the affair. So was the pin, because I suspected that wearing it on my date with Dalton had been my fatal mistake.

After leaving a message for him, I went outside to sit on the back porch. This was an ideal, secluded place to sort out the endless puzzle that had become my life in Maple Creek.

Because I'd lost my chance to solve the mystery of the landline phone, I turned my thoughts to Candace Ann's warning. Either she'd exaggerated the trouble being cooked up by Dale and Company or for some unknown reason she'd fabricated it.

Or… The summer sun had burned out Dale's lust for revenge. I was through with the class; they were through with me. In a few months they would target another hapless teacher with their malice. It was also possible that even as I contemplated their motives and plots, they were growing up.

I *did* want to see Candace Ann again, though. Who knew what she would reveal next?

WITH RELUCTANCE that took me by surprise, I picked the ruby pin up in a tissue and handed Dalton a small ziplock bag. I watched as he slipped the pin inside, sealed it, and wrote the date, time, and my name on the label.

I remembered the last time I'd seen it with the last rays of sunlight glancing off the rubies. They had reminded me of dark red eyes glittering with tears. Now I couldn't see it at all.

"I hate to part with this little pin," I said. "It's the only valuable piece of jewelry I own. Besides, I like it."

"You'll have it back eventually," he said. "Even if it turns out to be evidence. This woman said the police would know what to do with it?"

I nodded. "And since I'm on a first name basis with a policeman, I called you right away."

"First name basis, huh?" he said with a wink. "Is that all?"

"There's a bit more. *Do* you know what to do with it?"

"Give it to the lab. They'll find any trace evidence that's left."

"A lot of people handled it. The jeweler, the original owner, the person or people who handled it in the estate sale. Maybe Violet."

"I'll ask the lab to test it for DNA. It'll take a while, and I need a sample of your DNA to go with it for elimination."

By the time he'd taken a wipe on the inside of my cheek with a sterile cotton swab and recorded the pertinent information, I felt as if the romance had gone out of the evening and also felt a little sorry that I'd given him the pin. But I wanted to know what was going on in my house. If this was the best way to make that happen, so be it.

"It's maddening to have all these unanswered questions," I said. "Especially the landline. I almost wish it would ring again. I want to know how she did it."

"So do I." He picked up the receiver and listened for a minute. "Dead," he said.

"I have a theory. When the lightning struck the house and started a fire, it altered the phone in some bizarre way so that it works only part of the time and only for one person."

Said aloud, that sounded ridiculous. I felt my face go warm.

"I don't see how that's possible," Dalton said.

"Neither did the science teacher at Alcott, but my theory has a certain kind of demented logic."

He raised an eyebrow. "What exactly is demented logic?"

"The kind you'd find in a science-fiction story. Maybe I should use the phone in my story instead of the music box."

He smiled, no longer taking me seriously. "I have to go, Linnet. We'll try to get out of town for dinner again. I'll be in touch."

"When will you know something about the pin?"

"Can't say. Soon, I hope. I'll push the lab to start the test immediately."

I walked him to the door and watched him drive away with the ruby pin in his possession and a slender hope that it would prove to be an important clue.

Even though the caller hadn't mentioned Violet Julaine's music box—if it was her box—I decided to take another look at it. Had the two items been together because they were both broken? Or was there some other reason?

Wondering if I was overlooking something important, I sat on the sofa and studied the picture again. The Queen of Hearts, lovely and serene but oddly at home in the castle kitchen. The cherry tarts so realistically depicted that if it wasn't eight o'clock in the evening, I'd make a quick trip to the bakery. The Knave who resembled Ned spying on her through the window as he plotted his thievery.

"If only you could talk." I turned the box upside down and idly turned the wind-up mechanism to the right, wishing it wasn't broken.

To my surprise, it moved. Six turns, and a delicate melody began. Fairy music. *Believe Me If All Those Endearing Young Charms.*

Too stunned to move, I let the song play until its last notes faded; then I wound the mechanism again, and the music started over.

Enchantment, I thought. *Trickery,* insisted my rational side.

Find out what's going on here, I told myself. *While there's still time.*

TWENTY-TWO

Look for the simplest explanation first.

So said Rationality, and the simplest explanation was that I had been mistaken about the music box being broken. The wind-up mechanism might simply have frozen. Mechanical objects had a mind of their own, often stopping for no discernible reason, then starting again.

Like the landline phone.

By the next morning, the music box development had taken on the misty colors of a dream. As soon as I came downstairs, I turned the wind-up mechanism, expecting to meet resistance. Instead the delicate fairy notes of *Endearing Young Charms* rippled out into the silent living room.

So my theory explained this latest strangeness. It wasn't strange at all.

That's too easy. Delve deeper.

I might have listened to rationality if Tansy Stewart hadn't knocked at my door just then to inquire about my progress in getting the Gothic Writers back into the fold.

Hiding my amusement at her phrasing, I said, "Yesterday was a busy day. I had to work. Then I had company. Won't you come in?"

"Uh—no. I have a cake in the oven." She glanced back across the street at her house as if she expected to see smoke pouring through the open windows. When she turned around again, she focused her gaze on my geranium planter. Apparently Tansy hadn't overcome her reluctance to enter Violet Julaine's former home.

She took a backward step and leaned nonchalantly against

the railing. There we stood, I in the doorway, Tansy on the porch, while beyond the overhang, the rain began to fall.

"After we talked, I was so excited that I just couldn't wait," she said. "I made some calls myself. We have Ellen, Rob Leaver, and Josie on board. Annette thinks it would be too depressing to carry on without Violet. She won't be joining us."

"Who's left for me to call?" I asked.

"Doreen, Milla, and Loretta. Between you and me, I hope Doreen won't be interested. She's too abrasive."

"We'll be a small group."

"That's best for critiquing. Ellen's bringing two of her friends. She says they're serious about writing."

"Now we need a time and place," I said.

"I told them this Friday night at seven, unless you have a date. Do you?"

"Not tomorrow."

She nodded her approval. "As for place, I don't think we should meet at your house. No offense, but they might be spooked because of the murder. We want to make a fresh new start."

"I agree; I thought the same thing."

"So I'll host the first meeting. We won't have potluck dinner. Just soft drinks, coffee, and store-bought cookies. My treat."

"You should be in charge of organization, Tansy," I said. "You do it so well."

A faint blush stole over her face. "We don't need a leader once we get going, just someone to keep track of where the meetings are and who's bringing what to eat, but thanks for the compliment. Don't forget to tell the girls to bring their stories."

"I won't."

As Tansy dashed back to her house, dodging the raindrops, a major stumbling block rose up in my path. I didn't have a chapter to contribute. Nor a page. Nor even a paragraph. I'd better start writing. With the threat of severe weather hovering over Maple Creek, this was a good day to stay inside and work on my book.

I SAT ON THE BACK PORCH with a spiral notebook, a ballpoint, and my cell phone, while rain turned the backyard into a vast green wetland. This wasn't one of my more productive days. Secretly I hoped someone would discover my whereabouts and keep me company. In an hour, I'd talked to only one person and written a single line:

It was a dark and stormy day...

And that wasn't original. My muse hadn't responded to my plea for help. She wasn't concerned that I might arrive at a writers' meeting without a story in my hand.

Turning a page, I sketched beads of rain spilling down on a stylized row of tulips. Creation with a looming deadline had never been my forte.

Forget the day. Don't begin with weather.

I glanced down at the small pad under the cell phone in which I'd recorded contact information for the Gothic Writers. Contrary to Tansy's hopes, Doreen had accepted the invitation with glee. She was writing a vampire romance and had been longing for feedback. Loretta's line was constantly busy, but I'd left a message for Milla on her answering machine.

There wasn't anything else I could do for the group at the moment. That left my book, a mystery novel slanted for the younger girl reader to be filled with chilling apparitions that would later be exposed as a hoax.

I'd written that and a sketchy outline back in May, before my life at Alcott Middle School took a dangerous turn. None of my ideas seemed workable now, but Violet Julaine's music box had a strong hold on my imagination. All I needed was a plot to wrap around it.

What was that question so many writers used when planning a book? *What if?*

What if the music box had the power to transport my teenaged heroine, Lainie Lancaster, back to another era?

But I was writing a mystery, not a time travel. What if the music box was a clue to an old murder? Or if it held a treasure map?

I decided to begin with Lainie discovering an antique music box in the attic of her family's new house. It was a replica of the one Violet had owned and played the same sentimental love song. I'd already given Lainie a description, a history, and an assortment of adolescent problems. Surely I had enough material for a few pages.

I wrote one sentence, then another, and before long had an entire chapter in rough form. After a bit of revision, it was certainly good enough to present to the Gothic Writers, even if it ended up being ripped apart by the cutthroat Doreen.

When the cell phone rang, I had wandered so far into Lainie's world that at first I thought the ringing came from the landline.

"Hello," I said, happy to know that the doomsday caller didn't have this number.

"Hi, Linnet. It's Milla returning your call."

"Are you rested up from your drive home?" I asked.

"Not completely, but I'm in better shape."

"Tansy Stewart and I are getting the Gothic Writers together again," I said.

"That's nice."

I'd hoped that Milla would be excited about sharing her experiences with her fellow writers. From her tone I could tell that she wasn't.

"Would you like to be a part of the new group?" I asked.

"Well, Linnet, it's a good idea, but I'm past that point in my career," she said.

Her excuse, while understandable, felt like an insult. "I see."

I remembered the poised, polished author I'd first seen at the Tea Room, every blond hair in place, blue shirtwaist dress wrinkle free. She'd radiated professionalism and success. No wonder she didn't want to associate with amateurs.

"I have two online critique partners now and a good agent," Milla said. "Any more input would be extraneous. Too many opinions lead to a muddle. Besides I haven't started my new book yet."

"It's all right, Milla," I said.

"Are you sure?"

"Of course." I improvised. "We didn't want you to feel left out."

"I appreciate that." She paused, then said, "But it would be fun to see the girls again. Maybe I'll drop in."

"Good! We're meeting at Tansy Stewart's house tomorrow evening at seven. She's going to take care of the refreshments."

"I'll be there," she said. "About lunch. How does Saturday sound?"

"Perfect. We can hash over the meeting."

"It's a date. I'll stop by and pick you up around eleven-thirty."

While I had the phone in my hand, I dialed Loretta's number. Still hearing a busy signal, I snapped the case shut. Without an excuse to procrastinate, I turned back to my story.

ON FRIDAY EVENING, UNDAUNTED by another tornado watch, the Gothic Writers assembled in Tansy Stewart's living room, bringing their umbrellas, their work, and in the case of Rob Leaver's surprise guest, Captain Franklin, a gift of white wine.

"Violet's favorite—Chardonnay," he said, handing the bottle to Tansy, who looked uncertain.

"We're just having cookies," Tansy said. "Nothing fancy."

"Who says we can't drink a toast to Violet's memory?" he demanded.

Tansy set the bottle on a sideboard amid a Halloween-like display of black pillar candles, model castles, and a scowling gray gargoyle statue. "Not I."

While she passed around a plate of cookies, I found a seat next to Milla and studied the faces of the others. Did a killer sit in our midst, munching shortbread and chatting amiably with old acquaintances? The idea seemed ludicrous, but who knew what evil lurked behind ordinary appearances?

Ellen, for example. She'd appeared so gentle and ladylike at the Tea Room, but tonight she looked rather unsettling. In an apparent nod to the Gothic tradition, she wore a long black dress with a lace shawl and jet earrings. Her slender hands rested on her manuscript. I noticed that her fingernails were purplish-red, so deep a shade they almost matched her onyx ring.

Good grief. These people took Gothic seriously. But then here were Ellen's guests, Mary and Jane. Both were brunettes with shoulder-length bobs and both wore beige in various shades and forms.

Mary and Jane… Jane and Mary… I didn't need to remember who was who as they hadn't been part of the original group and were therefore beyond suspicion.

Concentrate on the people who knew Violet, I told myself. *The people Dalton suspects.*

Like Tansy, still holding the cookie plate, and Milla who had set a small Wonder Books shopping bag on the side table between us. It was filled to the top with bookmarks and planners, all bearing a replica of the *Capture My Heart* cover. She must plan on distributing them sometime this evening.

Milla Schoenherr. Stay away from her and you should be okay, the woman on the phone had said.

We couldn't have been sitting closer to each other.

Loretta and Josie shared a loveseat. They were happily whispering to each other, apparently catching up on a year's worth of news. Neither one fit the idea I'd formed of them. Josie was slender and graceful, a sylph in dark gray who kept playing with her black pendant. Loretta, plump and rosy cheeked, resembled a country maiden in an old-fashioned advertisement extolling the virtue of apples. She couldn't have looked more wholesome.

But appearances are deceiving. Everybody knows that.

Doreen was a surprise to me, possibly the youngest in the

group. Tanned and toned and all in white, she looked as if she'd just raced from a speedboat on Lake St. Clare to the meeting in Maple Creek.

One of these ladies might well have visited Violet on that cold February day and presented her with a gift of toxic tarts.

I moved on to the men. Chief Rob Leaver, Dalton's old mentor, had an abundance of silver hair, courtly manners, and a cane which he'd leaned against his chair. Captain Franklin—"Call me Frank," he'd said—was mildly attractive and appeared personable, but I couldn't imagine him as an aging Lothario.

Besides, slipping poison into pastry didn't strike me as a masculine method of murder. But, on second thought, was there a better way for a killer to deflect suspicion from himself?

"Except for Annette, it looks like we're all here," Tansy said.

The usual suspects.

The Captain had appointed himself unofficial co-host, leaving Tansy in a dither. Clearly she was accustomed to being in charge of her own ship.

"If you'll get the glasses, Ms. Stewart, I'll pour the wine," he said. "We'll start with a toast."

Quietly Tansy brought eight crystal goblets out of her china cabinet. The Captain opened the bottle and poured a measure of Chardonnay for each of us. We all raised our glasses.

"To Violet. Our friend who was cruelly done to death. May she rest in peace," he said in a loud clear voice as thunder rumbled over the roof.

"Oh my heavens," Tansy said with a shudder. "Do you suppose she heard that?"

"Let's hope so."

Doreen laughed. "Relax, Tansy. Did you forget we're Gothic writers? Ghosts and storms are our bread and butter?"

"We—we decided to welcome other genres in the new group," Tansy said, with a furtive glance at Milla who had set her untouched glass of wine on the side table. "Romance, science-fiction, whatever you're writing."

Doreen sipped her wine daintily. "Delicious, Frank. Violet would have loved it. She'd have loved this whole night. Doesn't it seem like she's right here in the room with us?"

"No," Milla said.

Loretta cast a wary glance at Doreen. "I'm looking forward to hearing another chapter of your book, Ellen. Did anyone ever find the body?"

"Oh yes, it was in the… Wait till I read the next installment."

Rob Leaver said, "Hard to believe it's been over a year, and they never solved Violet's murder."

"You should go back to the Department, Rob," Ellen said with a downward sweep of her thick dark lashes.

"Wish I could. I have a few ideas…"

Doreen neatly cut him off. "Remember our purpose here. Who'll go first?"

No one spoke.

"Linnet? Why don't you start? You're one of the new people."

So are Mary, Jane, and Frank.

As I glanced down at my chapter, suddenly convinced that it was ten pages of drivel, I felt a pang of belated sympathy for all those students who refused to give an oral book report. In spite of the wine and flickering candlelight, this gathering was a little like a class.

But I was a teacher, for heaven's sake.

"All right," I said. "It's a mystery for girls."

I started reading by the light of the Tiffany lamp behind my chair with rain for atmosphere and a deep courteous silence that would have been at home in a funeral parlor. It was all very Gothic, and when I came to the end, I waited uneasily for someone, anyone, to react.

"Very engrossing, Linnet," Milla said. "I never thought of a music box as being creepy, but you've made it work."

Ellen added her seal of approval. "You have the Gothic touch."

Rob tapped the floor with his cane. "I liked it, Linnet, but you could sharpen Lainie's motivation. Why does she go up to the attic? Just so she can find the music box?"

"She has to find it somewhere," I said.

"Ah, yes, but avoid contrivance at all costs. Maybe she hears a noise in the attic? Bats?"

Tansy gave an audible little shudder. "I wouldn't go exploring in an attic if I thought bats had nested there."

"You might want to work on Lainie's character a bit," Doreen said. "She doesn't act like any teenaged girl I know. Why don't you volunteer at the high school where you can observe real girls in action?"

Milla stifled a giggle.

"I can do that," I said. "Does anyone else have a comment?"

"You've made me want to read more," Ellen said. "That's the test of good writing. I'll go next," she added. "Linnet took us up to an attic. I invite you all to follow me down to the basement of Screaming Oaks, a plantation house on the bayou."

"Do they have basements in the South?" Doreen asked.

Ellen ignored her and adjusted her glasses.

Lightning streaked through the room, and it seemed to me that the candlelight cringed in the assault.

"Maybe we should move down to the basement," Josie said.

"We could..." Tansy didn't sound certain. "It's pretty messy down there, though. I haven't done my spring cleaning yet."

"A tornado watch isn't the same as a warning," Captain Franklin reminded us. "If you girls are worried, why don't you turn on the television, Ms. Stewart? See if there's any danger."

She did, and a game show came into focus with the tornado watch logo in the lower right corner.

"There, now," the Captain said. "We're safer here than out on the roads. Keep it on, Ms. Stewart, in case the situation changes. Just turn it to mute."

"I'll begin with a brief summary of what happened before," Ellen said.

I sat back and listened. Tansy's clock chimed the half hour. The rain on the windows grew louder. Soon I was drowning in a sea of spirits and werewolves and unholy creatures who prowled the night trolling for human prey.

Ellen's fictitious body lay rotting in an old steamer trunk. Rob had written about a detective who returned to earth as a ghost in the Great Depression. Frank's hero traveled in time back to the scenes of bloody battles for some reason that eluded me.

Josie and Loretta were proponents of the New Gothic—whatever that was, and newcomers Mary and Jane had crafted traditional mysteries with corpses galore and a dash of witchcraft. For me, the most frightening character was Doreen's green-faced vampire who haunted an imaginary Michigan island.

By nine-thirty when the meeting ended, I'd decided that, with the possible exception of the absent Annette, any one of Violet's friends had the imagination to concoct a bizarre murder plot and was clever enough to evade the authorities.

The problem now was to determine who had a motive.

TWENTY-THREE

THE LIGHT OF MY PORCH LAMP was a faint glimmer through slanting sheets of rain. Under the relative safety of Tansy's awning, I opened the umbrella and calculated my chances of making it across Beechnut Street without getting thoroughly soaked.

They were non-existent. Wishing I'd worn boots instead of heels, I braced myself for a mad dash to the shelter of my house.

I could see very little of what lay in front of me, only that the street and sections of low-lying sidewalk on either side had filled with water. They resembled a small lake. This was the kind of rapid flooding that turns cars into hydroplanes and ruins basements.

"Wait up, Linnet."

Ellen Trehearne came up quietly behind me. We were the last ones to leave Tansy's house, having stayed to help her move chairs back to their proper places and wash wine glasses.

"What a wild night!" Ellen took her car keys out of her purse. With a frown, she surveyed the short distance to her car, parked in Tansy's driveway. She didn't have an umbrella, only a long black raincoat with a voluminous hood.

"It's the wildest, but perfect for a Gothic gathering," I said.

"It was a good meeting. For once, people were on their best behavior, and I like our new additions."

"I'm looking forward to the next one." I raised the umbrella over my head as the wind blew a wave of rain in my face.

"Linnet," she said in a low voice, "I'd like to talk to you

in private. As soon as possible. Not now with the storm though."

"Sure. About…?"

"Violet's murder. Do you think we could meet somewhere?"

"I don't see why not. How about my house in the morning?"

"I'd rather not take a chance on anyone seeing me. Could you come to the Tea Room instead? It would look natural. Then we can arrange to meet somewhere else."

It all sounded rather cloak-and-dagger, in keeping with the dark tone of the Gothic Writers meeting. But the allusion to Violet's murder had immediately caught my attention.

"We close at four," she said.

"I'll be there around three-fifteen."

"Don't tell anyone where you're going," Ellen added.

"Okay, but why so mysterious?"

"Like I said, this is a private matter. Very private."

"We'll talk tomorrow then."

"And remember. Nobody can know."

With these ominous last words, she dashed across the muddy lawn to her car, and I splashed through the swirling water toward the light on my own porch.

WHILE WE'D BEEN IN TANSY'S living room drinking wine and listening to horror stories, the storm had intensified.

Straight line winds—if that's what they were—can be as dangerous as any tornado. They slammed into me, threatening to send me flying eastward with the wind. They turned the umbrella inside out and whipped my long hair around my face. With nothing to hold on to and zero visibility, I felt like a paper doll being blown into oblivion.

Drenched and breathless, I reached my porch at last and unlocked the door. Those last few yards to the pink Victorian had seemed a mile long.

Inside, I turned on lights, shed my wet clothes, and dried my hair, in that order. Then I slipped into a long robe and watched the storm from the front window, fascinated by its fury and the frantic swaying of the maples.

Beware of elms in thunder... The line from Archibald MacLeash's poem dropped into my mind.

Beware...

But there were no elms on Beechnut Street or anywhere else in Maple Creek. They'd succumbed to Dutch Elm disease decades ago, all those majestic trees I knew only from pictures, felled by an insidious bug.

Maybe one or two of them survived. You don't know. But you'd better know enough to beware of something.

A clap of thunder, too close and too loud, set my nerves into a tailspin. Ellen was right. It was a wild night, a dark and stormy night, and I was too wired, too much in the grip of the nightmare characters brought to life by the Gothic Writers, and too curious about Ellen's unusual request for a clandestine meeting, to go sleep.

Also the wine had given me a slight headache. Nothing too painful. Just a light persistent drumming on my temples.

I ran my hand along my forehead, trying to rub the hurt away. Something was tugging at me, trying to vocalize a plea for recognition. Something that had happened or been said tonight. Not Ellen's paranoia. Not Doreen's assessment of my heroine's credibility.

Go further back.

To Frank's toast? To Doreen's flippant comment about Violet being in the room with us? To…?

A lightning flash electrified the sky. Moving quickly away from the window, I settled in my favorite corner of the sofa, reliving the highlights of the evening, trying to catch whatever elusive strand danced just beyond my consciousness.

It was no use. I couldn't do it—unless it was Milla's refusal to think of Violet as a ghostly visitor. Was that it?

At eleven-thirty, with the tornado watch about to expire, I turned the first floor lights out and went upstairs to bed.

The worst of the storm had moved on. Rain continued to beat against the windows, but it was a soothing sound. Not soothing enough to lull me to sleep, though. My mind refused to turn itself off.

According to the forecasters, July was going to be a month of above average rainfall and violent weather. We were almost at the end of June. That reminded me of the date of my supposed death. June 21st was next week.

I turned listlessly on the bed, first lying on my right side, then on my left, then on my right again. Soon the sheet was hopelessly twisted around my body and the blanket was half on the floor.

How could I relax with an ax hovering over my head waiting to fall?

"I couldn't. But then I had no idea the ax was going to fall."

She drifted into the room, a slender form in a diaphanous lavender nightgown, and sat down in the Queen Anne's chair at the side of the bed.

"Poor Linnet. Can't you sleep?"

Her voice was soft and slightly accented, Scottish perhaps, like the voice of my mysterious caller. With her black hair, misty blue eyes set off by thick lashes, and fair complexion, she was beautiful.

How could I see all this detail when the room was dark?

"It's a small wonder, considering the company you keep," she said.

She reached out and touched my forehead. I sat up abruptly and wrenched away from her, in a futile attempt to evade her hand. "Who are you?" I demanded.

She drew back her hand. "You know who I am."

Who I am who I am who I am...

I reached over to turn on the lamp. The room flooded with pale light, and I was alone, just waking from a dream. Rather, coming out of a nightmare. My headache was worse, throbbing painfully where the dream woman had laid her hand, and it was cold, so cold under the lightweight blanket that I felt as if I were lying on a bed of ice.

I ran my hand over the crushed velvet seat of the Queen Anne chair. It was even colder than my blanket.

"Violet," I said to the empty room.

MORNING. SUNLIGHT. SANITY and freedom from the terrors of the night.

When I came downstairs the next morning, the room was bright with golden sunlight, and most of the water in the street had drained away.

Drowsily I opened the door to get the paper and scanned the headlines on the way to the kitchen. *Heat Wave Back On. 3000 Lose Power. Storm Takes Toll On City Trees.*

But not on Victorian Row. It looked the same as ever, stately nineteenth-century houses and lofty maples washed clean of dust. No traffic to speak of. A fresh sparkle on the gables and turrets and their gingerbread trim.

I set about preparing a special breakfast of French toast, fresh orange juice, and tea so hot it would burn my tongue and my throat.

If only it could burn away the memory of Violet Julaine strolling into my bedroom to inquire about my insomnia and make a caustic comment about the company I kept, a remark that could refer to practically anyone I'd come in contact with lately.

Bits of the nightmare still lingered in my mind, but they were fading quickly, unable to hold on to their power in the strong light of day.

Mostly I remember Violet's familiarity with my bedroom and being so cold.

Beating eggs, adding vanilla, dipping bread into the mixture, then into the frying pan, all of those ordinary down-to-earth activities, allowed me to view my nightmare dispassionately.

It wasn't unusual that I would dream of Violet. In a sense she had been at the Gothic Writers get together with us, a fondly remembered friend, the spirit founder to whom nobody had given a glass of Chardonnay.

It was a small wonder that I didn't dream of Doreen's green-faced vampire or Ellen's rotting corpse as well.

A small wonder considering the company I kept.

I turned my attention to breakfast and let what little I remembered of the dream dissolve like sugar in a cup of steaming tea.

After breakfast, I checked my cell phone. It told me that I had two unheard messages. I punched in the magic number and my password, as directed, and listened.

Milla couldn't make our lunch today. "I'm sorry, Linnet," she said. "Something came up. Catch you later."

How could so many things keep coming up in Milla's life? Well, that was the last date I'd make with her. I deleted the message.

The other one was happier. Sandra, was going to drive downstate with the puppy next week on June 21st. If that wasn't convenient, I should call her and make other arrangements.

That message I saved. It was only going to be inconvenient if I were dead, and I didn't plan to be.

Milla's cancellation left me several free hours until my late afternoon meeting with Ellen for which I had high hopes. I wondered, though, why she wanted to confide in someone she hardly knew. Incidentally, why, if she had information about the Julaine case, hadn't she talked to the police last year?

Speaking of the police, why was Dalton so quiet? What about my heart pin?

Call him, I told myself. *It's official business.*

I picked up the phone again but before I could dial the station, my doorbell rang three times with scarcely a second's pause between rings.

Masking my annoyance at the unknown visitor's impatience, I hurried to the living room and glanced through the window. Candace Ann stood on my porch with a basket in her hand.

I didn't care for this development.

Should I pretend that I was still asleep? It was only nine-thirty.

I let the curtain panel fall a second too late. She'd seen me. Grinning broadly, she waved and pointed to the basket.

I'd just lost one option, but there was another left. I grabbed my purse and car keys and opened the door.

"Good morning, Ms. Shellwin," she said. "I didn't wake you up, did I?"

"No. I'm on my way out. For an appointment."

"I got here just in time then. These are strawberries from my mom's garden. I picked them myself."

She shoved the basket at me. The berries were small and dark, still covered with moisture.

"They're so sweet," she said. "Just try one. Try it now."

"They look wonderful, but I can't. I just finished a big breakfast."

Her dark eyes held a shimmer that looked suspiciously like tears.

"But I'll have some for dessert tonight," I assured her. "I appreciate your thinking of me. Thank you."

Immediately she brightened, and I told myself that I had imagined the hint of tears. She was peering into my living room, past the umbrella stand, at the coffee table with its one adornment—the music box.

"I'll bet your house is as pretty inside as out," she said. "You can't just furnish one of these old mansions any old way. You need antiques and stuff."

I shifted the basket to my other hand and made a show of looking at my watch. "I'd like to give you a tour, but I'm going to be late for my meeting."

"I'd *love* that. Can we do it another time?"

"If you won't be too busy with your friends. What are you doing with all your free time this summer?"

"Just hanging out," she said. "Helping Mom in her garden." She took a deep breath. "I ran into Jimmy and Dale at the beach the other day."

"They missed the Board of Education meeting," I said pointedly.

Spots of color danced across her face. "Yeah, I guess, but they're still planning. They want to come up with something really good. It takes time."

I took a deep breath myself, feeling freer than I had for weeks. I'm not sure how I knew that Candace Ann was lying, but I did. Truly I had nothing to fear from vengeful former students because they didn't exist. Not as she had portrayed them.

How could I have been so gullible?

One question remained. Why had Candace Ann started this fabrication and continued to nurture it even now? Was it a pathetic bid for attention? A desire to be a teacher's summer pet?

A coffee mug, strawberries, torment. It didn't make sense.

I wanted to ask Candace Ann her motive outright, but I also wanted her gone. I didn't trust that puppy-dog adulation or play of emotion in her dark eyes. Now that I thought of it, where was her bike? Had she walked all the way to my house?

Maybe it wasn't a long walk. I didn't know anything about Candace Ann except that I didn't want to eat her berries.

Freshly baked cherry tarts with a teaspoon of arsenic? Fresh-picked strawberries in a basket with a dusting of poison that resembled dewdrops?

Probably not, but just to be safe…

I had no idea the ax was going to fall, the dream Violet had said.

Candace Ann was waiting, eyes a-glitter, for my response.

I had to say something. "It's all just talk, Candace Ann. Boys do that. Girls, too. It's part of being young. I don't think they're going to do anything."

"I do," she said.

TWENTY-FOUR

ELLEN'S MEETING PLACE was a small vegetarian restaurant with a whimsical name, The Leaf and Pod. Failing to find an entrée that interested me, I'd ordered a salad. Fortunately, I wasn't hungry.

Ellen surveyed her lettuce and tomato sandwich with delight. "I can't understand why this place isn't more popular," she said as an elderly couple came through the door, bringing the number of customers to seven.

"The menu isn't very extensive," I said.

"But it's healthy and inexpensive. What more could you want?"

"Pie and ice cream."

She grinned. "They have a delicious peach cobbler made with whole wheat flour and apple sauce."

I trailed my fork through various lettuces, searching for something as appealing as the mini blueberry muffin that had come with the salad. Not finding it, I came to the point of our meeting. "What do you know about Violet's murder, Ellen?"

"Nothing definite, but I have my suspicions," she said. "Ever since Violet died, I keep remembering little things she said. I didn't attach any importance to them at the time, but last night, seeing everyone together again, they came back to me."

Little things, then, stored in Ellen's memory all these months. They might be the very clues that had eluded the investigators.

"I didn't realize that you and Violet were close friends," I said.

"We were friends. Maybe not that close. After Violet got laid off from her newspaper job, she worked at the Tea Room until she developed pain in her knee. She still came to the restaurant for tea and muffins though. Along the way she found out that I was working on a book and invited me to join the Gothic Writers. We saw quite a lot of each other after that."

Ellen was eager to talk about Violet, unlike Tansy and Milla who rarely mentioned her. I leaned forward, more interested in what Ellen had to say than a bowl of garden greens.

"You know how bad the economy is these days," she said.

I nodded. "It seems like we're all on a sinking ship."

I had a mortgage, a car payment, and the usual bills; but I also had a job with the promise of a pension. I considered myself lucky but knew that anything could happen—anytime. Only a few weeks ago I had been worried about being tossed out of Alcott Middle School by a posse of liars.

Ellen said, "Violet was desperate for money. She had that enormous house to maintain and couldn't save enough to pay her summer tax bill. This was around Christmas, and she was already worried about it. She often said she'd do anything to keep Valentine Villa. Then a man entered the picture."

"A boyfriend?"

"I don't think so, and Violet never referred to him by name. He was going to make all of her money problems go away."

I smiled. "There's a man who can do that? Amazing."

"We used to joke about finding rich husbands on one of those Internet dating sites. Violet always said we'd probably end up with a man looking for a wealthy wife to take care of him."

"Did she find this man online?" I asked.

"Not as far as I know, but there was a man, someone she already knew, and there was some secret about him."

"Do you remember what she said?"

"Just this. One day she came to the Tea Room, all smiling and excited. I asked her if she had won the lottery. She said she'd found a way to get the money she needed and it was so easy she wondered why she hadn't thought about it before. I pressed her for details, but she clammed right up."

"Was it Captain Franklin, do you suppose?" I asked.

"Violet gave me the impression that he was a younger man."

"Well that wouldn't be Frank."

Nor Rob Leaver. There were only two males in the writing group. I'd have to look elsewhere for the man in Violet's life, the benefactor with the magical cash flow.

"Did you tell the police any of this?" I asked.

"No because I only started putting it together long afterward. A mystery man and a mysterious money source. Then two months later, Violet was dead. What do you think?"

"That maybe you should tell Lieutenant Gray now."

"But isn't it too late?"

"Not at all. The case is still open. There's a killer out there. Maybe you can help nab him."

"But it's so little. A comment here. Impressions there." She sighed and pulled the tall glass of iced tea closer. "If Violet's desire to have someone in her life led to her murder, that's truly tragic. Every woman needs a man, if only to take her out for an occasional dinner."

"I disagree. I can be happy whether I have a date or not."

My words bounced back to me, a taunting echo in the quiet restaurant. *Really, Linnet? How happy have you been lately?*

Happy enough, even with insidious forces and Candace Ann working against me. As for Dalton, wasn't I happier cruising the countryside with him than sitting on my back porch watching the rain fall?

Yes; and I'd better seize every bit of pleasure life offered before I grew old and my choices dwindled to one: The porch. Before the natural lights in my hair faded to gray and I found that I could no longer balance properly on a pair of high heels.

Ellen must have read my thoughts. "That's easy for you to say, Linnet. You're young and pretty, and you're dating the most eligible bachelor in town."

I gasped. "How did you know that?"

"There are few secrets in Maple Creek."

"I'm not actually going with Lieutenant Gray," I said. "We've been out to dinner a few times. That's all."

No one knew about those kisses at Marble Lake except for the still-at-large shooter. That was my secret.

"Whenever Dalton has been at my house, it's been for business," I added.

"Of course," she said, but her smile was knowing and sly. "I'd love to have even one romantic encounter, but I don't have a chance to meet men. The Tea Room isn't particularly male oriented."

"Neither is the Leaf and Pod, but there's the Blue Lion Inn and a roadhouse on the outskirts of town. It's called Hunter's. I'll bet they have loads of male customers."

"I applied for a waitressing job at both places. They want young women on the staff. Ah well…"

"You're not so old, Ellen," I said.

"I'm heading toward forty."

"Well stop. Go the other way. I thought you were around thirty."

She blushed, and for an instant looked young and vulnerable.

"Thank you. I'd like to think so."

"There's always the internet," I said. "That's the modern way for people to meet."

"Maybe I'll try it, if I get lonely enough."

I found a long curling piece of mystery vegetable and coaxed it out of the greens. It was unfamiliar. Crunchy. Bland in color and taste.

Ellen picked up her spoon and twirled the orange slice in her iced tea around in the glass. "So you think I should go to the police then? They won't laugh at me?"

"I'm sure they'll be grateful for any information you can give them. Please do it, Ellen."

"I will." She gave the orange slice another little spin around the glass. "I never wanted to believe that someone in our group killed Violet."

"I'm curious about something," I said. "Why are you telling me this?"

She looked surprised. "Why, because I know you're not the killer. You weren't in town when Violet was poisoned."

Actually I was, commuting an hour from my old house to Alcott, but as it didn't make any difference, I didn't mention it.

SOMETIMES A PROPER RESPONSE to an insult or unpleasant situation doesn't occur to me until weeks, months, and, in rare cases, even years have passed. In that way I was like Ellen, slow to realize the significance of the man-and-money aspect of Violet's murder.

As I drove home from the Leaf and Pod, a memory escaped from the last shadow of my nightmare—Violet strolling into my bedroom speaking with a slight accent. Like the woman on the phone.

Did this suggest that the caller was Violet trying to warn me from her grave about my impending death?

I almost burst out laughing. How many times does a dream contain a genuine clue? Then, if the caller were Violet in spirit form, if she sincerely wanted to help me, why wouldn't she have been more specific?

She could have said, "Next Thursday you're going to be shot to death while you water your flowerbeds. Lock yourself inside the house that day and ask your lieutenant to arrest (the shooter's name)."

"And by the way, that ruby heart pin was stolen. It's worth thousands of dollars, and the thief wants it back.... That's why you can't keep it."

Bring out your notebook, I told myself. *This is pure speculative fiction.*

THE NEW WEEK WAS GOING to be busy with the puppy's long-awaited arrival and the usual three Alcott meetings, one of them at my house. But Sunday promised to be quiet and peaceful.

Yesterday's sunny weather was expected to last until storms developed at the end of the week.

After breakfast, I took the *Tribune* out to the back porch and was engrossed in the *Travel* section when stealthy footsteps set off a silent alarm.

Candace Ann appeared at the end of the driveway, squinting in the brilliant sunlight. She wore a sleeveless floral dress, very unlike her typical attire, and an unusual bracelet—three strands of coral beads with an ornate clasp. It looked too tight for her wrist.

Her gaze came to rest on me in my back porch retreat, and she smiled brightly.

A knot of unease twisted itself around my throat. Each time Candace Ann stopped at my house, she came a little closer. This wasn't normal behavior, and I didn't like it. The screens separated us, but the porch had been built close to the driveway, only about three yards away.

I felt as if my private sanctuary had been invaded, which, of course, it had.

"Hey, Ms. Shellwin," she said.

"Good morning, Candace Ann." I made an effort to appear unruffled. "That's a pretty dress. You didn't ride your bike over, did you?"

She giggled. "Oh, no, I walked over."

"Do you live close by?"

She shrugged. "About fifteen minutes. I came to see how you liked your strawberries."

Strawberries… I'd thrown them out for the birds and sincerely hoped they'd gobbled them all up. I couldn't tell her that, of course, and didn't want her to see her berries strewn over the ground.

"I haven't seen such glorious strawberries in years," I said. "The ones at the supermarket look impressive, but they're tasteless."

"It's better to grow your own," she said. "Why don't you plant a garden? You have all this space back here."

"Gardening takes time that I don't have."

"I'd love to come over and help you."

I stared at her, wondering how to respond to this strange ffer and spare Candace Ann's feelings at the same time. She adn't moved, hadn't come any closer, but she kept shifting her veight from one foot to another.

All I had to do was issue an invitation and she'd be on the orch with me. The knot tightened. I touched my throat, tried o will it away.

What do you want? I longed to ask her that. *Don't you have nything better to do on a summer vacation day than seek out he company of your former ninth grade teacher?*

"Don't you wear jewelry in the summer?" she asked, saving ne the trouble of finding a diplomatic way to reject her offer.

"Not unless I'm going out," I said.

"You have such pretty necklaces and pins," she said. "Everyone says so. You should wear them all the time."

I shifted in the wicker chair, folded my paper with excesive rustling, and wondered how I could end this bizarre nterrogation.

"Do you think I could have that house tour now?" she sked.

I'd forgotten about the tour. And no, she couldn't have it. Not now. Not ever.

"Well, let's see..." With newspapers scattered all around me, could hardly claim that I had to leave for an appointment. But didn't want Candace Ann in my house, and I refused to feel nkind or inhospitable about that. In any event, it was risky or a teacher to invite a student into her home. Besides, I didn't now what this girl's intentions were.

Except at any minute I expected her to give me an update n Jimmy and Dale and their revenge plan.

"It's a mess today," I said. "I haven't had a chance to clean. The house needs to be seen when it looks its best."

"Oh, well... Later then. You promised."

I did?

"Are you using the mug I gave you?" she asked.

I couldn't tell her that I had taken it down to the basement, that her gifts made me so uneasy I didn't want them in my sight. There was so much I couldn't say to her, so much that needed to be said.

Don't give me anything, I thought. *Please. I don't want anything. Just to be left alone.*

"When school starts in the fall, mugs will come in handy," I said. "It's been way too hot for coffee."

"Yes, I guess…"

Inside the house a phone began to ring. It wasn't the landline but the cell, making so soft a trilling sound that I doubted if Candace Ann could hear it from the driveway.

"Excuse me," I said. "I have to get that."

Without waiting for her to answer, I hurried inside, feeling that I'd made a fortunate escape. From something.

Through the kitchen window, I saw Candace Ann walking slowly back down the driveway to the street.

Thank God, I thought, and snapped open the cell.

TWENTY-FIVE

"LINNET? DO YOU HAVE any plans for today?"

It was Dalton's voice on the cell phone, clear and brisk. Businesslike. Official business, that is.

I glanced at the Sunday papers, still strewn about the porch, and at Milla Schoenherr's book, not yet finished. "None. I'm just enjoying the day and trying to keep cool."

"Is it okay if I drop by later this afternoon? Around one?"

Okay? More than okay.

I couldn't think of anyone I'd rather see.

I'd finished reading the paper and started *Capture My Heart* but found I couldn't invest in Milla Schoenherr's lusty characters or concentrate on her extravaganza of passion. I kept glancing toward the driveway, expecting Candace Ann to return with some other bizarre comment or request.

"I'll be here all day," I said. "Do you have the DNA report on the ruby pin?

"Sorry. Not yet. I just wanted to see you."

"I'd like to see you too. Later then."

As soon as I set the phone down, I rushed inside to prepare for this welcome break in my Sunday routine. First I checked to see that I had plenty of soft drinks and beer on ice. The peach pies I'd baked for tomorrow's school meeting were cooling on the counter, and my new coffee percolator was clean and ready to turn out cups of the strong brew Dalton loved.

Then I changed into a dress that brought together all the colors of spring in a soft floral pattern. The day that had begun with an upset promised to end with a bang. A happy one.

Now, two hours later, Dalton frowned at his Pepsi can as I

told him about Candace Ann's visits. His grim expression gave the matter another layer, an even more unsettling one.

"If this girl is bothering you, I'll have a talk with her," he said. "What did you say her name was?" He opened his notebook and waited.

"Candace Ann Clayborne, but I don't think it's a good idea to involve the police. She'd say she was just being friendly. That could be true."

"It sounds more like stalking to me. If you think there's something unhealthy about this attachment to you, there probably is."

"Besides, I don't want to hurt her feelings," I added.

I gazed at the driveway where Candace Ann had stood earlier this morning and remembered our away-from-school encounters: Candace Ann staring up at my Valentine window in awe, then handing me a coffee mug inscribed "For my favorite teacher." Giving me a basket of homegrown strawberries and offering to help me tend my future garden. Strongly hinting for a tour of Valentine Villa that she seemed to believe I'd promised her.

And I remembered how I'd felt. Invaded. Uncomfortable. I had even dressed the truth in deception.

I'll use the mug for coffee in the fall when it isn't so hot. The strawberries are so much better than the supermarket variety. I can't let anyone see the house until I do some cleaning.

Could I have overreacted? I didn't think so. Still I wanted to be fair to her.

I cared deeply about my students, even those I would never teach again. But I believed in a deep separation between teachers and the young people in their care. Unconsciously—perhaps consciously—Candace Ann didn't. That was the problem.

"She's probably just lonely," I said. "In class, she didn't seem to have any special friends. I don't know what her home life is like."

"Even if they're unhappy, most kids don't hang around their old teachers."

At my look of dismay, he reached over and squeezed my hand. "Sorry, Linnet, I didn't mean to imply that you're old. Just that you're a teacher. Her former teacher."

I smiled, remembering Ellen Trehearne. "You're forgiven. After all, old is relative."

"Whatever you do, don't have her in your house when you two are alone," he added.

"I wouldn't dream of doing that."

"A high school journalism teacher downstate just got into major trouble being too chummy with her students. She invited her newspaper staff over for a pizza party and served them wine coolers. The parents found out. Now she might lose her job."

"She was foolish," I said. "She should have asked permission to have this party in school and brought in soft drinks."

"Agreed. Some people don't have an ounce of common sense, and teachers are easy targets. Her own editor blabbed about the wine coolers."

I remembered the promises of students who wanted to sneak out of the building before dismissal on test days, which was forbidden. "We won't say where we came from," they'd say. But the minute they were caught, they talked.

I'd only done that once when a freshman girl looked really sick. It turned out to be an elaborate act.

"In some ways you can't trust kids," I said.

Dalton sat back in the extra chair I'd brought from the front porch, as much at ease with me as I was with him. I felt better having confided in him. Still I wondered if I was doing the right thing in not setting Dalton on Candace Ann's trail.

The next time she comes to my house, if I feel the least bit threatened, I'll call him, I promised myself.

If I only knew what Candace Ann's private life was like. She had said very little about it. She'd missed a tutoring session because she had to baby-sit. For a younger sibling? A neighbor's child? I had no idea. In August she planned to visit her grandmother who lived in the south, and her mother grew strawberries. And somehow she always managed to run into Jimmy or Dale and ferret out their revenge plans.

But wait! I no longer believed that.

"Candace Ann is a mystery kid," I said, "But I know how I can find out more about her. She kept a journal."

At Alcott, all ninth grade English students did. It was a course requirement. I didn't read their entries, only graded them once a week on quantity—at least one paragraph written in ink every school day. To make sure that the journals wouldn't get lost or used for other classes, I kept them in my desk. At the end of the course, they were free to take them home, but few bothered to do so.

They were still there; I could easily access them. The office was always open during the day, and one of the secretaries would lend me a key to my room.

But should I do it?

"Here's the problem," I said. "I promised I wouldn't read the journals, but in this case, maybe I should. What do you think?"

"That my way is easier," he said.

"Forewarned is forearmed," I reminded him. "I wouldn't be doing this out of idle curiosity. Just to protect myself—if it becomes necessary."

"Don't do anything that might backfire on you."

I didn't intend to. Anyway, this was a distant Plan B, to be implemented only if Candace Ann became a real threat and before I called on Dalton to intervene.

"It's only a thought," I said, "and if I go ahead with it, no one will know."

But here was another problem. I was leery of entering the building with only a skeleton office staff on the premises. The last time I'd been on the second floor, the last day of school, someone else had been there, too, following me. Vanishing into the woodwork. It was unlikely that would happen again, although not impossible.

But what if this was the only way to find the answers I needed?

"Sometimes it seems that this school trouble is going to follow me around forever," I said. "Like a curse."

Dalton shook his Pepsi bottle, found it empty, and set it on the table next to Milla's book.

"Freedom is the solution, Linnet. The open road. New sights to see. New experiences. Getting away from it all."

I smiled. "You sound like a travel agent."

"I can make it happen. How about a nice long ride in the convertible? We can find a country inn for dinner and take our time coming home."

I would have been content to stay on the porch with Dalton for the rest of the day, breathing in the fragrance of the lilies that grew along the side of the house and the scent of cinnamon left over from the peach pies. Just talking or being silent, being with him, until the sun went down. And after.

But his idea was equally enticing. I felt as if he had just handed me a magic key.

"Which direction would we take?" I asked.

"North, south, east, or west. It's your call."

"Let me get my purse and lock up," I said.

I CHOSE NORTH, AND DALTON drove the Cadillac out of Maple Creek to the nearest northbound I-75 entrance. The wind buffeted us and muted the sound of Dalton's old-time tape a little, but I knew the lyrics by heart:

Love, love, tender love,/Hear my lonely cry/Moon and stars die up above/But without you, then so do I.

I loved the wind. It was the sound of summer blowing in, bringing us closer to June 21st. The first day of the new season, the day of my death. And how ironic was that? But here with Dalton, traveling to a magical place, the problems in my life seemed unreal. Even the Last One.

"I know a village where you'll swear you're traveling back in time," he said. "Nothing ever changes in Frederickville. There's a lake and an inn with the best chicken in Michigan. It's even better than what you'll get in Frankenmuth."

"Are we going there?" I asked.

"All roads lead to Frederickville," he said.

And I loved this romantic side of Dalton, one I was surprised to find behind his occasional austere manner. I loved being entertained by his knowledge of the little towns we drove through—the history of one, the obscure claim-to-fame of another, the five recent cougar sightings in a third.

He was always a policeman though, and at the end of our road trip, while we were sitting in a quaint country inn over plates of roast chicken and biscuits—pure comfort food—he said, "I've been thinking about everything that's happened to you, Linnet, trying to figure out who's behind it. The first was the attempted shooting by Carl Hogan at Alcott. Right?"

I nodded. "That's where we first met."

"Then the second shooting at Marble Lake when you were with me."

"No, the disconnected landline phone was next. I just didn't tell you about it when it first started ringing."

"Check—and that's still going on. Then the last day of school when you thought someone was following you down the hall. That's the only one that might have an innocent explanation. Now there's this girl, this Candy Ann."

"Candace Ann," I said. "This just occurred to me. Wouldn't most girls named Candace rather be called Candy?"

"Not if she wants to be unique."

That one word certainly described Candace Ann.

"So that's it," Dalton said.

"You forgot the ruby pin."

"Yes, the pin."

"Violet told me to take it to the police. She didn't say why."

He stared at me. "Violet who?"

I blushed. "It's what I named the caller."

I didn't tell him about the dream that had inspired me to give a dead woman's identity to the caller, and he seemed satisfied with my explanation.

I sat back, my fine dinner momentarily forgotten, trying to catch an elusive thought. A fly-by.

Dalton said, "Could any of these events be tied to Candace Ann?"

My first response would have been "No, of course not." But Dalton's question deserved consideration. Could Candace Ann have been a silent partner in the gun conspiracy? I hoped not. Could she have shot at us herself? I couldn't imagine that. And I'd long ago decided that the calls on the landline phone had no connection to the school.

"I simply can't see her stalking us on the beach," I said. "This is a freshman—she's probably fourteen years old. She rides a bike. Following me in a deserted hallway? Maybe. But I'm pretty sure she'd make herself known. She always wants attention. She takes a weird interest in what I'm doing, what I have..."

That was it! The pin! I caught the fly-by thought and held it tightly.

Candace Ann had asked me if I wore jewelry in the summer. She said everybody—presumably in the fourth hour class—thought I had nice jewelry. Specifically she'd mentioned necklaces and pins.

I'd worn necklaces and earrings, all inexpensive costume jewelry, to school, but never pins. The ruby Valentine heart was the only pin I owned.

Because I was sitting opposite a policeman, I told him what I'd remembered.

Dalton frowned again. He'd been frowning a lot since we'd begun to go out together, which wasn't a good sign. "This business is getting to be as puzzling a mystery as your phone calls. I want to tie it all together, but that's not easy to do."

"What we need are more clues," I said. "What we don't have is more time."

I thought, but didn't remind him, of what was supposed to happen on June 21st.

In that moment I made up my mind about reading Candace Ann's journal. Unethical or not, I was going to do it, and I'd ask someone, Beverly or Milla, to go with me. Just in case.

The connection between Candace Ann and the ruby heart pin was a tenuous one, but I couldn't afford to ignore it.

TWENTY-SIX

BEVERLY WAS THE FIRST to arrive for the meeting the next morning. She swept into the house with a foil-covered baking dish in her hands and a gleam of high excitement in her eyes.

"Have you heard the news?" she demanded, as I took the dish from her.

"Did something happen?" I asked.

"I should say something happened. Let's just put this in the oven on 'warm.' It's lasagna." She unfolded the foil and fussed with its edges. "Our famous authoress, Milla Schoenherr, has been accused of having sex with one of her students."

I almost dropped the dish.

"You're joking. Right?"

"I'd never joke about something so serious. It's in the morning paper."

In the kitchen, I placed the baking dish in the middle of the oven, set the temperature, and closed the door. These practical activities steadied me. Beverly's news had knocked me off balance.

She followed me back to the living room, expounding on Milla's beauty and grace and her reputation for aloofness with the high school staff.

"She never mingled with the others except when she had to," Beverly said.

"Who's she supposed to have had sex with?" I asked.

"Randy Galloway."

The name hung in the air. I came to a standstill in front of the sofa, reeling from yet another surprise, hoping that Beverly was mistaken or that there were two Randy Galloways in Maple Creek.

"Is that the man who came back to town for his class reunion?" I asked.

"The same. Okay. I stand corrected. Milla had sex with a *former* student. This happened ten years ago when he was in her eleventh grade lit class. Now he's suing her."

It seemed unreal. Randy Galloway, still remembered for his achievements in the classroom, on the football field, and in and out of the high school spotlight. The all-American golden boy with a secret as great as his reputation. The grown man who had showed a disturbing interest in my ruby heart pin. Cousin of the dangerous Garth McKay.

Connections were flying through the air, but I couldn't catch a single one.

"What does Milla say?" I asked.

"That he's making it all up. That she's innocent. What else can she say?"

"Maybe she is."

"Innocent or guilty, she'd better get a good lawyer," Beverly said. "Read the article. It's on the front page."

In the process of neatening the living room, I'd shoved the morning *Tribune* into the magazine stand. I read the story now, while Beverly hovered over my shoulder.

Randy Galloway, formerly of Maple Creek, now residing in Wyoming, is suing Ludmilla Schoenherr, an English teacher at Maple Creek High School, claiming that she seduced him when he was a student in her class ten years ago. Ms. Schoenherr was unavailable for comment.

"They don't tell you much in the paper, do they?" Beverly said.

"If Milla is unavailable for comment, how do you know she claims to be innocent?" I asked.

"Rae told me."

"And how does Rae know?"

"She heard it from somebody at the high school."

"I'd like to talk to Milla, to hear her side of the story," I said.

"So would a lot of people, I'll bet. The principal, the board members..."

Beverly turned the pages of the paper while the living room clock ticked away the minutes. Everything else was quiet. I sat still, remembering how Milla had talked about her past classes fondly, with a touch of nostalgia. She was the experienced teacher who had weathered all the storms. My mind still hadn't fully grasped the news, couldn't put Milla Schoenherr and Randy Galloway together as a couple.

But, if the story were true, that wasn't what they had been.

In my mind, I saw the handsome young man in the park with Garth McKay and Katherine Kale, not the high school junior he had once been. The minor. The child.

Why had he decided to break his silence now?

Beverly set the paper on the coffee table and I dropped it back into the magazine stand. "I still can't believe it," I said.

"Oh I can. Have you read Milla's book?"

"Not all of it."

"I wondered if she dredged up those hot sex scenes out of her imagination."

"But he was her student," I said. "That's so wrong."

"Sure it's wrong, but it happens. Here, there, everywhere. We live in evil times. What do we have to go with the lasagna?"

Beverly's mundane inquiry pulled me back to reality. To the prospect of the rest of the group appearing on my doorstep in ten or fifteen minutes. To the difficulty of wrenching my mind away from this shocking new development and applying it to short story selections for fourteen-year-olds and relevant composition topics.

"I baked peach pies and made a pasta salad," I said. "We have hot rolls. The guys are bringing the drinks. Oh, speaking of drinks..."

I'd forgotten the cooler filled with bottled water and juice. While Beverly picked up the paper again, her eyes riveted on the front page article, I brought it into the living room. Ned and Beverly had hosted comfortable, well-appointed meetings.

I didn't have a lakeside cottage or fancy outdoor furniture, but I wanted our third session to be at least as enjoyable as the previous ones.

It was a relief to deal with fruit juice and water, but now, with the refreshments set out, my thoughts turned back to Milla.

"If it really happened, why would Milla draw attention to herself by writing and publishing a sexy book under her own name? And she's stayed at Maple Creek High all these years. It doesn't make sense."

"Well, she was making good money," Beverly said. "She had tenure. As to the affair or whatever it was, only Milla and Randy know the whole story."

"I don't see how it could have stayed a secret all these years."

"Probably because no one else knew and neither of them talked—until now. Don't they say that eventually every secret comes out?"

"I suppose so."

I'd been going to invite Milla to accompany me to Alcott and stand guard while I read Candace Ann's journal. Obviously I wouldn't ask her now, but I still meant to try to contact her. Whether Milla was innocent or guilty, she was a fellow teacher, and she'd offered me friendship and advice—along with a few broken engagements.

But maybe she'd had an inkling of the disaster that was about to overtake her. She'd definitely been flustered at the appearance of Garth and Katherine when she'd seen them walking Garth's dog on Beechnut Street. Which made me wonder if Garth knew about the relationship between Milla and his young cousin and whether he knew about the lawsuit.

This made me suspect that perhaps Milla was guilty.

Stay away from Milla Schoenherr, and you should be okay, the caller had warned. Was this why? And what could Milla's dilemma possibly have to do with my supposed death?

Nothing, that I could see.

"Funny how all this came out now with Milla's book so

popular," Beverly said. "She's practically a celebrity. And who knows how much cash she's raking in?"

"I wonder if there's a connection."

"You mean that Randy's doing this because he wants her money?"

"It was just a thought."

But an inspired one. Randy had never told anyone what he did for a living, if anything. Supposedly he was hoping to stay in Maple Creek, and everybody needed money these days. But the prospect of winning a distant lawsuit wouldn't pay today's bills.

Where was the truth in this mess? I looked at it in another way.

Milla might well be guilty of seducing Maple Creek's golden boy, but she could also be the target of a liar who, for some reason, was determined to destroy her?

Randy Golden Galloway. Liar?

It didn't seem likely, but what did I know of these people? And, after all, I could so easily have been in Milla's place. Maybe that was why my sympathies had gone straight to her.

Alcott Middle School teacher Linnet Shellwin denied accusations that she had sex with a fourteen-year boy in her freshman class. Because of his age, the Tribune *isn't naming the alleged victim.*

One version of Dale's revenge plan, to be presented to the school board. Something mean. Beyond mean.

A chill wrapped itself round me. In that moment I forgot that I'd decided Dale's revenge plot was a product of Candace Ann's overheated imagination.

I shifted uneasily in my chair so that I was closer to the bay window and the sunlight. No one would believe such a vile story about me.

Would they?

My thoughts were traveling in fuzzy circles. I had to be alone to think this through, and that wouldn't happen for hours yet.

EVERYONE EXCEPT NED WANTED to talk about Milla Schoenherr and Randy Galloway. Everyone had an opinion; no one possessed genuine knowledge. But Rae's unnamed source at the high school claimed that Milla had been sighted at the airport in Flint.

"Getting out of Dodge," Arthur said. "That proves she's guilty."

"No it doesn't," I countered. "It's vacation time."

"You can't leave town if you're being sued, can you?" asked Beverly.

"That's if you've been charged with a crime," Rae said.

I checked to see that everyone had water or juice. "Doesn't it seem odd that somebody just happened to be at the airport when Milla was?"

"Not really," Beverly said. "It's closer to Maple Creek than Metro. Besides, like you said, Linnet, it's vacation time."

"Has anybody seen Randy?" Arthur asked.

No one had.

Finally Ned reined in his runaway group. "Let's continue this after lunch." The steel in his voice convinced us to find our partners and keep all discussion focused on the new course.

But when we broke at noon, the talk bounced back to Milla and Randy and took a strange new turn.

Arthur said, "Over the years I've heard similar stories about Maple Creek teachers and students. Flirtations and more. You know. I'm only surprised the district didn't cover it up."

He spooned more pasta salad onto his plate. "Delicious salad, Linnet. You're going to make some lucky man a great little wife."

While I tried to decide whether to thank him for the compliment or chide him for that sexist remark, Rae said, "You're not going to stop there, Arthur, I hope. What stories did the district cover up?"

He shrugged. "Oh, various scandals. Maple Creek High is like a little inbred community tucked away in the Michigan northwoods. Folks are related to one another, or they have history with one another, or they're just tolerant of certain people who know how to play the game."

"Like just about every coach we've ever had," Lou said.

"And that hot young business teacher, that redhead who was so popular with her male students. Lucy, Lacey, Lizzie… whatever. There were plenty of hushed-up incidents in those years."

Unfortunately Arthur couldn't remember the redhead's name or even the decade these wild activities took place. "But it doesn't matter," he said. "She moved out of state a long time ago."

"You can see how it happens," Lou said. "All that youth. Those raging hormones. Some of the teachers are only a little older than their students. A beautiful young teacher comes along…"

His glance strayed to me, and I looked away.

"Weekend trips to Mount Suzanne with the Ski Club, play practice, field trips, private tutoring sessions…"

"I didn't know the high school had a ski club," I said.

"It doesn't. I'm talking about the good old days. And I won't even get started on the goings-on between the adults. But what happens at Maple Creek High stays at Maple Creek High. That's the unwritten code."

Arthur nodded. "It's all in the family."

The school district Arthur and Lou described was vastly different from the one I worked in. I didn't believe it existed.

"If I got into some sort of romantic trouble, I think the district would throw me to the wolves," I said.

Lou's fleeting smile was difficult to read. "Probably. You're not one of the good old boys, Linnet."

Ned said, "Linnet isn't a boy, and you're talking nonsense, Lou. We have a close-knit school district true, but it isn't a hotbed of corruption and cover-up."

Lou bristled. "You don't really believe that, do you, Ned?"

"It's too late, now that Randy Galloway filed this suit and

it's been in the paper," Rae pointed out. "We'll just have to wait and see what happens."

"That's best," Arthur said.

"Back to work." Ned set his plate down. "We have a lot of ground to cover. When we're through for the day, maybe Linnet will give us a guided tour of this beautiful place. I've always admired it from the outside."

"And I'd like to know where Violet Julaine died," Rae said.

Ned frowned at her. "That's morbid, Rae."

"It was in a room on this floor," I said. "It's full of boxes now."

NED STOOD IN FRONT OF the Valentine window like Prince Charming posed for a greeting card illustration. The stained glass gave his face and fair hair a rosy glow. I wished I had a camera.

"I've always wondered what this room was like," Rae said.

"What do you think of it?" I asked, standing in the doorway. This was the last stop on my tour of the house and the only room that was still unfurnished.

"Well it's small, like a large closet, but I love the wallpaper."

Violet had chosen it. Tiny rose bouquets and pink stripes on a soft yellow background. It was very romantic, very Victorian.

"What are you going to use it for?" Rae asked.

"I'm not sure."

"You should fill it with Valentine memorabilia and one beautiful chair. Then you could look out at the treetops and unwind after a long day at Alcott."

"That sounds fine, except for the memorabilia," I said. "I don't want to be surrounded by things."

I cringed at a mental picture of what Valentine Villa must

have been like when Violet lived here, with walls painted pink or red or white and heart themed bric-a-brac at every turn.

"Besides, I don't have much time to sit and unwind," I said. "But this room needs special treatment. I'm in no hurry to furnish it."

Downstairs the landline phone rang.

I held my breath, counted rings, felt my heartbeat speed up.

Nobody reacted. No one said, "Aren't you going to get that, Linnet?" or "Don't you have an extension up here?" Rae joined Ned at the window for one last look at the view from the second story. The others were filing past me through the doorway.

Three more rings, and the phone was silent.

She—Violet—wasn't supposed to call again, but something had changed. It must be the news about Milla Schoenherr.

TWENTY-SEVEN

ALCOTT MIDDLE SCHOOL drowsed on its hill, a tired old building that needed a long rest to gather its strength for another year. I parked in the section reserved for administrators and office staff, alongside a mud-splattered Saturn. Unsecured by a chain, a shiny black bike leaned against the bicycle rack at the entrance.

Not Candace Ann's bike, unless she got a new one.

"The place looks spooky without the kids around," Beverly said. "I can see why you didn't want to come here alone."

I'd only told her that I needed something from my classroom and would appreciate company. She had quickly guessed my apprehension.

"It's safer when there's two of us," I said.

"Safer from what? This is Small Town, Michigan. What do you think is going to happen?"

"You never know. I'd just rather have someone with me."

I'd changed my mind about reading the journal at my desk. Beverly had readily agreed to accompany me, but she was clearly uncomfortable. I'd simply slip it into the large fabric purse I was carrying and take a textbook out of the room as a cover. Then in my own home I could peruse the entries in comfort without fear of someone discovering what I was doing.

I felt like a spy, but this still seemed like the best way to get a handle on the Candace Ann problem.

"Well, let's do this. Then we can go out for coffee and doughnuts," Beverly said. "I haven't had breakfast yet."

The sun was hot on my bare arms as we walked the short distance to the front door. I glanced at the high grass and weed-choked flowers that encircled the maples. Where were the members of the Go Green Club who had volunteered to take care of the grounds during the summer? Or the custodians?

"This," Beverly said, waving her hands at the neglected landscaping, "is a disgrace. Where does our tax money go?"

"Apparently not toward maintenance."

We went through the door, propped open to catch the breeze when it deigned to make an appearance. Inviting aromas of coffee and chocolate drifted out of the front office where a young woman in a prim pink dress sat at a desk idly turning the pages of a magazine. A radio played softly in the background. She seemed familiar, and when she looked up, I noticed a slight resemblance to Dwight Dunlap's secretary, Sara.

"What can I do for you?" the young woman asked.

"I'm Linnet Shellwin, the ninth grade teacher," I said. "I need to get something out of my desk. Could I have the key to my room please?"

"Sure thing, Ms. Shellwin."

She disappeared into a workroom opposite the principal's office and returned moments later with a key attached to a yellow index card. "Here you are."

"That was easy," Beverly said. "Shall I wait for you down here?"

"Why don't you come up with me?" I said, meaning, *Why don't we stay together?*

I wasn't fooling Beverly. As we left the office, her laughter echoed in the deserted hall. "Are you afraid of the Alcott Boogeyman, Linnet?"

I attempted a smile. "Maybe. Or one of his cousins."

"I don't like to do any climbing until I've had my coffee, but let's go."

I'd forgotten how many stairs there were to the second floor. We pushed our way up through hot, still air and emerged at the top of the staircase. On a bright, wholesome morning, the second floor was locked in gloom. Dust motes stirred in the meager sunlight, and the shadows were long and strange.

"The custodians must wait until September to clean," I said.

Beverly giggled. "Their motto: Why mop an uninhabited area?"

"Ned said they were going to paint the rooms this summer."

"Well they're not starting up here."

I surveyed the long hall with closed doors on either side, remembering stealthy footsteps following me. Remembering hoards of screaming boys and girls bursting through my classroom door—and the one with the loaded gun.

In this part of the building, the memories were thick.

"What a perfect place for a murder!" Beverly said. "It's dark and isolated with lots of places to hide a body."

"The girl downstairs would hear us screaming."

"Don't count on it. She's in her own world."

"Well no one's going to get murdered today," I said.

Beverly gasped. "Oh, Linnet, I forgot about your experience with that awful Carl Hogan. I'm so sorry."

"It's all right," I said. "I'm over it. Sort of."

I unlocked the door to my classroom and went straight to my desk while Beverly waited in the hall, fidgeting with the metal handles on her purse.

Now for some answers.

The journals had a drawer to themselves, the bottom right. They were all shapes and sizes: Traditional theme books, binders in rainbow colors, homemade tomes held together with paper fasteners.

They should be in alphabetical order but never were. I flipped through the fourth hour section and soon found the one belonging to Candace Ann. It was a small hardbound book with a jaunty snowman on the cover. I'd complimented her on her choice. She'd told me she found it in a Christmas clearance sale.

It was too pretty to be abandoned, but I was glad she'd left it behind.

I turned to the first page. The second semester course had begun at the end of January, the day after an ice storm had shut down the district. The first entry, neatly written in ink, described the view from the classroom window, which had been my suggestion for those who couldn't think of a topic of their own.

The ice is still on the tree branches. They glitter in the sunlight. When it gets warm enough, the ice will melt. The sky is grayish. That's all I can see.

"Did you find what you're looking for?" Beverly asked. "Because I think I hear that Boogeyman's footsteps."

"It might be Annabelle's skeleton, Almond, come out to see who's trespassing," I said.

"Too funny."

I closed Candace Ann's snowman book and slipped it into my purse. Then I took a paperback *Thesaurus* out of the middle drawer.

"I'm ready," I said. "Let's go."

Beverly stared at the book in my hand. "You came back here for a dictionary?"

"It's a *Thesaurus*, and I like this edition. It isn't as heavy as the one I have at home."

She started walking briskly toward the stairs. "Let's get out of here. Actually I *did* hear something. A scratching noise."

"Mice," I said and locked the door again.

AFTER COFFEE, DOUGHNUTS and more speculation about Maple Creek's new scandal and the whereabouts of Milla Schoenherr, Beverly and I went our separate ways. Beverly was driving downstate to buy a new dress. She had a special date on Saturday.

I went home and made myself comfortable on the back porch with a glass of lemonade and Candace Ann's journal. I could easily finish it while the heat was still bearable; and if the landline phone rang again, I'd be able to answer it in time.

Only… I hoped that Candace Ann wouldn't sneak up on me and find me invading her privacy.

Don't be silly, I told myself. *She won't be able to see what you're reading from the driveway.*

Unless she came up to the porch. She might do that.

With an exasperated sigh, I opened the journal. If Candace Ann showed up at my house with another manufactured excuse, I'd know for certain that her motives were suspect. I'd call Dalton. And for all she knew, I had a blank book of my own with a snowman on the cover.

I started reading.

Wednesday—Dale said hello to me in the hall. I think he likes me. Maybe he'll ask me to the Valentine Dance. I hope so. It's going to be early because of the winter break.

Thursday—I dropped my grammar yesterday, and a Valentine card fell out. I picked it up and put it back in my book. I don't think anybody saw me. I read it in Study Hall: Candy, sweet as chocolate, cute as a bee, you're the Valentine for me. There's no signature, but it must be for me. (Candy). How can I find out who put it in my book?

Friday—Dale sat with the new girl, Cecile, at lunch today. She's a flirt. I guess you could say she's pretty. Competition?

Monday—I don't want to write today I don't want to write today I don't want to write today I don't want to write today I don't want to write today.

Tuesday—I never know what to write about unless something happens. Sometimes Shellwin writes topics on the board for us. Today she wrote "Friendship." So I'm going to write about friends. Best friends. You need them. You can sit with them at lunch and call them on the phone. They'll help you with your homework. Friendship is good.

Wednesday—It's too noisy in here. I can't think with everybody shouting. Only a few kids are writing in their journals. Why should I? I don't have anything to write about anyway. Just—I hate noise. I hate noise. I hate noise. I wish she'd stop it. She never does. Aunt Alice says a good teacher would make the class be quiet.

Thursday—"Signs of Spring." This is Shellwin's topic. Dairy Land opens. I can wear a jacket to school. I can ride my bike. Flowers. Shellwin has a bouquet of tulips on her desk. Jimmy tipped the vase over, and our papers got wet. It was an accident, he said. Ha!

Friday—My favorite day of the week, but Shellwin gave us homework. Dawn is having a party. She didn't ask me yet. Dale's going.

Deciding that these teenaged ramblings were a waste of time, I began skipping entries. Dale appeared in most of them. Candace Ann had faithfully recorded what he had worn, where she had seen him, what he had been doing, who he was with, and anything else that struck her as memorable.

What, I wondered, was the ultimate purpose of this catalogue of trivia? And how surprised Dale would be to find himself immortalized in a classmate's journal.

I moved on, skimming paragraphs, then reading first sentences only, until I came to a recounting of one incident I could never forget.

Tuesday—Something finally happened to write about! Carl did it. He pulled a gun on Shellwin after school last night, but he wasn't fast enough. They got him and Adam too. I don't know what's going to happen to them now. Shellwin had this cop come talk to us. He wants information. He says we won't get in trouble. Whatever we say will be confidential. Like I believe that!

As I reread Candace Ann's entry, Carl's assault replayed itself in my mind in all its blood-bright detail. It seemed to me that she had known what Carl and Adam were going to do ahead of time, which gave credence to my theory that others in the class had been in on the Plot.

But Candace Ann?

The truth was in the journal. Ms. Shellwin, "My Favorite Teacher," becomes Shellwin. My narrow escape from death didn't merit a sentence.

Well, what did I expect? Remorse, perhaps? Gratitude that my life was spared?

Like I believed that.

Turning to the next page, I told myself, *You can't really know anyone. Not your friends, not your students. Especially not this girl.*

But she was telling me more about herself in this journal than she ever would in a face-to-face encounter.

I read on, glossing over descriptions of Dale's attire and witticisms, stopping when I came to an entry that was longer than the others and framed in little red sticker stars.

Monday—This was my best birthday ever! Last night I baked chocolate cupcakes to take to English class. Mom showed me how to write names in frosting on them. I had one for everybody. Shellwin let us have fifteen minutes of class time for a party. She's not supposed to let us eat in the room, but she made an exception because it was my birthday, she said. I'm kind of glad Carl didn't kill her. Dale said I could bake cupcakes for him anytime. How about that? I'm going to do it too! Oh, and I got lots of presents, three from the kids in class and one from Shellwin.

I stared at the neat handwriting, reread the entry, and tried to remember what had really happened on Candace Ann's birthday.

Nothing except English business as usual. No party. No food in class—ever. No presents.

I had wished Candace Ann a Happy Birthday and suggested that she pass out the cupcakes in the cafeteria. She'd objected but quietly set the plate under her desk.

With another sigh, I closed the journal. At some point, Candace Ann had turned from journaling to fiction. How could I believe anything she might write now?

TWENTY-EIGHT

EVEN IF CANDACE ANN HAD lost herself in fantasyland, I owed it to both of us to read what she'd written. Opening the journal again, I turned to the day after the imaginary birthday party. It wasn't exactly an entry, only a string of unconnected words designed to look legitimate and fool the teacher.

The rest of the entries were similar to the previous ones, with a thread of deep dissatisfaction running through them. Candace Ann hated the behavior of her classmates and my inability to control them. She even deplored the antics of Dale.

She duly noted the rare occasions when the class had a good day. On bad days, she recorded incidents I'd never been aware of. Frequently she quoted her Aunt Alice who had a poor opinion of teachers in general and of me in particular.

"That Shellwin woman shouldn't be teaching," Aunt Alice said. "There's too many teachers shouldn't be in the classroom. I say, 'Fire them all!'"

Candace Ann's crush on Dale gradually ripened into a friendship. She had a movie date with him and he invited her to a party. Fact or fiction? I couldn't tell, but the longer the entry, the more likely it was to be fabricated.

Candace Ann's attitude toward me pounded my fragile self-esteem into powder. She didn't respect me. According to her, no one in the class did. She blamed me for all the things she didn't learn; she ridiculed my failed attempts to keep the wildest fringe of the class in order. Now that I knew her true feelings, the gifts and friendly overtures took on an eerie significance.

What was she up to?

The last entry was a jubilant farewell to ninth grade, punctuated with fancy exclamation marks. I closed the journal. In a way, I wished I'd never taken it from my desk drawer. Since the first day of the course, I'd thought of the fourth hour as my worst class. Why didn't I realize that it was their worst class too?

If I couldn't provide a quiet learning environment for my students, then I should choose another career. Aunt Alice was right. But I didn't want to leave Alcott. More than anything, I wanted to go back to school in the fall, teach the new course we were developing, and do better with brand new groups.

Then do it, I told myself.

There were ways to capture students' attention and squash unacceptable behavior. I had books on classroom discipline from my Teaching Methods course and notes packed away in boxes where they weren't serving any purpose.

I was about to go inside and look for them when I heard Milla Schoenherr's voice coming from the front of the house. "Linnet… Are you in the yard?"

Abruptly I switched gears. "I'm on the back porch," I said. "Come join me."

The woman who appeared at the screen door was scarcely recognizable as the Milla Schoenherr I knew. Her hair, now dyed black, was cut in a short pageboy, and she wore oversized sunglasses. In a plain white dress, she looked like a celebrity hiding from the public glare.

That could well be what she was doing.

"You look glamorous this morning," I said.

She ventured a weak smile. "That's too bad. I was aiming for nondescript."

"You'll never be nondescript, Milla."

"I'm so tired of people staring at me," she said. "Everyone. People I don't even know. They know me."

She ran her hand through her hair, frowning. It had the hard glitter of ice that Candace Ann had described in her journal. "I thought a change of appearance would help."

"And has it?"

"Not much, and I don't like my hair this short. I should have bought a wig instead of having it cut."

She dropped wearily into the guest chair, took off the sunglasses, and slipped them into her white leather clutch. "I guess you heard about my trouble," she said.

"Yes, and I'm sorry. If you say you didn't do anything wrong, Milla, I believe you. No questions asked."

Her smile was slow and sad. "You're sweet, Linnet, but it's true. Does that change your mind about me?"

"It's your affair, Milla." I felt my face grow warm at the unintentional gaffe. "Your business, I mean."

"Yes, it is. But you don't understand how it could have happened, do you?"

What could I do but answer truthfully?

"No. I mean, I can't see myself being physically attracted to a boy in my class."

"Well, your students are younger than mine."

By two years.

"Even so. They're children." Realizing how censorious that sounded, I fell silent.

She gazed out at the rolling expanse of lawn, as if scenes from the past were forming in the shade of the weeping willow tree.

Finally she said, "I never thought of Randy Galloway as a child. There was something about him. Some irresistible thing… The first time I saw him, I was attracted to him. And he seemed older, much older, than sixteen to me."

"He grew into a very handsome man," I said.

She smiled. "He looked the same at sixteen, the year he was in my class. The Drama Club put on a play that spring, *Our Town*. Randy had a minor part. I was the sponsor. The rehearsals brought us together, and somehow, we drifted into a relationship."

"Drifted?" I said.

"It just happened. It wasn't planned. I was a little lonely. So was he. After a while, I convinced myself that in five or ten years, the age difference wouldn't matter. Suppose we met for the first time today. Randy's twenty-six; I'm thirty-six. That isn't so unusual."

"But the gap between sixteen and twenty-six is insurmountable," I said. "And a sixteen-year-old boy is a minor."

She couldn't deny that—didn't even try to.

"Did Randy care for you too?" I asked.

"He said he was in love with me."

"And now he's changed his mind."

She looked down at her hands. She had an elegant French manicurc, and she wore a ring, an aquamarine in a gold setting.

"Randy has changed completely," she said. "He's rewritten our history. Now he says I took advantage of him, says I ruined his life. That I'm the worst kind of monster. He called me a predator. He looked at me with such disgust. I was devastated."

"I'm sorry."

"But once we were in love, and it was wonderful." Her voice hardened. "I think somebody pushed him to file this lawsuit. Probably that cousin of his, Garth McKay. Randy always idolized him."

"What are you going to do?" I asked.

"What can I do? I can't change the facts. Whatever happens will happen. But I didn't come here to talk about Randy and me."

She opened her clutch and took out a glittering pin shaped like a floating heart.

"I'm here to make a trade, if you're willing," she said. "The stones are diamonds."

I stared at the pin, too stunned by the abrupt change in subject to react.

"Go ahead and put it on," she said. "It'll be like you're wearing stars."

I took the pin and let it rest in my palm. Its stones caught the sun's rays and danced in the light.

"It's beautiful, but I don't understand," I said. "What do you want to trade it for?"

"The ruby Valentine pin," she said. "The one you were wearing the other night."

"But why?"

"Because it belongs to me."

I tried to give Milla's pin back to her, but she kept her hands folded in her lap.

"I still don't understand," I said. "That pin was part of Violet Julaine's estate sale. How can you say it's yours?"

Just for the record, the caller had said, *that wasn't Violet Julaine's pin.*

"I guess I'd better explain," Milla said. "I wore the pin over to Violet's house one day, and it must have fallen off my sweater. I thought I'd lost it in the snow. Then I ran into you that night at the Blue Lion, and there it was, on your dress."

"How do you know it's the same pin?"

"It is."

Remembering Randy Galloway's interest in it when I met him in the park, I believed her. Possibly he'd given the pin to her when he thought he loved her. Perhaps it really had belonged to his mother originally. And he'd stared at it, red stones glittering on my white dress, and wondered how I'd acquired it.

"Why didn't you tell me this at the time?" I demanded.

"You were on a date with a cop. I couldn't very well accuse you of stealing my pin."

I bit back an angry retort. "I didn't steal it."

She took a figurative backward step. "No, no, of course you didn't. The point is, it should never have been with Violet's things in the first place. When someone dies and she has something of yours, you're out of luck. But now that you know what happened..."

She trailed off. I didn't say anything. In truth, I didn't know what to say.

But Milla did. "The ruby pin is valuable, but this one is worth much more."

"Then why are you willing to part with it?" I asked.

"The diamond pin is just something I bought for myself, but the ruby heart has sentimental value to me. Now that I know it wasn't lost, I want it back. Please, Linnet. If you want a Valentine pin with red in it, there's plenty of jewelry for sale around Valentine's Day. You can buy yourself something else."

I'd let this fiasco go on long enough.

"Please take your pin back, Milla," I said. "A trade won't be possible. I don't have the ruby heart."

She stared at me while I tried to decide what to tell her. In the end there was only the truth, discreetly edited.

"The police took it. They think it might be evidence in the Julaine murder case."

The color drained instantly from Milla's face. "Why do they think that?"

"They didn't say. All I know is they're examining it for DNA evidence. I suppose I'll get it back eventually."

And when that happened, I knew I'd never trade it for Milla's starry diamond heart. I didn't believe that she was being entirely truthful with me.

About her illicit love affair with Randy—oh yes. About her desire to have her ruby pin back. Yes. But about losing it in Violet's house? Maybe, but there was more to the story.

My mind served up a series of unsavory images: Milla wearing a snow-white sweater to show off her Valentine pin. Red and white in honor of Valentine's Day. Milla with a box of poisoned cherry tarts in her hand and a false smile on her face. Milla, the elusive Queen of Hearts.

My images didn't mesh with Ellen Trehearne's tale of a mystery man and money, but if they were true, I'd blithely invited a killer into Valentine Villa. Well, onto its porch. I had to get rid of her.

"I'm sorry, but I can't help you, Milla," I said in my best This-conversation-is-over tone.

"You could—if you wanted to."

"I can't imagine how."

I still held the diamond pin. She snatched it out of my hand and dropped it into her clutch bag.

"I *am* sorry," I said. "You could speak to Lieutenant Gray, I suppose. There's nothing I can do."

"No one can help me now," she said.

I INTENDED TO CALL DALTON, but a few minutes after Milla stalked off—literally in a huff, without saying goodbye—the landline phone rang. It was as if it had waited for my company to leave.

I rushed into the kitchen and picked up the receiver, wondering what the caller—Violet—would have to say about this latest development. I didn't doubt that she was aware of what had just transpired on my porch.

She didn't bother with a greeting. "You know now, don't you? You know why I told you to stay away from Milla Schoenherr. But you didn't listen to me."

So my suspicions were true. Confirmed by the phantom caller. At what point had I begun to believe in the impossible?

"She's a killer, and she's getting desperate," she added.

"No harm's done," I said. "She won't come back. Did you think she was going to murder me?"

"She considered it—if that was the only way she could make the evidence disappear. But now the jig is up. Her DNA has to be all over that pin. Your lieutenant will find that out soon enough."

"But just because her pin turned up in Violet's house doesn't mean that she killed her," I pointed out.

"What matters is that Milla *thinks* it incriminates her. She's coming unraveled. Couldn't you tell?"

"It's a good thing I gave the pin to Dalton then," I said.

"It's a good thing you listened to me."

"So I'm not going to die on the twenty-first of June?"

"Not by Milla Schoenherr's hand. You could still be hit

by a truck or struck by lightning, but Milla's going in another direction now."

"Thank God."

"Let me congratulate you, Linnet. You've outwitted death and backed a murderess into a corner. That's quite an accomplishment. I'll say goodbye now."

"Wait!" I cried. "Tell me how you made this dead phone work. Tell me why you cared what happened to me. Tell me who you are."

Her soft laughter drowned in a ripple of static with her last words.

"You know who I am," she said.

TWENTY-NINE

IT WAS A BLESSING TO CUT the fear loose and watch it fly away; a sweet conclusion to sit in the magical wishing alcove of the Blue Lion and watch the candlelight turn Dalton's cornflower blue eyes to shining jewels. And it was a pleasure to be happy.

I was going to live. I had nothing to fear but being hit by a truck or struck by lightning.

Dalton was frowning into his Merlot. Not that he was unhappy or annoyed. No doubt he was as relieved as I was, only obviously befuddled by certain aspects of my story.

Like the voice on the phone. All right. The voice of Violet Julaine. No matter how the information about her identity had come my way, I accepted it.

Dalton, perhaps less so. He believed me, but his practical, objective side remained in charge. I'd handed him a perfectly good suspect, and his reaction was disappointingly low key.

"Very interesting, Linnet." He made a tent of his hands over the wine glass. "I'll certainly talk to Ms. Schoenherr again, but, like you said, her possible DNA on the ruby pin and the fact that it was found in Violet Julaine's house doesn't add up to Milla as the killer."

"But what if she thinks it does?"

She's coming unraveled, Violet had said. *Couldn't you tell?*

"If her conscience is catching up with her, then she'll crack," Dalton said. "Could be this business with Galloway sent her over the edge."

"You always thought Violet Julaine's killer was a member of the Gothic Writers group," I reminded him.

He nodded. "Ms. Schoenherr had opportunity. They all did. Now give me her motive."

"The caller didn't tell me," I said. "Milla knows."

"I'll have to convince her that it's in her best interests to talk. And if she's the one who shot at us..."

I shuddered at the steel in his voice.

He could coerce a confession out of Milla, I suspected, and in such a way that Milla would think he was doing her a favor.

"You'd better hurry before she leaves town," I said.

"I will—first thing tomorrow. What did you learn from the journal?"

I'd never expected that question. "I didn't tell you that I was going to read it. Did I?"

"I know you by now," he said. "Did you find out anything about this Candace Ann?"

I hesitated. Candace Ann's scathing comments still burned in my memory and would for a long time. I didn't intend to reveal them to anyone; and in the fall, if their owners didn't come to claim the journals, I'd destroy them. No one could complain. They'd been told to take them home.

Dalton was waiting for his answer, regarding me over the flickering candlelight, all business now. Police business.

I said, "I learned that Candace Ann, like so many of her kind, lives in a dream world. The purpose of keeping a journal is to record thoughts and feelings. I guess no one said they had to be true. We teachers assumed they would be."

"Just that?"

"I'm not exactly one of her favorite people, which makes me wonder why she's gone out of her way to visit me."

"I wonder too," he said.

It still troubled me. "Apparently Candace Ann craves attention. But why would she look for it from a teacher she doesn't particularly like? That's me, by the way. Pretty much in her own words."

"I'm going to keep Candace Ann on the backburner," Dalton

said. "As for this other matter with the pin, it looks like you're off the hook. How are you going to celebrate?"

"Oh... With all good things. First my new collie puppy, Caramel. Her breeder is driving her down to Maple Creek tomorrow afternoon. Then..."

Tomorrow was the first day of summer, no longer a day to dread. I knew who my would-be killer was and felt that she was contained.

So easily?

Yes. Milla Schoenherr was coming unhinged. The woman in the shadows with the gun. Following me and Dalton to Marble Lake. Firing at us. Trailing me on the second floor of Alcott. All to kill me so that the evidence of the ruby heart pin would die with me.

Milla had no need to kill me now. She never had. She must have been unbalanced for a long time.

Somehow, that didn't seem right, even when I viewed Milla as a woman driven by circumstances to desperate, illogical measures.

I picked up my wine glass, but didn't drink. Something—one tiny piece—didn't fit in the neat little scenario Violet and I had concocted.

"Then?" prompted Dalton.

"Then I'd like you to come over and meet my puppy," I said. "My little Caramel."

"Sure I will, but I was thinking of something more celebratory. Just for you and me. Something major."

His sparkling eyes suggested a host of glorious possibilities.

"You work the details out, and I'll go along with it," I said. "It'll be more fun that way."

THE TWENTY-FIRST OF JUNE, and I was alive and likely to stay that way for many years to come. Furthermore Dalton was in my life, and I was happy about that.

Love, love, tender love,/Where are you tonight?

As I poured pancake batter into the griddle, I hummed the melody from Dalton's vintage tape, knowing that I'd hear it again soon. I knew where Dalton would be tonight. With me, en route to a surprise.

The morning was as perfect as the first day of summer should be, with cerulean skies, golden sunshine, and a sweet breeze to cool the hot air. It was difficult to believe the forecast in the morning paper: *Storms. At times severe.*

In other words, *Batten down the hatches. Beware of elms in thunder.*

Dalton planned to talk to Milla Schoenherr today and call me afterwards. In the meantime I had a large chunk of the day free. Everything was ready to welcome Caramel to her new home this afternoon. My notes were in order for tomorrow's meeting at Lou's condo. I'd found my books on classroom discipline and organized them for quick reading. I'd already read one line:

"Keep your students busy and you won't have discipline problems." Written by one who had never met my fourth hour class. I hoped his other suggestions would be more helpful. As for that one, I'd already tried it.

I ate breakfast slowly, determined to hold on to my happy mood while it seemed equally determined to slip away.

The journal lay on the kitchen table, taunting me with its brutal assessment of my worth as a teacher.

I hate noise. She can't keep them quiet. That Ms. Shellwin shouldn't be teaching. I say "Fire them all." She never does anything...

I didn't want Candace Ann's book in my house, didn't want to see that jolly snowman face with its mocking smile.

Take it back to the school and resist the urge to read any one else's journal, unless you want to make yourself miserable. Just know that they all hate you.

The sooner the journal was in its proper place, the better. I'd take it back now and, since it was such a beautiful day, walk the short distance to the school. On the way home I'd stop at Dairy Land for an ice cream cone. To celebrate summer and love.

I couldn't ask Beverly to accompany me again, but there was no need to, now that Milla was nearing the end of her reign of terror. Gathering my purse and the paperback *Thesaurus,* I decided on a plan: Tell whoever was at the desk that I'd picked up the wrong book by mistake yesterday. It sounded unlikely, definitely a fabrication, but a part-time secretary wouldn't be likely to question it. She wouldn't care.

So I set out, eager to be rid of the journal, hoping that I would soon be rid of Candace Ann as well.

The streets were quiet. No children played in their yards, but colored chalk drawings decorated the sidewalks. A large black cat watched me with baleful green eyes from a front porch, and sprinklers drenched the lawns. From an unseen fountain, I heard a soothing splash of falling water.

Small Town, Michigan, aka Maple Creek. Something evil had happened here over a year ago, but the killer was even now writhing in a trap of her own making. With Dalton watching over us all, I expected only good things for the future.

Savoring the breeze and a renewed euphoria, I walked on. Just imagine. No more phantom calls on the disconnected phone. No more looking over my shoulder at the slightest noise. No more Candace Ann, for if she came to my house again for whatever reason, I'd tell her that I couldn't have company at this time and close the door.

Rude? Yes. But she already had a low opinion of me, and, with luck, we'd never have to deal with each other again.

Alcott Middle School looked old and tired and warm, its dark red bricks baking in the sun. It would be hot inside, except in the front office where the windows were open and the fans would do their best to cool the air.

Three cars were parked in the reserved section this morning, and the black bike leaned on the bicycle rack, once again unsecured, as if daring anyone to approach it. The front door was again propped open, and coffee and chocolate aromas drifted out with the strains of music.

The sense of déjà vu was as strong as the sunlight.

The girl who resembled Sara was working today, separating onion-thin papers of different colors into four stacks.

"Good morning," she said. "Ms…I forget your name."

"Linnet Shellwin." I smiled, apologetically, I hoped. "I'm sorry to bother you, but could I borrow my room key again? I picked up the wrong book yesterday."

She looked at the *Thesaurus*, then looked at me.

"I wanted *Bartlett's Quotations,*" I said quickly. "They have the same cover."

Please believe that, I thought. *Although I wouldn't.*

"Just a minute," she said and left me alone in the office.

A scent of lemon overrode the coffee-and-chocolate aromas. Probably furniture polish. The front office, the only part of the building a casual visitor would see, must have received a cleaning. I rested my hand on Sara's desk. Yes, the furniture had been dusted, and I heard the distant roar of a power motor, bringing the scent of freshly mowed grass in through the open windows.

The old building was slowly coming to life again.

"Here you go," the Sara look-alike said. "Watch your step on the floor, Ms. Shellwin. It's just been polished."

I thanked her and, clutching the key, climbed the steps to the second story, once again pushing up through hot stagnant air. When I reached the top of the stairs, I glanced down the hall, fighting off a vestige of my past discomfort.

Apparently the custodian hadn't reached the upper level yet. Still I walked carefully, noting footprints in the dust. Many footprints. Mine and Beverly's leading to and away from my room. Others, larger than ours, going in different directions.

The view was as uninviting as ever, filled with shadows and narrow strips of light forcing their way through the window at the end of the hall.

And it was quiet. Too quiet for comfort. I could hear my

breathing, and my footsteps clumping across to my classroom door. I could almost hear my heart beating.

Casting off a feeling of unease—for I had no need to fear Milla now—I unlocked the door and crossed to my desk, dropping the *Thesaurus* on its dust-coated surface. Then I pulled open the lower desk drawer. I found the fourth hour section, found Maria Edmond's bright red notebook, and dropped Candace Ann's book behind it.

That's done. Thank heavens. That's over. Get out of here.

My hand lingered on Maria's journal. Was it crammed with poison, too, with a thousand and one variations of "I hate Shellwin?"

Unable to resist the temptation, I lifted it out of its slot and quickly turned the pages, skimming the neat entries. A description of the view from the window. Ice-crusted branches and gray sky; beauty and loneliness. Lyrics of Nancy's favorite song. The highlights of the Valentine dance. A surprise A on a science quiz. A bad day in gym.

No complaints about an out-of-control class and an inept instructor.

Heartened, I replaced Maria's journal and closed the drawer. I felt vindicated. Not everyone thought I was worthless.

Out in the hall, I heard footsteps. Heavy. Measured. Loud. Growing louder.

Hastily I threw my purse over my shoulder and pushed the chair back.

A hulking form with a familiar face filled the doorway. A mocking voice said, "Morning, Teach. Ready for your lesson?"

THIRTY

IT WAS CARL HOGAN, back from wherever he'd been and looking more dangerous than ever. In his beefy hand he held a gun. It was pointed at my head.

"Carl..." I closed my own hand on my purse, remembering how I had distracted him before by hurling textbooks and other objects at him.

Now the books were all stored away for the summer. I had only the purse.

"I'm not Carl," he said in a tinny voice that sounded as if it came from a machine.

I saw then that he had a bulkier build than Carl with coarser features and a florid complexion. His eyes were small and cold.

"Who are you?" I demanded.

"Caulfield Hogan." He made a grotesque bow. "Summer custodial staff. At your service, ma'am."

"Hogan?"

"Carl's brother," he said. "You don't know me. I was before your time."

"Well, Caulfield Hogan, you'd better get out of here before I call for help. There's a buzzer inside the drawer. All I have to do is press it and someone will come running."

"A panic button? Sure there is. Every room has one."

His sneer mocked my feeble lie. He drew closer to me, waving the gun in the air. A wave of alcohol and garlic swept over me. "I came to finish what Carl started," he said.

My heart began to race, and I felt the cold closing in on me. There was no panic button, of course. And how many people were in the building? Three? Four? None on this floor, except my assailant and me.

I said, “Carl is a disturbed kid who made a serious mistake. He needs help.”

“Sure he does, and you had to see that they threw the book at him, didn’t you? Couldn’t trouble yourself to speak for him. Never contacted his family. Didn’t even answer his letter.”

“What letter?”

“The one he wrote to apologize. But you didn’t care what happened to him. And you call yourself a teacher.”

“Yes, I do. Give me the gun—Caulfield. You can walk out of here and no one will know about this.”

His eerie cackle resounded in the silent room. “That isn’t the plan.”

Thunder steamrolled across the sky. Since I’d entered the classroom, the clouds had grown perceptibly darker. Now they filled the windows with their purplish bulk, and the room swam in deep shadow.

Caulfield advanced toward me as Carl once had, the gun steady in his hands, his stare hard and purposeful. I held my ground at the desk. There was no point in looking for a weapon. Everything had been put away for the summer. Every last pair of scissors, the staplers, the heavy paper-cutter. I had never been more vulnerable.

“So—just go while you can,” I said.

“Fat chance, lady.” He raised the gun. “Move it.”

“Where?”

“In there.” He pointed to the closet.

Just as Carl had.

The cold crawled through my body. It froze my voice, made it sound strange to me, high pitched, filled with panic.

“You’re crazy,” I said.

“Sure I am. It runs in the family.”

“Well, I’m not going anywhere.” I summoned my last bit of bravado. “You’ll have to shoot me and someone will hear the shot. You won’t get away.”

He laughed, a chilling devil's sound heard more often in nightmares than in life. "You *are* stupid, Ms. Shellwin. Did you ever hear of silencers?"

As he moved the gun just a little, I noticed the bulky cylinder on its muzzle.

He laughed again and pulled the trigger.

I HEARD A MUFFLED THUD...

Silencer.

Pain broke my arm apart. I cried out, and darkness settled over me.

I SAT ON A HARD TILE FLOOR, my right leg bent at an awkward angle, my back braced against a wall. The merest slit of light showed between the bottom of the door and the floor. Not enough to see properly by.

My head was literally splitting, and the pain in my arm was severe. I tried to move it and heard a feeble whimper that must have come from somebody else.

Awareness came slowly. Remembering the shot, I touched my head, expecting my hand to be covered with warm, wet blood. It was dry. I moved my hand down my arm. In darkness, I let my hands skim lightly over a rigid, stiff groove. There was no blood here either, but shreds of my rayon sleeve were stuck to the edge of the wound. I felt broken.

The pain grew steadily worse—from my waist all the way up to my head—and I had a more serious problem.

Caulfield, the mad janitor, had locked me in the closet where I would stay until fall when the new ninth grade teacher unlocked the door to unpack supplies and found a body.

Hold on! Maybe Caulfield hadn't locked the door. I forced myself to stand, turned the knob, pulled it desperately forward. My hopes crashed in fragments around me. The closet was locked. I couldn't open it from inside.

"Help!" Through my pain, I pounded on the door. "Somebody! Help me!"

In answer, thunder crashed across the sky.

"Somebody—please help me."

Anybody.

My voice sounded weak, incapable of penetrating a wooden barrier and traveling all the way down to the first floor where the people were.

No use. It's no use.

I had only one encouraging thought. Maybe Caulfield Hogan meant only to scare me. Otherwise, he would have shot me in a vital spot. He'd come back in a few hours and open the door. Meanwhile this closet could kill me—this tiny space with its unyielding door that I had opened and closed every school day since the room had been assigned to me.

That wouldn't—couldn't—happen. I would be missed. The girl downstairs who looked like Sara would investigate when I didn't return the key. Wouldn't she? Sandra expected to find me home waiting for the puppy. She'd know something was wrong. But what would she do then? And Dalton had planned a special evening for us tonight, a surprise. When he didn't find me at home, he'd look for me.

That I could count on. Couldn't I?

The coldness that had invaded my very soul turned my body to a block of ice. I began to shake uncontrollably.

Get hold of yourself get hold of yourself get hold of yourself.

My cell phone! I'd been holding my purse when Caulfield shot at me. I imagined him tossing me into the closet like a bag of trash, a limp body still holding the purse.

Look for it. You can dial "O" for Operator in the dark. Tell her what happened. Wait for rescue.

I felt along the floor and the shelves, identifying what I could. Dust pan. Broom. A package of notebook paper, its smooth packaging unbroken. Leftover boxes of pens and pencils. The books I kept on my desk. Plastic bookends. A large glass vase. My calendar already turned to September.

Poor Ms. Shellwin. She died in June. Oh, well, we know not the day nor the hour, as the Good Book says.

Nothing felt like a purse.

I sat back on the floor and leaned my head against the wall. Trying to ignore a sudden overwhelming desire for something to drink, I reviewed my chances.

Realistically now…

Even if Sara remembered me, she'd assume I'd left the building, taking the key with me. She might check to see that the room was locked. Or not. I didn't know how conscientious she was. Sandra… I couldn't hold back my tears at the thought of my collie puppy coming to an empty home with no one to welcome her.

And Dalton. When he realized that I was missing, he'd mount a search, but he'd never think that I'd take the journal back to Alcott. He would question Milla Schoenherr, the most obvious culprit. Whatever he did would take time that I might not have.

I took a deep breath realizing that this closed-in space had very little air, and it wasn't circulating. Before long, I would have none at all. I had no water, no food; and when I used the last of the oxygen, I would die.

Like one of Edgar Allan Poe's doomed characters, entombed while still alive.

No! No…

I made myself harness my runaway terror. There was a tiny space between the floor and the door's bottom. Air could circulate to some degree. My life wouldn't end like this, with untimely death at the hands of a crazed avenger, unless I starved to death. There must be something I could do.

You're a teacher. You've taught a whole unit on survival skills. Think of something! Okay. You're locked in a closet in an almost deserted building. How do you get out? Scream? Pound on the door?

I'd done that. What else?

Thunder rumbled outside. If the storm proved to be severe,

the office staff, including the custodians, would go home early. Caulfield had probably already left the school. He'd stay away from the second floor for a few days, perhaps work outside on the grounds, then steal upstairs and check to make sure that I was dead.

He'd alert the principal. Hogan was just summer custodial help. No one would connect him to the murder. My murder.

How long would it take someone to die of starvation? How long before the other custodians moved up to the second floor?

A sudden realization forced every desperate thought out of my head. It was the twenty-first day of June, and I was going to die. Not at the hands of Milla Schoenherr, as Violet had predicted. Instead I was destined to be the victim of a man I'd never even met. Caulfield Hogan. Brother of the misguided Carl.

Why had Violet never mentioned Caulfield Hogan, the real danger?

Breathe. Breathe sparingly. Take one long, sweet breath. Make it last.

I wanted water desperately—and food.

You don't need either one yet, I told myself. *You just had pancakes and orange juice.*

It was raining out, rain pounding against the old windows. There was a candy bar in my purse, but my purse wasn't here. Water and food. Both were beyond my reach.

My thoughts ran free, following their own dark, diverse paths, giving me all the reasons I was going to die and all the reasons I might survive.

I closed my eyes. How good it felt not to struggle. Just for a minute.

Don't ration your air. Breathe. Relax. Something will happen.

I HEARD MUSIC, my favorite song from Dalton's vintage tape. Love, love, tender love/Hear my lonely cry…

When the man and the time were right, true love was possible. Add one wrong ingredient, and you had a deadly mix. Poison in the cherry tarts. Tainted love. Deadly love.

Milla's affair with Randy Galloway had turned toxic. My relationship never would because it was right. Dalton and I were adults, compatible and free of prior entanglements. Society would smile on us as Dalton smiled at me now.

He took my hand in his own and held it. "Don't you know that I love you, Linnet? We're going to have a happy future together. Now, try the door again."

I touched the knob, and the door dissolved in a spray of dark powder. I stepped out into the classroom. Lightning sizzled across the sky.

"You could still be hit by a truck or struck by lightning," Violet had said.

Or I could be interred in a schoolroom closet by a madman.

I stood at the window, watching the trees on the hill bend low in the force of the wind. Turning to face the class, I said, "For your first journal topic, describe what you see when you look out the window. Use specific and concrete words only."

They had wide, diabolical grins on their faces. A few were laughing. Someone groaned. Jimmy was shouting.

"For example," I said, "I see...

Elms in thunder.

Beware of elms in thunder.

Beware...

Lightning flashed in the darkness. The windows dissolved as the closet door had, and the black vortex swept me up in its gritty embrace and bore me away.

"SHE'S IN THERE! I know it! Hurry!"

The girl's voice reached me across a dim, distant landscape.

A key turned smoothly in the lock, and the door swung free. I opened my eyes to a dazzle of brightness. The classroom lights were on, and someone held a large lantern flashlight, swinging it back and forth in my face.

"My God. Linnet!" Dwight Dunlap stood over me, tall and strong, in savior mode.

I opened my mouth to speak but found that I couldn't.

He helped me to my feet, and I collapsed against his chest, shaking. My legs might have been made of straw. I felt the stuffing falling out of my body, leaving me as weightless as a wraith.

"You're hurt! Let's get you into a chair. Saralynn, call 911. Call the police station."

With them was a man I didn't know in a green Alcott Ravens jacket and a Detroit Tigers baseball hat worn backwards and…

Candace Ann. Tears streamed down her face, and her hair hung in limp, wet strands.

"I told you so," she said. "Didn't I tell you?"

Dwight sent her an impatient look. "Yes you did, Candace Ann. Now move out of the way."

"Tell him what?" I wanted to say.

"Saralynn, get Ms. Shellwin some water."

She hadn't moved. "What do you want me to do first?" she asked.

"Get the water."

Dwight led me to the desk and picked up the chair that had fallen over on its side. I sank into it gratefully. He examined my arm and exclaimed over the shreds of white rayon clinging to the skin.

"What happened?" he demanded.

Reaching into a reserve of strength, I found the ability to speak. "Caulfield Hogan shot me. I think the bullet grazed me."

"Hogan!" he echoed.

From where I sat, I could see the large classroom clock. It was nine-thirty. I'd been in the closet for almost twelve hours.

Saralynn still hadn't moved. *I need water,* I thought. "Could you get my water?"

"I'm sorry, Ms. Shellwin," Candace Ann blubbered. "I didn't want him to hurt you."

Dwight's furious voice cut into the silence. "You knew about this, Candace Ann, and you didn't tell anyone. You're as guilty as Hogan is."

"He talked about it. Caulfield always talked. I didn't want Ms. Shellwin to die."

"I never liked that Hogan," the man in the green jacket spat out. "He's been nothing but trouble since he signed on."

"Come along, Candace Ann," Saralynn said. "You can wait in the office."

"Am I in trouble?" she asked.

"It depends on what you did," Dwight said. "Go along with Saralynn now."

Saralynn laid her hand on Candace Ann's shoulder. "It'll be all right, honey. Let's go get some tissue and that water."

"Wait!" Candace Ann looked directly at me. "Ms. Shellwin. I really am sorry. Can you ever forgive me?"

I wanted to know the answers to about a dozen questions first but didn't have the energy to ask them yet.

"I guess so," I said.

That was the most I could give her.

THIRTY-ONE

WHILE I'D BEEN LOCKED in the closet, life went on without me, and my worst imaginings failed to materialize. Sandra left a note for me tucked in the screen door: "Did you get the date wrong? I'll swing by with the pup after lunch tomorrow."

That was today.

Caulfield Hogan had been apprehended in a bar downstate bragging about how he'd taught a certain teacher a lesson. He was currently in custody, soon to learn a lesson of his own.

As for Dalton, he merely postponed our special evening until the weekend. "We have more to celebrate now." He leaned over my narrow hospital bed in the Emergency Room and laid his hand on my forehead.

Best of all, two doctors had pronounced me in good shape—considering—and discharged me after I'd spent a long, sleepless night reliving my escape from death.

Life was good, I decided, as I paid the cab driver and walked up to my front porch on legs that grew stronger with every step. The pink Victorian had never looked more beautiful to me, rain-washed and sparkling in the morning sunlight, with its Valentine window shining like a magnificent pink jewel.

Life was indeed good, even with Tansy Stewart dashing across the street before I unlocked my door to get the news of my ordeal firsthand.

I gave her a capsule summary of what had transpired, promising that we'd get together for coffee and more details in a day or two.

"But how did you know?" I asked.

"Through the grapevine. Everybody knows."

Well, I was living in Maple Creek, where life was peaceful again, even with my cell phone ringing softly from the depths of my purse. From now on, that was the only phone that would ring in Valentine Villa.

I gave Tansy a quick smile, let myself in the house and opened the cell, wondering who would welcome me home next.

"Oh, Linnet, how are you? It's Beverly."

Her subdued tone suggested that something was wrong.

"I survived," I said, "but it wasn't easy."

"Did you hear the news about Milla Schoenherr?"

"No. What happened now?"

"She's gone," Beverly said.

"Do you mean she left town?"

"No. She left this world. Milla took her own life yesterday."

I sank into the sofa, feeling a new weakness steal over me. Maybe I wasn't completely recovered after all.

"Because of the trouble with Randy Galloway?" I asked.

"Apparently. What else could it be?"

"But she couldn't go to jail for that, could she? Not for an old he said/she said incident that was never reported to the police?"

"No, but she could stand to lose a lot of money if Randy wins his lawsuit. She'd have to say goodbye to her reputation. Maybe even her job. A judge could forbid her to work with young people again. Her permanent certificate could be rescinded. A lot of bad things could happen."

Deadly love, I thought. It had certainly been lethal for Milla. One mistake had set the stage for her world to come crashing down on her.

"How did she do it?" I asked.

"She swallowed pills. Pain killers, tranquillizers, antibiotics—every pill she had in the house, all at once. So I heard. Her neighbor got worried when she couldn't reach her by phone and called the police."

Just like Tansy and Violet.

"Poor Milla," I said. "She should have stood up and faced this down."

"Is that what you would have done?" Beverly asked.

"Yes."

"So would I. I don't understand why Milla just gave up."

She's coming unraveled, Violet had said.

It was the only logical explanation, but I remembered Milla as I'd first seen her, proudly signing copies of *Capture My Heart* in front of the Tea Room. She'd seemed so polished and serene. Positively unflappable. She couldn't have known what was waiting for her around the bend, would never have imagined that Randy would come home to Maple Creek and turn on her.

"By the way," Beverly said, "Ned changed the meeting to tomorrow so you can join us. He figured you'd need a day to recuperate."

"That's good. I didn't want to miss one."

She paused, and when she spoke, I could detect a critical note in her voice. "You should have called me if you wanted to go back to the school, Linnet. If there were two of us, that Caulfield creature wouldn't have done what he did."

I recalled the footsteps I'd heard on the last day of school and the shots fired at Dalton and me at Marble Lake. Who else could the stalker-shooter have been?

"He was going to find a way to get to me one way or another," I said. "I just thank God it's over."

BUT IT WASN'T OVER. WOULD it ever be?

The day's mail included a letter addressed to Ms. Violet Julaine.

From someone who didn't know she'd been dead for over a year? I didn't think so. Not stopping to debate the legality of reading someone else's mail, even if she was dead, I took the letter over to the sofa where the light was brightest. My hands trembled as I ripped open the envelope. Inside was a single sheet of paper, covered with ragged handwriting.

Dear Violet,

I'm sorry for what I did to you, but I had to protect myself. You should never have tried to blackmail me. We were friends, and friends don't betray each other. But I'm sorry. As it turned out, you weren't the only one who knew my secret, so it didn't have to happen. Rest in peace, Violet. I forgive you.

Sincerely,
Milla.

Milla forgave Violet? For trying to blackmail her? For making Milla kill her? The world seemed to have slipped out of its orbit.

As for Violet, I wondered why she would accept a gift of food from a woman she'd recently tried to blackmail. Did Violet think that Milla would so easily forgive, forget, and bring her a gift of baked goods for Valentine's Day?

Oh, well, only Violet could answer that question. Somehow I knew that I'd never hear from her again.

I folded the paper and replaced it in the envelope to give to Dalton tonight. Ellen Trehearne had been right.

I set the letter on the coffee table. Was there no end to the weird happenings at Valentine Villa? A landline phone straight from the Twilight Zone, a haunted music box, and now a letter from a killer to the woman she'd poisoned. And why had Milla sent her apology to Valentine Villa? To be read by Violet's ghost?

It didn't make sense. By the time Milla gathered all her bottles of pills together, she must have completely lost touch with reality.

One question tugged at me. Besides Violet, who knew about Milla and Randy Galloway?

Almost certainly Garth McKay. Maybe Katherine Kale who was close to Garth.

I couldn't think of anyone else.

CANDACE ANN HAD THE ANSWER.

I saw her through the bay window and almost didn't go to the door. I didn't want to see her today, or any day, but in the end curiosity overcame my anger.

She had brought a bouquet of daisies for me, some white, others painted an unlikely shade of blue.

"These are for you, Ms. Shellwin," she said. "I want you to know that I'm *so* sorry."

Deciding to be magnanimous, I said, "Let's forget about it, Candace Ann."

I took the flowers with one hand and kept the other on the door, not moving aside, not smiling. Offering her no encouragement. Just a brief "thank you" for the flowers.

"Are you going to be all right?" she asked.

"The doctors say I'm fine."

Her dark eyes glistened with tears.

"And you call yourself a teacher," Caulfield Hogan had said.

"Yes, I do."

Candace Ann was my student, but she had stepped over an invisible line. Still, she had saved my life by alerting Dwight Dunlap to my danger, but she'd also let Caulfield lock me in the closet, where I might have died.

My feeling toward her couldn't be more ambivalent.

"Caulfield isn't all bad," she said. "Neither is Carl."

"It's interesting you'd stick up for a pair of criminals," I said.

"They're my cousins. My kin."

"Those two? I didn't know."

"We grew up together," she said. "All my life I've heard

their mom, my Aunt Alice, talk against teachers. Caulfield had a hard time in school. They made it harder for him, and he dropped out in his sophomore year. Then there was Carl. He was always in trouble."

"I know." Carl had been one of the most disruptive boys I'd ever taught. Or tried to teach.

"Nobody ever helped Carl," Candace Ann said. "They didn't want him in their classes. They did everything they could to get rid of him. Aunt Alice said some of the teachers were worse than Caulfield even. Like Ms. Schoenherr at the high school. My aunt said she was pure evil, and someday she was going to let her know exactly what she thought of her."

I didn't want to talk about Milla with Candace Ann or anyone, for that matter. Instead of responding to her revelation, I said, "What Caulfield Hogan did…? Was that the mean plan you kept warning me about?"

"Oh, no," she said. "I—I just made that up."

"But why?"

She stared down at her feet. "I don't know. It made things more exciting."

"Not for me it didn't."

She bit her lip—hard. "I'm sorry. I overheard Caulfield talking with his friends about what he was going to do to you. I know I should have told someone, but…I didn't. I'm sorry."

I felt as if I were drowning in apologies. Everyone with the possible exception of Caulfield Hogan and his toxic mother, Alice, was sorry for something.

"I think I'd better go lie down now," I said.

"You said you were okay."

"I'm just a little tired."

"All right. See you." She nodded and walked slowly to the sidewalk. I watched as she got on her bike and rode away.

I didn't think she'd ever come to the pink Victorian again, and that was fine with me. But she *had* saved my life, and yes, I could forgive her.

SOON AFTER CANDACE ANN LEFT, Dwight Dunlap and Saralynn came to see me, bringing me a two-pound box of chocolates and a card signed by several faculty members—the ones who hadn't left town for the summer. This gave me a chance to ask him a question that had been troubling me.

"Why didn't somebody recognize Caulfield Hogan when he applied for the summer job? He looked so much like Carl."

"I don't know, Linnet. Frankly, I don't think there's that much of a resemblance. I wasn't principal here when Caulfield was a student."

"What about MacGregor?"

"MacGregor's been here for years, but he never saw the new man," Saralynn said. "He's on sick leave."

"Well, I guess it didn't matter," I said.

"What matters is that you're all right," she said brightly.

"And don't worry, Linnet," Dwight added. "Next year will be better."

THE BLUE TRUCK PULLED into my driveway at exactly three o'clock. I'd been waiting for Sandra to bring her to me for hours. Now her arrival seemed unreal, like a wondrous fairytale unfolding before my eyes. I'd wanted a dog of my own for so long. Not just any dog. A collie puppy.

I hurried outside as Sandra stepped down and came around the front of the truck to its bed.

Caramel stood up in her small crate, her head tilted to one side, beautiful eyes bright with curiosity. She looked exactly like the pictures Sandra had sent me. A little dark sable Lassie whose fur glistened in the sun.

"Welcome, baby girl," I said softly.

She wagged her tail.

"Did she make the trip all right?" I asked.

"Like a trouper." Sandra slipped a red puppy lead over her head and led her down onto the lawn.

"She's so beautiful," I said. "Can I hold her?"

Sandra smiled. "She's your dog now. Puppy, meet your mistress."

"Caramel," I said as I picked her up, uncaring about the pain that still lingered in my arm in spite of the pills. She swept her little pink tongue over my cheek.

The name was right. Her coat had all the colors of autumn blended together, but, more than anything, she reminded me of melted caramel, spilled in the sun. Caramel with marshmallow for a ruff.

My little caramel sundae, I thought as I set her down in the backyard and watched her amble away on short legs, nose poking in the grass, exploring her new surroundings.

I felt the sting of tears in my eyes. This was a beginning. It so easily could have been an end.

"Let's go check out your toys, baby," I said.

"And I'll be on my way," Sandra said. "I have to drive to Ohio this afternoon."

I looked up from my puppy, startled. For a moment, I'd forgotten that Sandra was still here.

CARAMEL PREFERRED VIOLET'S Queen of Hearts music box to her bright new toys. When I caught her trying to nudge it off the coffee table with her nose, I quickly shoved a toy parrot in front of her and set the music box on a high bookshelf.

"Listen to the music, Caramel," I said, turning the wind-up mechanism. It was frozen in place.

Well, I was done with seeing supernatural properties in every object I owned. The music box had simply stopped working for a while. One day it would start again. In the meantime, Caramel's attention turned to a plastic basket filled with toys and chews. She pulled them out one by one and began to drag the basket around, growling a play growl and slamming it into the furniture.

That was how Dalton found us, surrounded by dozens of plush toy animals that chirruped, quacked, meowed, and panted.

"Your living room looks like a toy store," he said with a broad grin.

"The kitchen is neater. Let's go in there."

Dalton settled himself at the kitchen table. I brought out a can of Pepsi, his favorite, and filled Caramel's bowl with fresh water.

"I still can't figure out what made that phone ring." He lifted the receiver and listened. "Dead as dead can be."

"It served its purpose. I'm going to assume that somehow Violet Julaine found a way to communicate with me from wherever she is."

It was my old lightning strike theory. I'd grown comfortable with it. And along the way, I'd worked something else out in my mind. The brain emits energy. The phone is an electrical device that works on energy. Why couldn't psychic energy—Violet, that is—make the phone ring?

I was perfectly happy with my expanded theory and felt no need for validation from Annabelle or even Dalton.

Dalton shook his head. "I can't come up with a better explanation, but there has to be one."

"I wonder why Violet didn't warn me about Caulfield. Maybe she only knew what Milla was going to do."

"Tunnel vision," he said. "And maybe we should stop trying to explain the inexplicable."

"You're right. I'm going to paint the kitchen. I'll take the phone out and spackle in the space. That was my plan before life got so crazy."

"That's what I'd do." Dalton took a swig of Pepsi and reached down to pet Caramel who was lying with her head on an enormous boot toy she'd dragged in from the living room.

"Are you going to stay in teaching?" he asked.

"Yes. I couldn't possibly have another year like this one."

"That's good."

"I'm a survivor," I added.

"Yes, you are."

"Now that we agree on that, let's talk about us."

"Us?"

"You and me and the future." He stood and pulled me up into his arms. "That is, if you'd like to share it with me."

I searched his eyes and knew he was serious. "Oh, I would."

He had said those words, or similar ones, in a dream while I'd been locked in the closet. He told me he loved me, and his love had dissolved the closet door.

Perhaps I wasn't through with the supernatural after all. But this wasn't the right time for a discussion of portents and messages in dreams.

Dalton pulled me close and held me, and we let our kisses burn out the last of the darkness. I moved my head back, searching his eyes one more time. Just to be sure.

"So I guess it's on to the future then."

"Starting now." His blue eyes sparked with promise.

"Starting now," I said.